SHIFTING SANDS

SHIFTING SANDS

Anne Worboys

Chivers Press • G.K. Hall & Co.
Bath, England   Thorndike, Maine USA

This Large Print edition is published by Chivers Press, England, and by
G.K. Hall & Co., USA.

Published in 1999 in the U.K. by arrangement with Severn House
Publishers Ltd.

Published in 1999 in the U.S. by arrangement with Chivers Press Ltd.

U.K. Hardcover   ISBN 0–7540–3832–7 (Chivers Large Print)
U.K. Softcover   ISBN 0–7540–3833–5 (Camden Large Print)
U.S. Softcover   ISBN 0–7838–8102–9 (Nightingale Series Edition)

British Library Cataloguing in Publication Data available

Library of Congress Cataloging-in-Publication Data

Worboys, Anne.
    Shifting sands / Anne Worboys.
        p.   (large print)   cm.
     ISBN 0–7838–8102–9 (lg. print : sc : alk. paper)
     1. Large type books.   I. Title.
    [PR6073.O667S55   1999]
    823'.914—dc21   99–22230

CHAPTER ONE

'I don't believe this.' Susanne did a double-take, closed her eyes then opened them again. 'Pleased to announce . . . winner of a luxury cruise for two down the Nile.' A shiny brochure slid out of the envelope on to the floor. She picked it up. *Cruise of a lifetime!* shouted the large black print that lay over a backdrop of red sun and palm trees, emerald green and brown; a sky of unbelievable brilliance. The advertising department had had a field day. She took a moment to gather her startled wits then shouted, 'Vita!'

Her mother, never one to hurry, wandered elegantly downstairs carrying a Ralph Lauren gown over one arm and a Gina Frattini trouser suit over the other. Vita Landseer was a beauty. Her ash-blonde hair was drawn away from her face and folded into a pleat at the back of her head with total disregard for fashion. Her fingernails were salmon-coloured, her lipstick pale and glossy. Fifteen hours a day, whether anyone was due to call or not, she presented a picture of perfect grooming. She looked very much what she now was, a *vendeuse*. Never mind that she operated from a cottage down a lonely cart track and that the high-class clothes she sold were not new.

Susanne waved the letter under her

1

mother's nose. 'Tell me if I'm hallucinating.'

Vita laughed and carried on into the little oak-beamed sitting room. 'I'm sure you're not.' She headed for a free-standing rail of clothes that looked as though it had lost its way among the occasional tables with their family photos, antique bookcases, and watercolours. 'This is an impossible situation,' she muttered. 'I'm going to have to find premises. Turn on the light, dear, will you? The trouble with these picturesque cottages is they don't let enough light in.'

Susanne yelled, 'Mother! Were you listening? I have something to tell you.' She came to the door holding the letter in her hand. A flick of the switch and the room glowed with soft light from standard lamps with pale shades. 'Remember that mindless questionnaire I filled in in an idle moment— some marketing concern wanting to know if I prefer margarine to butter? Where do you buy your cosmetics, Boots or chain stores? All that kind of thing, and they offered a whole lot of prizes.'

Vita wasn't sure she remembered. 'Could you lower your voice, dear?'

'Remember you said, "Throw it away. Nobody wins those things."? Remember saying that?'

Vita turned, laughing. 'Yes. Yes, of course I would say that. I never have believed anyone does. I mean, do they ever publish—'

2

'I've won a cruise down the Nile for two.'

Her mother stared at her. Then she sat down, hard, on one of the chairs salvaged from the Grange Hill bankruptcy sale.

Little Hammer, the cottage that Harvey Bevin, their neighbour, had let to Vita at a peppercorn rent, had been built by Harvey's ancestor in the seventeenth century and was originally intended to house farm workers. Now, with its red hanging tiles, mullioned windows and fringe of wisteria vine, it had evolved into a Grade Two listed *Des Res*, though the kind of people who were Vita's associates when she was the rather grand chatelaine of Grange Hill, looked upon it as 'quaint'.

Those were the people who saw her enforced move to the cottage as at the very least an embarrassment, at worst a humiliation. Some of them had turned away, not knowing how to deal with it. Some made excuses saying you couldn't have an extra woman at a dinner party. Others came with diffident offers of help. One of these brought a Versace suit.

'I've put on weight,' the woman said, avoiding Vita's eyes. 'I can't wear it and it would be such a pity to waste it.'

Susanne, when she heard, was breathless with indignation but Vita, endowed as she was with grace and humility—the humility had come in very handy in recent months—had

3

accepted the outfit. 'I shall sell it,' she said, 'and no one will be any the wiser.'

She placed an advertisement in *The Lady*.

Forty-one women wanted the Versace suit, scarcely worn, and selling at a third of the shop price. The telephone rang for weeks. Vita examined her own wardrobe. She and Darren had attended Ascot and Glyndebourne. They went to weddings and elegant city functions. Would she ever have an opportunity to wear her own smart clothes again? Tentatively, she offered them and they, too, were snapped up.

A month later, when requests were still pouring in, she rang round her better off friends and acquaintances asking if they had anything they would like to off-load. For those women who lived their social life in a restricted circle, now she came to think of it, there was a limited number of times they could appear in the same suit or dress. The response to her enquiries was gratifying. A hobby emerged. Within a short time the hobby became a business and wardrobes in Little Hammer filled up until they overflowed.

Busy businesswomen who hadn't the time to shop arrived in the evening to try her clothes on. Friends and neighbours formed a habit of dropping by for coffee and to get advice on style. Vita's elegance became a symbol for her success. She gave women ideas for putting together a look. She found it was fun helping them feel good about their appearance. Word spread. She acquired well-known customers, went on local radio, and inevitably became over-worked. What had begun as a reaction to a charitable hand-out became a monster, spiralling out of control.

Vita's clientele was now ranging further and further afield. Women were willing to drive across counties for her bargains. But she hadn't lost track of the fact that hers was a luxury trade. At the first sign of a depression purveyors of designer clothes could sink without trace. Women could dress, when they had to, from chain stores.

'Vita!' said Susanne. 'Come out of your trance. Look at this.' She thrust a paper under her mother's nose.

Vita took it. She read aloud, 'Award to Ms Susanne Landseer, a trip for two down the Nile from Aswan to Cairo.' She looked up, her eyes round as pennies. 'You don't think it's an elaborate joke?'

'Joke? Why should it be? Somebody has to win these things. Why not me?'

Vita rubbed her forehead thoughtfully. 'Why not indeed?' she managed at last.

'Funny this should arrive the very day I leave my job. Don't you think that's funny, Mum?'

'Don't call me Mum,' Vita murmured automatically, scanning the rest of the letter. 'Well, well!' she managed as she reached the bottom of the page, then added, thinking of all

5

they had both been through, 'You deserve a bit of luck.'

'Thanks. You too.' They smiled at each other. 'But what I said was, funny it should arrive the very day my job goes *Phut*! I'm at a loose end. I can actually go.'

'Life's full of coincidences, dear. You'll find that as you go along.'

Susanne didn't believe in coincidences. She believed things happened when they were meant to happen and they brought with them choices. 'Maybe it was meant to be,' she said, recognising not only that there was now a choice to be made, but that the choice could be far reaching. 'Who will I take?'

Vita recognised that she was speaking to herself but she answered anyway. 'Sleep on it,' she advised.

Susanne looked down at her mother's hands that were lying in her lap. 'Why have you crossed your fingers?'

Vita swiftly uncrossed them, but said nothing. She, too, was thinking about lean, handsome Nigel Danvers, though with cynicism. Since the Landseer women came down in the world, Nigel had been conspicuously avoiding Susanne. Vita wasn't surprised. She had always suspected, anyway, that when he had made a name for himself as a trainer he would look for a partner among the daughters of rich racing men. That was the way Nigel's kind operated. They went for the main chance.

Susanne leaned against the clothes rack, hand on hip, frowning at her mother. 'I said, why did you cross your fingers?'

Vita was aware that her independent daughter didn't care for her to show her protective side. She rose elegantly from her chair. 'Write out a few names and put them in a hat,' she said lightly. 'You've got plenty of friends. I'm sure any one of them would be delighted to be offered a free trip down the Nile.' She turned towards the door then turned back and stood frowning at the rail of clothes. 'It really does look awful in here. Could you manage to squeeze another into your room?'

It was on the tip of Susanne's tongue to say that most of the people who visited now came for shopping, but she stopped herself in time. Vita hadn't made the mental adjustment to complement her transition from grand lady of Grange Hill to Little Hammer. 'I could make a bit of space by decking myself out for the cruise,' she said, teasing.

'Feel free.'

'What! Are you serious?'

'If you can find something to fit you.' Vita shrugged and went off to the little kitchen to start preparing their dinner.

*   *   *

Since Harvey Bevin's wife died a year ago he

had fallen into the habit of walking over the fields in the early evening to spend a half-hour with his tenant. He had to have his whisky and Vita knew he hated drinking alone. Harvey was a countryman born and bred. He lived in tweeds, discarding them only in the hottest weather for an open-necked shirt and smart chinos. His cheeks were ruddy, roughened by all weathers for he was a huntsman as well as a racing man.

When Susanne was a child he had allowed her to keep her pony at his racing stables and later, when she became a proficient rider, taught more by his stable lads and the jockeys he employed than by the riding school where she went for lessons, he invited her to join them when they exercised the racing string in the early mornings. Inevitably, when she outgrew her pony, it was not replaced.

Since taking a job in London she came home most weekends. It was wonderful in the park at five o'clock in the morning with the sun still low in the sky, the big oaks and chestnuts glinting in its rays; squirrels scampering up and down the gnarled old tree trunks; a fox slipping silently into the rhododendrons that grew wild in the valleys. There was exhilaration in galloping with the wind in her face and the thunder of horses' hooves in her ears.

And there was Nigel.

Nigel had been employed at various stables

around Newmarket for some years. He was a fearless and very accomplished rider, but too tall for a jockey. That left him with a career as a trainer. He came to train Harvey's horses. When the Landseer family lived in the big house he had been a frequent visitor there.

Harvey's ruddy face lit up when Susanne answered the door. 'I thought that was you I saw skimming along the road on a bike. Home for the weekend?'

Susanne gave him a hug. 'I've left my job. I've joined the great ranks of the unemployed,' she said lightheartedly.

He looked concerned, then smiled tentatively. 'You don't exactly appear to be downcast.'

She turned and led him inside. 'Harvey, dear, you must know what's going on in the city these days, firms restructuring, people shifting sideways, it's happening to lots of people, all the time. What I've been offered within the company doesn't suit me so I've bolted.' Amazing how things could change. In the space of half an hour she had gone from being jobless and depressed to a free woman racing across the world at someone else's expense. 'Don't worry, I'll find a gap to slide into,' she said. 'Sit down and I'll get Vita.'

Inevitably, Vita had heard them for voices carried right through the tiny cottage. She came in from the dining-room where she had been sorting through her stock and immediately

9

began apologising for the rail of clothes in the drawing-room.

'My dear, I'm so pleased the business is such a success,' Harvey replied expansively. 'You deserve it.'

Vita's embarrassment ebbed. 'The good news is that I'll soon be able to pay you a decent rent.'

He waved her offer away. 'Let the arrangement stand in the meantime. Of course, if you get frightfully rich . . .'

Vita laughed and headed for the corner cabinet where she kept the Waterford glass, relic of grander days. 'After thirty years as a dependant I'm enjoying earning my own living, but it's not the kind of business in which one makes a fortune. Now let me get you a drink.' There was always plenty of liquor on offer at Little Hammer for in a moment of inspired anger Susanne had emptied the drinks cupboard at Grange Hill and removed as much liquor from the cellars as she had dared.

'Thanks.' He crossed the worn Turkish carpet and settled in one of the comfortable loose-covered chairs. These were Harvey's furnishings, taken from the attics of Hammer Place. After a prolonged battle with the receivers, Vita had added a few pieces inherited from her parents, a small Victorian desk, a piecrust table and a valuable glass fronted seventeenth century bookcase. Even before the rail of clothes had been wheeled in, the room had a cluttered look. But then, as Vita said in those dark moments when reaction set in, it was a comfort to have some of her old friends round her.

'I'm glad you're down,' their guest said, accepting a glass of whisky from his hostess, nodding his thanks. 'I've got a new gelding, and two of the staff are off. Were you thinking of riding out with us in the morning?'

'Yes. Yes, I was.'

'Good. I'd like you to try him.'

Susanne said, 'Great.' Vita gave her a gin and tonic and she mouthed her thanks. 'Tell me about him.'

'He cost me an arm and a leg.' Harvey wore the benign countenance of a man who has an arm and a leg to spare. 'But he's worth every inch.'

Susanne poked her finger into the piece of lemon floating in her glass. 'What's his name?'

'Silver Penny.'

'I like that.' She turned it over on her tongue. 'It's got a fast sound.'

'He goes like the wind.'

'That's my second bit of luck today.' She told him in lilting tones about the trip down the Nile.

Caught with his whisky to his lips, Harvey made a noise half way between a gasp and a gulp. He hurriedly set his glass on a little piecrust table, coughed, slapped his palms on his knees and eyed her in astonishment. 'Well I'm blessed! Amazing! Hearty congratulations. I'm pleased for you.'

'Thanks.'

His eyes had taken on a distant look. 'Dolores suggested once that we go on a cruise. A little run round the Med. It didn't come to anything. I'm sorry now. She might have enjoyed it.'

'She'd understand you couldn't take a horse,' said Susanne comfortingly.

'That's about the strength of it. Ah well.' He lifted his head. 'It's a pity you can't take someone with you, but I daresay you'll have no trouble finding friends on board.'

'The prize is for two. If you could manage without your horse I'd take you.'

But Harvey the quiet countryman wasn't at home with sophisticated teasing. 'That'd set the gossips raging.' He swiftly changed the subject. 'So what's this about space, Vita? I hope you won't go. I'd be lost now without my walk across the fields for my drink. Old boys get attached to habits.' He smiled at them both in his fond, fatherly way. 'I wonder if we could find you a showroom in the village.'

Vita said swiftly, 'That's committing myself. I can't be sure the business is going to keep expanding. I'm not worried about the buyers but it'll be a while before I can be sure the sources are durable. At least while the stuff is contained here in the cottage I'm safe if they dry up. You know I've nothing in the bank.'

12

'Come, come,' he protested sitting up erect in his low seat. 'I'm behind you. Give me another glass of this stuff and we'll talk about it.'

Vita said adamantly, 'I can't lean on you, Harvey. You've been far too kind and generous already.'

He swirled his topped-up drink round the glass. 'I'm a businessman. I don't give anything away.'

They smiled at him, knowing he did.

Susanne left them talking, went to her room and stood looking idly at the clothes rack that was taking up half the inner wall space. Beautiful gowns by Ungaro and Amanda Wakeley. A wonderful silky purple coat by Thierry Mugler. Two by Nina Ricci. She fingered them lovingly, considering whether to take up her mother's offer to help herself to the stock when she went off on the cruise. She decided against, but all the same she found herself sliding the hangers along, looking at the garments, thinking of Nigel. Thinking of herself and Nigel on the deck of a riverboat under a canopy of stars. Thinking how impressed he would be by such clothes and what marvellous company he would be on a cruise down the Nile.

Forget it, she muttered. When her father ran off with his blonde secretary Nigel had been sympathetic, but when bankruptcy loomed and the family had to leave Grange

13

Hill he had begun to edge away. Their visits to the pub came to a halt. And mysteriously, when they were together, there were always other people around.

Next morning she biked over to Hammer Place, her haversack stuffed with carrots, their green tops wet with dew. It was dawn and the birds in Grange Hill copse were singing. She had the lanes to herself except for a badger on the way back to the hide after its night ramblings. The white-painted wooden gate stood open. She spun in and pedalled up the long drive to the stables. Out on her right was the big Georgian manor house where Harvey Bevin now lived alone, and beyond that the park.

Nigel was waiting for her, standing with thumbs stuck in the waist of his riding trousers. His thin face was sun-browned from the long summer. He looked just right this morning in the arched doorway against a backdrop of bales of straw.

'I've saddled Silver Penny for you,' he said, smiling at her. His teeth were very white in his tanned face.

'Thanks.' She hid her surprise. He had never done this for her before. She took her bike round the back of the stables then hurried back pushing her long hair up under her hard hat.

He was still waiting when she returned, slapping his riding crop against his polished

14

boots. They went together into the stables that were full of the noise of impatient hooves and the rattle of metal bits, the thump and squeak of saddles coming down off their trees, the chatter of the busy stable hands. 'Why didn't you come last week?' he asked, smiling, solicitous. 'I missed you.'

'I'm dead flattered.'

'You know I always miss you when you're not here.'

She recognised when he gave her arm a little shake that she had sounded touchy. 'We've had problems,' she said. 'Vita's business has not only taken off, it's getting out of hand.' They were going down the row of stalls, glancing in at horses impatiently rustling round in their straw, whinneying, wanting to be out and away. She stopped talking because she could see Nigel wasn't listening.

He paused at a stall where a handsome bay stood with his head over the door, bright-eyed and anxious to greet them. 'Silver Penny,' he said addressing the horse, 'meet my chum Susanne who's going to ride you this morning.'

'I say, he is handsome!' Shining bay coat. Long black mane and tail.

'Give her a good run, now,' Nigel went on, still talking to the horse. 'She's a great friend of mine. I'll expect you to put your best foot forward.' He patted the horse affectionately on the flank. That was one of Nigel's endearing characteristics. He was genuinely

15

fond of the animals he trained.

Susanne pulled a carrot out of her pocket. Silver Penny's velvet nostrils quivered. He delicately took the carrot in his teeth and chewed it noisily, spattering saliva. Then he nudged her hand open, looking for more. She emptied her pockets, laughing. 'You do know what you like, don't you?'

'All us chaps know what we like.' Nigel lifted her free hand and kissed it. Susanne wanted to say it was a bit early in the morning but she didn't. A kiss is a kiss whatever the hour when delivered by a man you could love if only he wanted you to. She smiled at him and opened the stall door. The stable hands were emerging in hard hats and shining boots, all ready to go. Nigel, following close behind with the tall Samovar on a loose rein, legged Susanne into the saddle. Silver Penny danced round in a circle.

Harvey Bevin emerged from the big house, strode across the courtyard and took his stallion from one of the girls. He glanced at Susanne. 'Keep a tight hold on him until we get to the gallops. He'll take advantage if he senses you're not in control.' He went to the mounting block and climbed up into the saddle. 'There's nothing he likes better than to show the rest of us his heels.'

They trotted out into the park, eight of them. Nigel jogged up beside Susanne. 'Okay?' he asked.

16

'Okay.' She looked down at her hands, firmly on the reins, feeling uncomfortable with Nigel's close attention that had not been turned on her for a long time. Harvey lengthened his horse's stride. The rest of the group followed. Susanne stayed back. When the leader broke into a canter she gradually let out the reins. Silver Penny had a long stride. He bounded ahead effortlessly, straight through the centre of the group and out to the front as though this was where he belonged, at the head.

'Hang on to him, Susanne. Don't let him get away.'

'I won't,' she shouted back. They cantered down the hill into the valley with the wind in their faces. The gallops began at the bottom of the park and ran, flanked by big leafy trees, for several miles.

She reached the foot of the valley first and drew rein. Harvey came up beside her. 'What d'you think?'

'He's wonderful. So smooth. And he's got a lovely soft mouth.'

'I thought you'd be pleased with him. Right! Ready to let rip?' He looked at her consideringly.

She nodded.

'If he gets out of hand just keep going. Give him his head.'

'Don't worry.'

They persuaded the excited animals into

17

line.

'Right! Away!'

Silver Penny streaked out in front, neck at full stretch, hooves moving like pistons. Behind them the thunder of hooves receded. Susanne and her mount were alone with the trees and the wind and the pale morning sun coming up over the horizon. They raced for the head of the valley. She turned in her saddle. The horses were in a line with Nigel on Samovar at the front, galloping flat out, yet gradually falling back. 'You're going to win the Grand National, you clever thing,' she said, bending over to pat Silver Penny's silky neck. The wind hurled her words behind them.

At the head of the valley she pulled up easily.

Nigel swept in beside her. 'Jockey of the year!' He stood up in his stirrups and waved his whip in the air.

Susanne's senses were singing.

'I'm thinking of entering him for The Oaks,' Harvey said as he drew rein. The horses stamped around, snorting, tossing their heads, sweating. 'What do you think?'

'I think, yes. He's a goer all right. I'll come and watch him win.'

'You're a good rider, Susanne,' Nigel said as they clambered up the steep slope to the ridge that ran parallel with the gallops. 'I wouldn't let just anybody ride him.'

She looked at him with puzzled eyes. Who

was 'just anybody'? And weren't they all good riders? You wouldn't get a chance on Harvey's horses if you weren't. As they reached the spine she let out the reins and Silver Penny fled along the track. She headed him for a fallen log. He gathered up his haunches and rose effortlessly. Behind her she could hear the beat of hooves. She gave the gelding his head, knowing it was Nigel trying to catch up. Silver Penny out-distanced him with ease.

Back at the stables as they were dismounting Nigel said, speaking casually as though he was in the habit of taking her to glamorous restaurants, 'How would you like to come out to dinner at The Weavers tonight?'

She blinked. The Weavers, a sixteenth-century inn situated on the other side of the forest, had recently been converted to a high-class restaurant.

'Well?' He smiled down at her.

She was getting her breath.

'Not to your taste?' He gave her a whimsical look.

She thought, this has got to be something to do with Silver Penny. 'Yes,' she said breathlessly. 'Yes, I'd love to.'

He rubbed his hands together, looking pleased. 'I'll pick you up at seven-thirty, then.'

She wondered as she cycled home if Harvey, through Nigel, was offering her a job. It was less disturbing to think about that than about the fact that Nigel, after all this time, was paying her attention again.

CHAPTER TWO

Susanne chose her outfit carefully. She didn't
have many clothes. Most of them were suitable
for the office: the jade suit had been bought
for a wedding and worn only once afterwards,
to the firm's Christmas lunch.

Vita was preparing her own meal in the
small, cluttered kitchen. She looked up as
Susanne came in, well-brushed hair swinging
on her shoulders, creating a drift of perfume.
Before she could stop herself she said,
critically, 'Aren't you a bit overdressed for the
pub?' That was where Nigel had taken
Susanne in the good days before their family
fell on hard times.

'I'm going to The Weavers.'

'Oh.' She quickly hid her surprise.

Susanne went to wait by the front door. Vita
had never interfered in her life, but she wasn't
good at hiding her feelings. She hadn't seemed
to care when her own dinner party invitations
dried up—*My dear, there's the awkwardness of
the uneven numbers*—but she had been angry
on Susanne's behalf when Nigel stopped
ringing.

Five minutes later he came down the
drive, swung round and began backing up

precariously close to the rosemary bed. Susanne went out to direct him. The circle of gravel at the front of the cottage was inadequate for the kind of car Nigel drove, a 1975 Toyota Celica. It wasn't vintage, but it was special. He had done it up himself in his spare time, and maintained it himself. It had pace and elegance and that, he said, was what he wanted from a car. He did indeed, thought Susanne, look absolutely right behind its wheel.

He swung the car round, sending gravel flying, and jumped out to open her door. Not expecting this courtesy, Susanne had already opened it herself and was settling into the passenger seat. He held his own door wide a moment while glancing pointedly at the front door of the cottage, looking innocent, and puzzled.

She felt guilty. Vita would have been polite if she had asked him in. She was always polite to Susanne's friends. She said apologetically, 'Mother's tied up, otherwise I'd have asked you in for a drink.'

He lowered himself into the driver's seat and started the engine again.

*   *   *

The cow bell that hung over the front door at Little Hammer sent its sweet notes ringing down the hall. Vita went to answer it. 'Gilbert!'

she cried with pleasure, holding out her hands to Darren's cousin.

Gilbert Ellis, in his capacity as a solicitor, kept an eye on Vita's affairs. In his role as Darren's cousin he kept in touch with both of them, hoping that one day he might manage to bring husband and wife back together. He was a chubby man of slightly less than medium height, bald and with startling, wild-looking eyebrows over piercing eyes. He was dressed in office clothes: navy-blue striped suit and tie.

'An impulse visit,' he told her. 'I hope it's not inconvenient. I was scooting up the road on my way home when I suddenly thought, we haven't seen you for ages. So I rolled down the drive—'

'Farm track,' Vita interrupted wryly as she backed away into the tiny hall, holding the door wide. 'Harvey's talking about having it done up before someone breaks a spring. I'm delighted to see you, Gilbert. Come in. I've been neglectful of old friends and I'm sorry, but I've been busy. I'll tell you about it.'

They went into the sitting-room together. Both pairs of eyes turned towards the rail of clothes standing before the bookcase in the corner, Vita's obsessively and with embarrassment, his in surprise.

'This really is too shaming,' she said holding her hands briefly over her face. 'My stock has overflowed. Both of the bedrooms are cluttered and you should see the dining-room!

22

We're eating in the kitchen.'

'Don't worry, don't worry. Why should I mind?'

'No, I'm sure you don't.' She flung her hands wide in a gesture of helplessness. 'I'm having to come to terms with the reality of my position. Susanne, thankfully, didn't bring her escort in. Now your arrival has shown me that something just has to be done.'

He came into the room, looked round, chose a chair. 'Who's she going out with?'

Vita flopped down on a window seat looking depressed. 'This, I hope, is a one-off. She's gone to dinner with Nigel Danvers.'

'Young Danvers!' The black brows shot up.

In Vita's mind she was thinking this was an unlikely reaction unless there was some very good reason why Susanne should not be out with Nigel. 'Why should you be astonished?'

He stared at the beamed ceiling. 'None of my business, I s'pose.'

Vita shifted uncomfortably on the long cushion. 'You're her godfather,' she ventured.

Gilbert scratched his head and stared down at his well-polished shoes. 'Mind if I take my jacket off?'

'Do.' She could see, and was immediately disturbed by the fact, that he needed a moment in which to think. He folded his jacket carefully, laid it over a chair arm and sat down again.

'I thought Danvers dropped her when you

23

moved down here.'

'He did.'

'So it's on again?'

Vita noted the careful presentation of the question. She fingered the leaf design on the cushion. 'I'm sure you'd tell me if there was anything I ought to know. Wouldn't you?'

Gilbert placed his elbows on the chair arms, steepled his fingers and made a sissing sound through his teeth. 'Susanne is twenty-six, Vita.'

She shifted impatiently, gesturing with both hands. 'A very young twenty-six, so far as men are concerned. Girls who spend all their spare time round animals don't become very sophisticated. We—Darren and I—thought when Nigel came to Hammer Place that his attraction was tied up with their shared interests. She used to spend entire weekends over there, mucking out with the stable hands, feeding the horses, checking the tack. And as you know, they often went out together. Then, suddenly, he wasn't there.'

'And his disappearance coincided with Darren's bankruptcy. Yes, I know,' Gilbert added baldly. 'Well, life's like that, Vita. You've found out a bit about it yourself.'

Vita sighed sharply, not for herself but for the whole uncomfortable situation. 'Yes, she's grown up. But she's had a pretty rough time lately. When things are going wrong, that's when people are vulnerable.' She told him how Susanne's job in London had folded.

24

'Is she upset about that?'

'Not really. She saw it coming. But it's disturbing for her. She can do without being taken up by Nigel Danvers and dropped again when it suits him.'

Gilbert considered. She could see he knew something. It was in the narrowing of his blue eyes, the way he held his breath then let it out again. He made his decision and sat forward in his chair.

'You'll know of Colin Cheviot?'

'He owns Stirling Boy.' Everybody in the racing world was talking about Stirling Boy for he had had an unprecedented number of wins during the past year.

'Yes. He's building up his stud. And he's looking for a young trainer. Charlie Brooks is due to retire. He's got his eye on young Nigel.'

'Oh!' Her immediate reaction was that Harvey would be sorry to lose him.

'He's been taking out Colin's daughter. Over a period. Some months.'

'Maybe they've fallen out.'

'If they have, then Colin doesn't know. He's a client of mine. He was in the office yesterday. He talked about marriage.'

Vita's face went still as she waited for him to go on.

'That would be a very nice arrangement for him. Whatever one might think of young Danvers he's got a future. He's the best young trainer in these parts. If Colin got him for a

25

son-in-law . . . well, that's what he was hinting.'

Vita said edgily, 'Maybe he's not interested.'

'Oh, he's interested, all right. He and the girl are seeing a lot of each other. He's playing hard to get. But Colin'll get him, as soon as the price is right. Harvey Bevin can't afford to pay him what he deserves and Colin can. And there are no sons. Young Danvers is no fool,' said Gilbert. 'He'll be taking the lack of an heir into account.'

'So it wasn't the bankruptcy.'

'Oh yes it was,' said her visitor cynically. 'That was when he started to look around.'

She jumped up. 'I'm so sorry, Gilbert. I offered you a drink. What will you have?'

'Vodka, thanks, if you've got it.'

'We've got everything.' She was about to add, 'from the Grange Hill cellar' when she remembered Gilbert was Darren's cousin. Vita went to the corner cupboard for glasses, then brought the bottle and a plate of salted nuts from the kitchen. There wasn't room in this little sitting-room for a drinks cabinet.

'To change to a more cheerful subject,' she said as she came back through the door. 'Susanne's won a cruise for two down the Nile. Ice?'

'Don't bother. Won a cruise down the Nile?' Gilbert looked bemused. 'How do you do that?'

She told him about it.

'Is she taking you with her?'

26

'Me! Taking me? Not likely. I should have such a dull daughter!' Vita's laughter rang out.

'Oh, I don't know.' He helped himself to a handful of nuts. 'You get on well together. Why not?'

'Come on, Gilbert. Young people don't take their mothers on romantic cruises.'

He shrugged. 'I think they ought to. The world would be a better place for it. Who's she taking, then?'

'It's only just happened. She's scarcely come to terms with it. She hasn't even telephoned the organisers.'

Gilbert eyed her speculatively. 'Does young Danvers know about this?'

She was silent, remembering that Susanne had gone riding that morning. She remembered, too, that they had told Harvey the news last night. A dart of suspicion lanced through her mind. 'I suppose he could know.'

Gilbert sought thoughtfully among the nuts for a cashew, found one and raised his eyes, took another sip of his vodka then said ruminatively, gazing at the ceiling, 'I was a young opportunist myself, once. I know how they think. I'd have seen this as a way of getting myself a trip I couldn't afford, and at the same time a means of bringing Colin Cheviot to heel. Where have they gone to eat?'

'The Weavers.'

He looked at his watch. 'It just occurs to me, Felicity will have gone to bridge by now,

27

leaving me a cold dish in the 'fridge. Let's go to The Weavers and have a decent meal.'

'No, really, Gilbert!' Vita began to laugh, but ruefully. 'You can't do that. I'd be delighted to go to a pub with you.'

'Come on,' said her visitor, heaving himself out of his chair, 'we're going to eat at The Weavers.'

'My dear,' Vita protested, 'as you pointed out yourself, Susanne is twenty-six. She can look after herself.'

He stepped close to her and wagged a finger in front of her nose. 'You pointed up the fact that I'm her godfather, implying responsibilities. If she's thinking of making a fool of herself tonight, then I'm darned sure I'm going to be there to nip it in the bud.'

*   *   *

Susanne was lifting a glass of champagne to her lips when a familiar voice said, 'Hello, you two.'

She put her glass down and looked up. 'Gilbert!'

He was standing by the table, hands in pockets, smiling benignly down at her. Behind him Vita stood, looking embarrassed. 'So,' Gilbert said heartily, pushing his chin out, pulling it in again, hurrumphing, 'congratulations are in order, I'm told. You're off on a pleasure cruise. And taking Vita with you.'

Susanne's startled eyes went to her mother's face.

'He's teasing,' she said, looking as though she would like to disappear through the floor. Susanne turned back to Nigel. 'Meet my godfather, Gilbert Ellis. Nigel Danvers, Gilbert.'

The two men nodded. 'I think we've met at the Cheviots,' Gilbert said, looking hard at Nigel.

Nigel stared straight ahead.

'Isn't that so? Met at the Cheviots, didn't we?'

'Gilbert dropped in unexpectedly,' put in Vita, breaking the awkward silence, 'and insisted on taking me out. Felicity's playing bridge. If we'd known you were here of course we wouldn't have dreamt of coming.' She took a pinch of Gilbert's navy-blue sleeve between finger and thumb and attempted to lead him away, 'We'd better go somewhere else, Gilbert, dear.'

'I don't think we need to run away,' Gilbert said affably. He addressed the head waiter who had come to meet them. 'Could you seat us somewhere out of sight of these young people? What about that table behind the King Post?'

The waiter nodded and led the way. Vita fled after him. 'Congratulations again,' Gilbert said. 'Glad you're taking your mother. She could do with a break.'

He caught up with Vita behind the King Post. 'Oh, Gilbert!'

'Slipped off my tongue,' he said unrepentantly as he sat down in the chair the waiter had pulled out for him. 'Put the cat among the pigeons, though, didn't I? No real harm done. Susanne's got free will. And a brain. It'll be interesting to see what she makes of it.'

Susanne, not knowing what to make of the incident, turned to Nigel. He was looking directly in front of him at some point mid-table, right over the single rose in its slender vase. 'What the hell was that about?'

'I'm sorry,' she said. 'It's not like him—'

'I don't mean him coming here,' Nigel made no effort to hide his annoyance. 'I mean, your taking your mother on this cruise.'

She saw sharp lines of disappointment in the turn-down of his mouth, anger in a cleft running from his nose to his chin. But hadn't she known since this morning, though refusing to accept it, that Harvey had spilt the beans? It had been blindingly obvious in Nigel's grooming and tacking up Silver Penny, something he had never done for her before, in his solicitude when they were riding. In his congratulations though he knew she was perfectly capable of handling the new horse. And finally it had been there in his invitation to this expensive restaurant. He had never taken her to anything more glamourous than a pub before. She had known, but she hadn't cared. She had been intoxicated by the thought of Nigel and herself standing on the deck of a river boat on the Nile with that great red sun going down behind the palm trees.

'Why was he banging on about the Cheviots?' she asked, by-passing his question because she didn't know how to answer it.

'God knows.'

'Roberta Cheviot?' She wasn't such a fool as to imagine he had gone to bed with a book since dropping her. So why was she angry now? Not angry, she acceded. Aggrieved that Gilbert had spiked her foolish dream? No. He had only turned it round. It could still be saved.

'I've taken her out. Yes.' Nigel was gathering himself together again. 'And I've taken you out. And I've been to parties at the Cheviots. As he said, he met me there.'

She smiled at him, wanting to be forgiven for her godfather's interference.

But Nigel didn't see the smile. He had lifted the champagne bottle from its bed of ice and was measuring with his eyes the amount left in the bottle. 'Here, let me top your glass up. So your mother wasn't all that busy,' he said. 'I thought you meant she was busy with her secondhand clothes.' He looked up into her startled eyes. 'Well, they are secondhand, aren't they?' he asked innocently. His own

31

eyes were running accusingly over her Miss Selfridge two-piece.

She raised her eyes and took a sip. 'I buy my own clothes from chain stores,' she said stiffly. 'Vita's business is with designer labels.' She hadn't meant to sound resentful. Or apologetic. The evening was deteriorating; falling about her ears.

'But secondhand,' he persisted, looking into her eyes, wanting her to shamefully admit that which he had made shameful.

Choosing her tone very carefully she said, 'If you wanted to call them secondhand, you could.'

'What would you call them?'

'Designer, and Couture, and Home-based Shopping are the words we use. There's no need to spoil the evening just because a mistake has been made.'

'Mistake?' He looked surprised.

There was nothing to lose now. 'Let's be honest with each other, Nigel,' she said. 'You thought I might ask you to come with me to Egypt.'

Nigel ignored her hands, extended so that he might take them in his, a gesture of conciliation.

'How blunt you are tonight. I certainly didn't expect you to take your old mother.'

'She's forty-seven,' said Susanne, containing the disappointment in a carefully judged reply. 'Precisely nineteen years older than you.'

'That's what I said. Old enough to be my mother, too.' At last he took hold of her fingers and lifted them. 'I was a bastard, wasn't I?' He gave her his most winning smile and kissed the back of her hand. 'No hard feelings?'

She looked at the fan of soft, shining hair that had fallen on his forehead, hardened her heart and made herself say, 'I'm afraid you've blown it, Nigel.'

A flicker of a thoughtful smile hovered round his mouth. She could tell he was reading her uncertainty, perhaps even her longing. 'We could wipe the slate clean and start again. Let's have another bottle of champers.' He swung round in his chair. 'Waiter!'

She pointed out that he was driving.

'I drive better drunk than sober.'

'Faster. Don't you mean faster? I wish you wouldn't, Nigel.' Out of the corner of her eye she saw Vita and Gilbert making a discreet exit.

'Better,' he insisted. He turned to the hovering wine waiter. 'Another bottle, please.'

She protested, 'I don't want to drink any more and I don't want you to drink the whole bottle.'

'Relax and have fun. Come on. You're too serious. You mustn't let life become a great worry.' He was urging her to smile at him while the waiter went through the elaborate ritual of uncorking the champagne. They saw the other diners turn their way, smilingly, as the cork shot into the air. It was hard not to smile back, though that was admitting there was a celebration. The waiter re-filled her glass.

'To us,' said Nigel, holding his glass towards her, indicating that she raise hers.

The bubbles caught in her nose.

'Great stuff,' he said.

He was right, of course. She took a sip, though knowing she had had as much as she could reasonably carry. Another sip and her head grew light. She allowed herself to remember the dream. They loitered over dinner.

He was relentless in his wooing. He was light-hearted. He said amusing things about their friends. He talked of Silver Penny's chances at Newmarket. He reminded her that they had a great deal in common. He said regretfully he'd never travelled. 'Never had enough money,' he said.

She thought of dancing with him on deck under a tropical moon. She saw Egypt bathed in a golden glow. The two of them, arms entwined on the deck of a glamorous, white-painted ship. She heard soft music in the distance. All her life there would be the memory of this handsome, fun man sharing a holiday with her under a tropical moon. A little voice in the back of her mind whispered that he could be unkind. Had been very unkind about Vita's business. But he would be lovely to her on the cruise because he wanted so badly to go.

He leaned towards her. Looked into her eyes. 'You're not really taking your mother on the Nile, are you?' He sounded incredulous, as though he was seeing in his mind's eye an old lady labouring across the deck of the river boat in an outlandish array of secondhand clothes.

Susanne suddenly saw him very, very clearly and she was angry. Angry with herself for the delusion she had allowed. She could not be angry with him for being what he was. 'This evening isn't working on any level,' she said. 'I think I'd like to go home. But I won't bother you.' She pushed her chair back and stood up. 'I'll get a taxi,' she said.

His hand came out in a rapid and decisive movement. 'That you will not. You'll sit there while I call for the bill.'

She thought it best to comply. She didn't want a scene. She sat mutely and his hand withdrew. The waiter came and discreetly placed a saucer in front of him with the bill folded. He flipped it open. A spasm of anger contorted his features

'I'll pay my share,' she offered, recognising he had expected a return on his investment. Ignoring her, he slapped down his credit card. She didn't want to get into the car with him but she did. She felt the evening had to be tidied up decently.

He drove as he rode, with an air of knowing exactly what he was doing. Neither of them spoke. Gilbert had parked his car considerately on the edge of the grass leaving them room to turn. He swung violently round, backed with a speed that left her gasping, then straightened up facing the cart track. She slid out of her seat. 'I'm sorry,' she said. 'I'm really very sorry that the evening turned out like this.'

He didn't look at her. He hadn't let the car out of gear. He roared away without a backward glance.

The door leading from the hall into the sitting-room lay open. She couldn't get to the stairs without being seen. She heaved a sharp sigh and went to stand in the doorway.

Her godfather was leaning back in one of the big chairs, his hands behind his head. Her mother, looking strained, was sitting bolt upright on the edge of the sofa, her hands awkwardly in her lap.

'Darling, do come in,' she said. 'Gilbert wants to say he's sorry.'

'He doesn't look sorry,' she said.

'Your mother speaks for herself. She's sorry I was such a crass, interfering bore.'

Susanne gave him a level look. 'Then why?'

'You'll thank me one day. As your godfather I'm responsible for seeing you don't make a fool of yourself.'

'I thought you were responsible for my

36

religious education.'

'Don't be angry, Susie.'

'I am,' she said. 'Why can't you leave me to make my own mistakes? It could have been fun.'

She saw their faces change. Thought they were going to laugh. She couldn't bear it. She turned abruptly, hit her head on the door frame and burst into tears.

*   *   *

'Don't be ridiculous,' Vita said the next morning, laughing as she filled the electric kettle at the tiny sink. 'Of course I'm not going with you.'

Outside the early morning mist was clearing. A late swallow swooped past the window. 'As a matter of fact, you are. Punishment for interfering.' Susanne, at the scrubbed table, took a large mouthful of egg. The early morning ride gave her a lusty appetite. Nigel had taken part in the work-out, Harvey had not appeared. She had been looking forward to riding Silver Penny again but Nigel appropriated him without a word of explanation. To be fair, he did not owe her one. She regretted having been thrust into a position where she could view this darker side of the man she had admired so much. She was sorry to have made an enemy of him. She half expected him to say she needn't come again, but he didn't. Hadn't the right, anyway. But even if she had to appeal to Harvey for help, Nigel could make things difficult. He was in charge.

'You've got masses of friends,' said Vita reaching for the cornflakes.

'Friends with jobs. It's November. They've all used up their hols. You,' said Susanne with soft force, 'are coming with me. We'll help ourselves to your stock.' She nearly said secondhand clothes but stopped herself in time. She sat back in her chair, pushed her hands down into the pockets of her jodhpurs and continued, 'So, fortified with clothes we can't afford, let's go off on this cruise we can't afford and swan around like millionaries. It'll probably be the last time we have an opportunity to cut a dash. Only remember not to give our address to any of the tycoons we meet. They wouldn't want to risk their Rolls Royces on our farm track.'

Vita set about clearing the table. Butter in the fridge. Salt in the cupboard. Dishes in the sink. She opened the window to clear the smell of stale bacon and egg. When that was done she stood with both hands on the table looking down at her daughter. 'I'm sorry about what happened, dear. I'm sure Gilbert would have found a more tactful way to deal with the matter if he'd had time to think about it. He only had your interests at heart.'

'He could have fooled me. He doesn't like

Nigel.'

Vita thought carefully before she spoke. 'Gilbert believes Nigel is an opportunist.'

'Opportunists can be good fun.'

Vita went back to her chair and sat down again. She put her elbows on the table and her chin in her hands. The electric kettle let out a shriek then turned itself off. 'Listen, dear, I didn't want to tell you this but I can see I have to.'

'More bad news?'

She told Susanne what Gilbert had told her about Nigel's plans.

Susanne heard her out, blank-faced.

'I think you might be rather, let's say, upset, if he took this trip with you then came back and married Roberta Cheviot. Look dear,' she leaned forward, her eyes large and apologetic, 'you know I don't like interfering, but you might not like the gossip. And Roberta's hardly going to like it, either.'

Susanne stared at an oak beam in the low ceiling.

'I'll leave you to think about it.' Vita tactfully left the room.

'Sod it!' said Susanne under her breath. She felt better after that.

*   *   *

Vita's argument that a girl didn't take her mother on a romantic cruise began to take on a different shape. 'Let's face it,' Susanne said, 'you're the attractive one. I might get a rich stepfather out of this. If I had one of those he'd have the right to stop Gilbert interfering in my life.'

After a while they found themselves, though still at loggerheads on the issue, laughing about it. 'And I couldn't go off in Valentino and Féraud creations in the company of a girlfriend wearing Dorothy Perkins. Think of the awkwardness.'

'You've got other men friends.'

'We might have to share a cabin.' Susanne widened her eyes, prepared to shock. 'There's no one I especially want to sleep with except the two-timing opportunist.'

'Ring up and find out.'

She returned from telephoning to say yes, they would have to share a cabin. 'That leaves you, Vita. In the present climate, if one shares a room with a girlfriend one will almost certainly be suspected of lesbianism. I don't think even the most sophisticated Nile cruiser would think I might be having sexual relations with my mother.'

Vita put a hand to her head in that way she had when things had gone beyond where she could cope. 'I don't know how to talk to you when you're in this mood.'

Susanne put an arm through hers and led her towards the dining-room that had become a salon. 'Let's go and look at some clothes. I'm

40

getting enthusiastic about the idea of getting you off with a rich widower.'

'Surely you know cruises are full of rich women looking for husbands. Rich widowers don't last long on their own,' her mother retorted.

'None of the rich widows will be as handsome as you in an Ungaro shift, darling.' Susanne was quite certain of that.

She examined the fabrics, letting them slide silkily through her fingers. The red of the Danish flag, the salmon of a flamingo's feathery neck. The delicate blue of a robin's egg. Such lovely clothes they were. She realised she had never looked closely at them before. They had been Vita's business, not part of her hurrying, scurrying business world. Now she recognised their potential even in the way the material draped on a hanger.

'The trouble is,' she muttered as she chose a plain lavender silk with 'exclusive' written into its slinky folds, 'how does one go back to Miss Selfridge or Marks and Spencer afterwards?'

Vita gave her a buttoned-up smile. 'You'll manage.'

Even prepared in her mind, Susanne was surprised at what the Ungaro shift did for her. She scarcely recognised the woman looking back from the mirror. She had been going to have her hair cut. Now she changed her mind. These clothes called for long hair, well-groomed. The outdoor look, the business girl

41

look, had fallen away.

'I don't see myself mucking out the stables in this,' she called across the tiny passage.

Vita came and stood in the doorway wearing a Louis Féraud two piece. 'You do look expensive!'

'Don't I just!' Susanne grinned. Vita herself was elegance personified except for the crumple of anxiety in her face.

'Would you like a last opportunity to change your mind?'

'Don't want to share a cabin with me? Is that it?' Susanne gave her a sly, teasing glance.

Vita looked embarrassed. 'Mothers and daughters simply don't go holidaying together in this day and age.'

'You can do anything in this day and age,' Susanne retorted. She felt she was stepping out into the unknown.

CHAPTER THREE

Gilbert and Felicity drove them to Heathrow. The M25 was blocked so they were late arriving. 'Don't worry,' Gilbert told them confidently as he unloaded their bags out of the boot of his BMW at the entrance to Departures. 'Tour people always ask you to come early. It saves them stress, never mind that you have to stand around for hours.'

'Good of you to take your mother,' he whispered as he kissed Susanne goodbye. 'She deserves a holiday.'

'Oh, sure. No problem.' She wondered if he had forgotten who got them into this ridiculous situation.

They knew immediately they walked into the waiting group in the departure lounge that they were in the wrong clothes. Marks and Spencer would have been adequate. These middle-aged to elderly people—what would Nigel have made of them? Susanne wondered—wouldn't recognise a Fellini trouser suit but they saw the difference, saw the glossy look expensive clothes convey, and were overawed. They turned away, talking busily to each other, casting surreptitious glances at the newcomers when they thought they weren't looking. The people who had given the prize had omitted to say this was a cut-price package.

The archaeologist, a rangy young man with fair hair flopping over a freckled forehead loped up and introduced himself. 'I'm Peter Quest.' He was grinning all over his face at finding someone of his own generation to talk to. He hovered round Susanne, not talking much, mainly looking at her as though she was the icing on his tour cake.

Vita saved her by inviting her along to the Duty Free. 'So who's made a conquest?' she taunted Susanne good-humouredly. 'Not the phoney rich divorcée.'

'Ugh,' said Susanne.

*   *   *

The sand hills were by turns red, cinnamon-coloured and pale beige. They ran in a great sweep east from the snaking Nile to the Red Sea. From where they sat in the plane they could glimpse the entrance to the Suez Canal.

They changed planes in Cairo for the flight on to Luxor. The young archaeologist seated himself across the aisle from Susanne and asked her if was her first trip to Egypt.

Susanne nodded. 'I've been all over the place back-packing but I imagine one doesn't do that here.'

He was horrified at the idea. 'I should think not. You'd soon get into trouble.' His eyes roved down the length of her, from her shining fair hair to her frail sandals. There had been necessary purchases. One didn't wear Doc Martens with a silk Versace suit. 'You don't look the type to back-pack,' he said.

'What's the type?' she asked him straightforwardly.

'Er ...' he looked her over again and uttered an embarrassed little laugh.

'You should see me in ragged old jeans with my hair shoved up under one of those straw hats with corks dangling from the brim. I look the part all right. A cartoon Aussie. And when

44

I got to India I took to the sari like a duck to water.'

His wide-set eyes, mouse-coloured, moved up to her pale blonde hair. 'Nobody would take you for an Indian, that's for sure.' He asked her where else she had been.

'All the places back-packers go. There's a lot to see between England and New Zealand. My father gave me a lump sum for my twenty-first birthday and I chose to blow it that way.'

'Whew!' The mouse eyes were full of wary admiration. 'No regrets?'

'Absolutely not.' Of course there were regrets. She could have helped out when things went wrong, but that wasn't the kind of thing one told a stranger. 'I could have put it into shares and they could have dropped,' she said lightly. 'No one can take that adventure away from me.'

'No,' he said. 'Er . . .no.'

'You haven't done anything like that?'

'Archaeology has terrific potential for travel. I've got a lifetime of digging in foreign places ahead of me. And ancient civilisations don't threaten you like real life.' He seemed pleased about that.

Vita, half listening, with her head in her paperback thought with a feeling of regret that this young man wasn't going to interest Susanne. A pity. A little romance on the rebound might have been a good thing.

They came down at Luxor into a world of

45

sand and sand-coloured airport buildings. When the doors were opened the heat struck up from the landing strip and poured into the cabin. Passengers squirmed in their seats, fanned themselves with newspapers. The archaeologist produced a magazine from his canvas bag and waved it in front of his face. 'It's not like this all the time. I hope you've brought something warm for the evenings,' he said. 'It can get jolly cold when the sun goes down.'

'I know. We've brought wraps.' Vita had hung on to a cashmere stole, relic of better times, and Susanne had found a quilted jacket among the designer stock. She vigorously fanned her face with her paperback, blowing the incipient embarrassment away, hoping the rest of the party weren't going to show them up by appearing in white woolly cardigans.

The plane took off again, to the relief of all.

'Look below,' said Peter pointing out of the window as they circled over Aswan. 'You can see the dam now. One of the largest man-made structures in the world.' And there it was, its great granite blocks hedging on one side the vast, calm lake whilst from the other spurted a raging torrent. The passengers were eagerly stretching over one another in order to see out of the windows.

'It's nearly three miles wide and three hundred and sixty feet high. Seventeen times bigger than the Great Pyramid of Cheops.'

He had all the facts. Susanne hoped he wasn't going to feel impelled to unload them on her. They came in to land. She reached up into the luggage rack and brought out the two big hats. A good plain straw for her, designed by Valentino and one slightly more elegant for Vita by Philip Treacy. Looking at them now with a nervous and newly critical eye, Susanne told herself firmly that good straws would look equally at home on the Nile as at Ascot. Vita put hers on and Susanne carried her model in her hand. As they descended the steps the heat came up to meet them, hot as a furnace. She hurriedly put the hat on her head.

Long, white-railed decks, big windows. *Phoenix* sat on the waters of the Nile like one of those Mississippi paddle steamers that were familiar from Hollywood films. One could imagine lovely southern belles in crinolines holding parasols and taking their ease on the deck. Mint juleps dispensed by black plantation slaves. The tourists waited on the concrete strip, more of a footpath than a landing stage, to be led aboard. The archaeologist came up. 'This is as far as the boats can go,' he said then pointed upstream. 'The cataract's that way. If you want to go south to Wadi Halfa or Khartoum you change boats here, but it's not so interesting as the stretch we're going on.'

'Another time,' said Vita, knowing there would never be another time. She was

47

remembering the first-class hotels she had stayed in in glamorous cities all round the world. Darren had not been adventurous. He would never have thought of taking her on a riverboat cruise on the Nile. Their travels took them to meet business people. They ate good meals and drank good wines and wore formal clothes. Darren, she remembered, looking at Peter in his khaki-coloured cotton shirt that was open at the neck, and his loose cotton trousers, had never looked like that. She was gratified to realise she could now think of her errant husband with a degree of dispassion. Susanne was right, she thought. Right about us both. We needed this. There was something eminently relaxing about being far beyond the clawing reach of one's responsibilities and disappointments.

As they prepared to descend the steps to the gang-plank, small boys with dark faces and big black eyes clustered round offering for sale little carved figures, scarabs, nuts and sweets.

'You have to bargain,' Peter said, again hovering at Susanne's side. He reminded her of a friendly crane, all wings and legs. 'Never pay the asking price,' was his next bit of information, 'a third is about right.'

Vita bought a scarab without having to bargain. Even as she examined the stone the price dropped. 'Fifty *piastres*, forty. Twenty.' She saw the anxiety behind the eagerness in their handsome, dirty little faces and her heart melted. 'Right, I'll have this one,' she said and produced some coins. 'Oh Lord, that was a mistake,' she wailed as a clamorous crowd of children descended upon her. Tenacious little brown hands grasped her forearms, trays of polished stones were pushed under her nose. She couldn't move ahead. A tall man in a long white gown with a scarlet turban on the back of his head came up the steps and shooed the little pedlars away. They made their way down on to the gangplank.

The crew were lined up to welcome them aboard, all dignified and elegant in striped cotton gowns that reached down to their feet. Uniform white caps of folded cotton sat on their heads. They smiled, exposing gleaming white teeth. A bright-faced boy with enormous brown eyes took Susanne and Vita up two companionways to the top deck and flung open the door of a cabin situated immediately behind the deck house.

'Good cabin?' he asked anxiously, those wonderful eyes searching their faces for incipient signs of displeasure. 'Good for you?'

'Indeed it is,' Vita agreed, recognising that as the boat sailed back down the river towards Cairo they would have a view ahead as well as out over the desert. Susanne went inside and looked round. There were two beds, and in the narrow space between them, a mat. In the corner, a wardrobe, and a small chest of drawers. A door led into a tiny bathroom.

'Good cabin,' repeated the boy, thrusting out his hand. '*Baksheesh* for good cabin.'

Vita dropped some local currency into his little palm and he retreated smiling broadly.

'Have you sorted out your *piastres* from your ten p's?'

'I don't think I have,' Vita replied. 'He did seem faintly surprised. And very pleased. We had better find out about tipping.'

'It's called *baksheesh*.'

'That's what he said.' She turned the word over her tongue.

They unpacked their clothes, their faces crumpling with anxiety. They were going to look like a couple of orchids in a bed of garden weeds. And they weren't going to make friends. That had been evident at Heathrow. Vita's eyes rested on the vast cashmere shawl that was designed to swirl round her shoulders and trail its corners down to the hem of her skirt. 'Oh God!' she muttered. And then, 'I'm going to take a shower.' There was no air conditioning on *Phoenix*, only a fan in the ceiling. The cabin was very hot. She switched the fan on.

Susanne wandered out on deck and stood looking across at the bank where pedlars in their tiny turbans and long grubby *galabiyas* still hung around hopefully. She tried to imagine Nigel here, and failed. The sand and the brown waters of the Nile had come between them. She wondered why she had

50

allowed Gilbert and Vita to see that she had been in love with him, then remembered it had been the truth at the time. But she wasn't in love now. From this distance she could see him quite, quite clearly. She thought, he belongs with Harvey's horses. He was part of the package. Funny I had to come to Egypt to see that.

'Your turn,' Vita called. 'You'd better get started. We've only a few moments before lunch.'

Susanne came back inside, negotiated her way past Vita in the narrow space between the bed ends and the wall, tossed her clothes on to a bed and entered the bathroom. Soap here. Towel precariously placed there. This must be the smallest handbasin in the world. She stepped under a spray of cold water with a great sigh of relief.

Vita was standing by the door looking svelte in a Karen Millen cotton sheath. Susanne stopped to stare at her. 'The trouble with you,' she said, trying not to sound apprehensive, 'is that even in your raggedy gardening jeans with a woolly hat on your head you manage to look expensive.'

Vita glanced down at her slender body and shook her head ruefully.

'We could always tell them the truth. I mean that I won the trip in a competition that could have been done by a five year old. Dad's bankrupt. We deal in secondhand clothes.'

'Do you have to be quite so brutal?' Vita stared at her in shocked surprise.

'No. It's something Nigel said. I thought it might be useful in helping to get a perspective.'

Vita looked disheartened. 'Get dressed. I can hear them rolling in to lunch.'

Maybe Nigel's rudeness had a place in the scheme of things, Susanne thought as she slid her own sheath off the hanger, conspicuously ignoring the label. Nothing exists except what's in the mind. It's only a few steps from Vita's business to the High Street Oxfam. I shall instil into my mind the fact that I could have bought this at Oxfam. It was worth a try.

The other members of the party were already seated when they arrived at the door of the dining-room. They found an empty table by the door and sat down. Nobody was looking at them. They weren't wanted at anyone's table. They were too different. They sat back, idly watching the waiters as they moved round soundlessly in their handsome, gold-embroidered kaftans and soft leather sandals.

'It's rather like being on a film set,' Vita said, musing.

The archaeologist, coming to join them, overheard her words. 'It's all very unreal. You're not going to be here long enough to come to terms with it, so don't try. The waiters are Nubians. They're darker, grander and a good deal taller than the locals. They come

52

from the south. May I sit with you?'

It was left to Vita to indicate the chair beside her. This is how it is to be, Susanne thought. And there will be sly smiles and knowing looks from the rest of the party. She resigned herself to what seemed inevitable. Peter pulled out the chair opposite and sat down. He had a pleasant enough face, dotted with freckles, and pale hair. Sandy, she would have said in England but they weren't in England now and the sandhills they had flown over were quite a different colour. 'By the way,' he said eagerly as he unfolded his napkin, 'you will remember not to drink the water, won't you?'

Susanne folded her arms on the table. 'And we won't put ice blocks in our drinks because they're made from water, and we won't eat salad because the kitchen hands may have washed it in the Nile.'

He grinned uncertainly and she was sorry. If she was to have his undivided attention for the next ten days, short of anaesthetising herself mentally, she was going to have to accustom herself to his facts and figures. She smiled at him kindly and he grinned back.

'Got it in one. If in doubt, consult me,' he said bossily. 'I shan't be far away. I'm going to offer to take a group ashore after lunch. Do you want to sleep off the journey, or would you like to join me?'

'I'll have a rest,' said Vita.

Susanne said impatiently, 'She's got a mother-and-daughter complex. She thinks I don't like her breathing down my neck when in fact there's nothing I like better. Of course she will not have a rest.'

'I can see who's in charge,' said Peter archly. Susanne looked away. He rose, tapped the table with his spoon and made his announcement about the trip to the *souk*, then asked for a show of hands. Vita counted them and decided as there would be a crowd, she would go after all.

A vast Egyptian with his long white *galabiya* stretched over his egg-shaped stomach had made an appearance in the doorway. He wore a red fez and wonderful embroidered slippers.

'That's Hassan. Our guide for the tour.' Peter jumped up to greet him.

Filling the doorway, Hassan looked benignly over the company. He told them about himself. That he spoke perfect English, as was indeed obvious. That he had travelled up and down the Nile for forty years. That he was born of Bedouin stock.

'Bedouins are nomads of the desert,' Peter intervened knowledgeably.

He finished by warning them to be careful of the food. 'Nearly everyone gets gyppy tummy,' he said. 'I get it myself sometimes. And watch that dangerous sun.'

He offered to negotiate for them with shopkeepers in the *souks*. 'You have to recognise that they must live, but also that they are rascals. And that's enough for the moment,' he said. 'There's a lot of time ahead of us.' He looked forward to making new friends. Then he progressed through the dining room in the wake of a waiter, like a ship in full sail.

Peter said, 'He's a famous character. We're lucky to have him. He has a fund of stories and he's good company. Don't offer him a drink. He's a Muslim. Muslims don't drink.'

'You forget I walked through India.'

'No, I didn't forget. I didn't believe it,' he said.

'Why not?'

'Come on Susanne, let's face it, you're not the type.' He noted her annoyed expression and added hurriedly, 'I believe you've been to India. But not walking.'

'Let's go out on deck,' said Vita briskly and they rose from their seats.

'I'm going to get awfully tired of this,' said Susanne as they turned their backs on the dining room.

*   *   *

Hassan, the impressive Egyptian guide, gathered the party together and led them ashore where a row of horse-drawn carriages awaited them. Susanne climbed aboard and was disconcerted when Peter followed her. She called to her mother but Vita had already turned tactfully away. Susanne muttered 'Damn,' under her breath, knowing she would be stuck with the archaeologist all afternoon.

The heat was overwhelming. It came down from a white-hot sky and was reflected up from the stones. Bare-footed men in the ubiquitous dirty white *galabiya* scattered as they passed. So many people! And nearly all men. Where were the women?

Peter was quick to explain that the women were at home. Egyptian females had little freedom. Those who were in the street were heavily veiled, as though the faces beneath those huge dark eyes were too private to be exposed to the view of strangers. Or, as Peter was convinced, they were some man's exclusive private property.

They left the carriages on the outskirts of the *souk* and, led by Hassan, entered the busy, enclosed lanes where tiny, dark shops proliferated. It was blessedly cool there, but only for a few moments. They soon realised they had exchanged one kind of heat for another. Here the crush of humanity was overwhelming, the air turgid, smelling of dust and sweat. Salesmen cajoled them.

'Jewellery? You want jewellery?' Susanne turned aside into a dark cave of a shop and was immediately, and rather frighteningly, surrounded by eager men, hemmed in by their black eyes, their little red fezzes, their long bodies slim in grubby white *galabiyas*.

'You buy?' They thrust under her nose trays full of wonderful yellow gold and glowing desert stones.

She forgot her initial fear. There was a necklace that might have graced the slim neck of Cleopatra or Nefertiti, jewelled pendants fashioned as strange creatures with a human head, a bird's wing, a fish's tail. Gleaming scarabs. Enchanted, she picked up one after another.

'You buy? You rich English,' said one of the men with disarming certainty. 'You buy.'

She ran her fingers over the intricately wrought handle of a dagger, its fine gilt lattice work, its tiny, sturdy decorative bands. Her fingers lovingly stroked a ring of rich red carnelian, feeling the life in the stones.

A strident English voice behind her said, 'Hey! What's going on here?' The anxious salesmen fell back as Peter thrust his way through. 'You're not buying that tourist junk, are you?' he enquired robustly. 'It's not real gold, you know.'

The magic went. The Egyptians regarded her in silence with sad eyes. One of them ventured, 'Real desert stones.'

'I think you'll find they're flawed,' said Peter.

Though he spoke in a low voice now and the Egyptians may not have understood him, Susanne turned away, embarrassed.

'You'd better stay with the crowd,' advised Peter, taking a proprietary grip of her arm and leading her back into the *souk*. 'Hassan has taken your mother with the others to a tailor's shop.' He glanced at Susanne's closed face and added with a slightly apologetic air, 'Of course, there's no reason why you shouldn't waste your money any way you like, but I think you'll find when you get home the stuff will look pretty silly with English clothes.'

'Thank you,' she replied, trying not to feel impatient with him.

At the tailor's shop the group were chattering excitedly, fingering the fine cotton on display. 'The best cotton in the world,' as Peter said knowledgeably. 'They can make up a garment by evening. They work fast when there's a boat in.'

'A couple of kaftans might solve our problem.' Susanne looked sideways at her mother.

'Problem?' asked Peter.

'Just a joke,' she said hurriedly. 'I really would like one of those. They strike me as a good cover up for the sun on deck.'

Women in the party gathered round, exclaiming. How much would it cost, in this material? In this? Susanne fingered a long robe made of thin cotton material patterned in inch wide stripes.

'What I'd do with it afterwards I can't imagine.' She looked musingly at the range of shapeless garments on show, caught Peter's shrewd glance and said impatiently, 'I'm not one of those ladies of leisure who drift around in long robes for half the morning. I'm up at five o'clock exercising horses. And after that it's to work.'

'Sure.'

She glared at him, briefly met his amused eyes and glanced away only to meet the anxious black eyes of one of the salesmen. 'You buy kaftan? Ladies like kaftan. I measure.'

Already several of their party had succumbed and with a great deal of laughter were submitting to the energetic attentions of men with tape measures. 'Yes, I think I might,' said Susanne. 'Let's have a bit of fancy dress.'

Vita added, 'Why not?' They were urged into the dark interior of the shop. Susanne chose a cinnamon stripe on a cream background. It flattered her skin and would match her hat. Vita chose black and white. A sinewy little man with quick fingers and darting black eyes bustled from one to another, measuring them from back of neck to foot, making suggestions, anxious to please.

'Ready tonight.'

'No, no. We'll be here for a day or two.'

'We bring to boat tomorrow? Breakfast time we come to boat?'

'Oh, all right. But don't stay up all night.'

'I don't think his English is up to that,' said

59

Peter, 'but they'll stay up all night if they have to. They're after business. The tourist boats are a godsend to them.'

They wandered on through the *souk*, in and out of the tiny stores, refusing urgent invitations from vendors of sticky sweets who were carelessly brushing flies from open trays of enticing looking fudge.

'Remember what Hassan said,' Vita murmured. 'Be careful what you eat.'

He beamed approvingly. 'The food is good on board. You do not need this.'

'My mouth is watering, but don't worry, I can be strong-minded.'

They emerged into the different heat of the outdoor afternoon and took a gharry back to the boat. Passengers were lolling on the sun-deck beneath shady umbrellas. The same group of sharp-eyed pedlars hung around at the top of the granite steps urging them to buy silver necklaces, scarabs, strings of beads. The same ragged, dirty children who had been playing in the dust leaped up to run after them, holding out trinkets in the palms of their grubby little hands. The tired travellers shook them off, too discomfited by the heat to protest.

'See you in the bar before dinner,' Peter said. 'I'll buy you a drink.'

Resenting his proprietary air, Susanne replied, 'I'll be in the bar, but you don't have to stand me a drink.' She saw two of the passengers who were watching them exchange arch glances. 'They're all determined we're going to have a love affair,' she muttered to Vita as they climbed the steps to their cabin.

'You'll have to come to terms with it. Anyway, he is very nice.' In her mind Vita was comparing him with Nigel Danvers and finding Peter rather more to her taste.

Susanne opened the door to the cabin, stepped in and flung herself on the bed. She pulled the thin cotton material of her dress away from her chest. 'I'll stretch out while you have first turn in the shower.'

Vita stood looking down at her thoughtfully. 'I'm sure you'd enjoy his company if you gave him a chance.' She picked up the tour brochure. 'He's got quite an impressive pedigree. Listen to this.' She read out, *'Peter Quest, M.A. PH.D. Studied Egyptology at Cambridge. Has excavated at Sakkara. Contributes to various archaeological and historical publications. Lectures in Egyptian hieroglyphics at the University of—'*

'Enough, Mother.' She called Vita that when she showed her maternal side. 'And I'd prefer you to be a companion rather than judge and jury.'

Vita threw a towel at her. 'You'll feel better when you've had a shower.'

Susanne washed her hair and combed it back from her face, careless and uncaring of its effect. She looked at the Louis Féraud dinner

61

dress she had chosen randomly, for the umpteenth time wishing she hadn't raided Vita's stock, hating this false position they found themselves in; hating Peter for saying 'Sure,' in a tone that meant he knew very well she was rich so there was no point in her protesting. She knew she ought to be able to laugh about it but she couldn't.

She went with restless footsteps out on deck. The sun was going down, a startling, flame-coloured ball in an opaque sky, streaked magnificently with vermilion and gold. In the foreground, tall palms stood starkly like black velvet cut-outs against the wild colours behind. She held her breath, thinking she had never seen anything so grand, nor so unreal. Graceful *feluccas*, the Egyptian sailing-boats, slid across the darkening waters of the Nile.

Someone came quietly along the deck and paused beside her. Feeling her nerves sharpen, she looked round, expecting to see Peter but it was the tall Egyptian with the warm brown eyes and fatherly manner who had been introduced to her earlier as the boat's manager.

'Captain?' she had queried.

'No. They call him the manager.'

He said engagingly, 'It is nice to have someone so young on board. We do not have many girls of your age. You are happy with the boat, Miss Landseer?'

'I think it's wonderful, Mr Abdou.' She

62

smiled up at him, glad of his undemanding company.

'There are newer boats with air conditioning and more facilities,' Abdou said, 'but I do not apologise for *Phoenix*. It keeps its guests close to the country. People who come with me experience the real Egypt. You do not do that from an air-conditioned saloon on a fast boat.'

She wondered if he was being tactful, endeavouring to make her feel good about not being on one of the exclusive package tours, but a glance at his kindly brown face told her he meant what he said. 'I'm sure that's right,' she replied. She lifted one hand to the sun. 'Did you ever see anything like that?'

He nodded, smiling. 'Often. I am lucky enough to see it every evening. But I never get used to it.' He turned to look across to the riverbank and Susanne's eyes followed his. A man, formally dressed in navy blue suit, white shirt and tie, was wandering idly, hands in pockets, along the river path. Though his manner was idle he stood erect, back straight and head high. Her mind flew to the ancient Egyptian kings she had seen pictured in the brochures. He had the same way of standing, as though he was held erect by an invisible thread that led direct to the sky.

'Who is he?' she asked, sensing the manager knew; that this man was someone everyone knew. He had an air of one who is accustomed to being recognised. He had paused and now

63

he stood, feet apart, appraising the *Phoenix*, smiling faintly.

'That man,' said Abdou, 'is Captain Saheed, the son of General Saheed, one of our most famous citizens.'

'What is he famous for?'

'He owns and breeds the best horses in Egypt. This son of his is one of the country's best riders.' He glanced down at her. 'Your mother was telling me that you're a very good rider yourself.'

'Not at a national level. But yes, I ride. Tell me about him.'

'He's descended from our royal family, which you may know had to go into exile in nineteen fifty-two. This . . .'

Susanne did not hear the rest of his sentence for at that moment the man looked up. Her eyes met his, seemed to envelop her, seemed to look right through her, and at the same time, contain her. She heard Abdou say, 'I will go down and ask him if he would like to come aboard.'

Susanne shook herself out of her trance and swung round. The door to her cabin was closed. She opened it and called to Vita. Her voice sounded urgent to her own ears though there was no urgency. There was no reply. She went into the bathroom and looked in the small mirror over the handbasin. Wide, dazed eyes looked back at her. She glanced down at her dress, looked back at her carelessly combed hair; picked up a lipstick; put it down again. She had a sense of something having happened. Something beyond her control.

CHAPTER FOUR

She swung away from the mirror without doing anything to her hair, without regret at not having made the best of herself. Her mind had gone somewhere else. She began to descend the outside steps.

On the deck below, outside the bar, Peter was waiting. 'Ah, here you are,' he said. 'Now, what are you going to have to drink?' He took her arm and led her, unprotesting, inside. She could hear voices coming up from the deck below. Mr Abdou's familiar tones, then a firm, rich voice, somehow accentless.

'I said, what will you have?'

She started. 'Sorry. Tonic.'

'In what?' He grinned, conscious of being witty.

She shook the strangeness away. 'Gin . . . er . . . thanks.'

He led her over to the bar. A group of people moved aside to let them through, smiling approvingly because the only young woman on board had teamed up with the young archaeologist. She felt she had moved beyond them and their fatuous smiles. She was standing on the brink of something she did not as yet understand. Someone spoke to her and she answered. Peter handed her a glass. 'Say when.'

She stared without seeing at the tonic going in to the glass.

'Hey, do you really want to drown it?' Peter was looking at her with a puzzled expression. 'You haven't got sunstroke have you?'

Susanne made a tremendous effort to pull herself together and, laughing, she held up her glass. Someone said, 'Here's to a wonderful trip.' Then Abdou came in with the visitor and all heads turned.

General Saheed's son was not tall by English standards. His height was in the way he held himself, with inborn pride, as though in his mind he was the tallest man in the room. Chatter in the bar stopped abruptly. The two men crossed the threshold. The visitor inclined his head faintly, an eagle's head, a falcon's head, looking down from away up there where he dwelt, to include everyone in the room.

Now that he was close to her Susanne saw his eyes were of a surprising blue, not sapphire, not cornflower, not any blue she had ever seen and they were almond-shaped, like the kohl-rimmed eyes of the ancient Pharaohs. In place of the kohl this man had the thickest lashes she had ever seen, as beautiful as any woman's. Those eyes again met hers and continued to hold her gaze as he walked with

66

the manager towards the bar. The barman dropped what he was doing and sidled swiftly along to serve Abdou and his guest.

'Who the dickens is that?' asked Peter. 'Someone very important, obviously.'

She told him what Abdou had said. 'What! A relation of King Farouk? I shouldn't think that would be anything to be proud of,' Peter commented disparagingly. 'He was a dissolute rascal. D'you know your Egyptian history?'

'I shouldn't think this man had been born when his dissolute rascal of an ancestor was thrown out,' someone put in. 'We've had a few kings in the past whom we're not very proud of. Heh?'

They both turned. It was a military-looking man who had spoken. A solid-looking man with white sideboards, a fierce expression and twinkly eyes. Vita, who was standing by him, introduced them. 'Colonel Alison. My daughter.' Then Abdou and the visitor came away from the bar carrying their drinks. Susanne remembered Peter saying they should not offer Hassan a drink because his religion did not allow for it. Weren't all Egyptians Muslims? She looked at the glass of whisky in the visitor's hand. Then she lifted her eyes.

He was looking directly at her while speaking to Abdou. Together, they came forward.

'Captain Saheed, may I present Miss Landseer,' said the manager courteously and

Saheed held out his hand. A ripple of surprised interest went round the room when Abdou did not proceed to introduce him to anyone else. And Saheed held her hand far too long. She tried to withdraw it, felt his fingers close. Then Abdou said urbanely, 'And this is our official archaeologist, Mr Quest. Mrs Landseer. Colonel Alison.' Saheed reluctantly released Susanne's fingers and shook the others by the hand, then rested those amazing eyes on her again.

'Miss Landseer also rides,' said Abdou. 'She has been telling me about it.'

'When you are in Cairo you must come riding with me in the desert. I have a stable full of Arab horses.'

'Yes,' she returned promptly. 'I would love to.' She was glowing inside; standing on tiptoes in her mind.

'You are a good rider?'

'Yes,' she replied with total confidence. Had he taken in what she said? His eyes did not leave her face. She felt blinded by their blue gaze. Hypnotised. She felt if he turned and walked out of the bar she would be powerless to prevent herself from following him. Abdou led his attention away to some other passengers who were lining up, watching and listening, hoping to be introduced.

Peter said sourly, 'You seem to have made a hit. I'd be careful, if I were you.'

She asked, laughing, 'Because he has a

68

dissolute ancestor?'

'He's probably married, and dissolute himself. I wouldn't like to think of you going out alone in the desert with an Egyptian, whoever he was. I wouldn't trust him an inch.'

'Because he's a foreigner?' She looked under her lashes at him. 'Vita read out your pedigree on the brochure. You dig abroad. You must be accustomed to foreigners.'

'Cheap labour,' he retorted. 'Not the cousins of kings.'

'Look what you've missed.' She spun round to hide her face from him, thinking that the warmth moving out from her heart must be felt, or seen like a rosy cloud. At that moment Hassan, the enormous guide, came into the bar, like a star in musical comedy, she thought delightedly, in his red evening robe, his black face gleaming beneath the startlingly white turban-like headdress. Colours had become more intense in her eye and mind. He made his way to Peter, stopped in front of him, spoke.

Peter's face fell.

'What!' she heard him exclaim in a voice of disbelief. Then, 'Oh, hell!' He glanced at his watch then looked round the room. 'I'd better make an announcement. I s'pose most people are here now.' He stepped over to the bar, picked up a bottle opener and banged on the wood. The lively chatter faded. Everyone turned to look his way.

'Some of you have booked on the flight to Abu Simbel tomorrow. I'm afraid there's a hitch,' he said. 'We may not be able to go.' A murmur of disappointment floated round the room. He apologised, saying he would naturally do what he could. 'But we haven't got any details yet, only a message that the plane isn't available.'

The tour manager hurried to consult with him. People fell into little groups, expressing their disappointment. The majority of the passengers had paid extra to see the reconstructed temples of Rameses II and Nefertiti.

A voice behind Susanne asked, 'You are disappointed, Miss Landseer?'

She turned and looked full into the Egyptian's face. There was again that *frisson* of excitement. 'No, actually I'm not going, so it doesn't affect me.'

He nodded and smiled, exposing a perfect set of white teeth. 'I will see what I can do. My father is not without influence. He is here at the Cataract Hotel today to arrange for a visit by foreign royalty. We are to have dinner with a head of government at nine this evening. That is why I am dressed like this.' He indicated his impeccable suit. 'My father was busy with his papers and I grew bored with waiting for time to pass, so I took a stroll down river.' He paused, then added softly, 'And found you.'

70

She felt he had written the words on her heart.

'Tonight, I will get my father to look into this matter of the plane,' he said. 'If anyone can arrange a replacement, I'm sure he can.' He spoke as though the waving of a magic wand was to him an everyday occurrence.

'Peter would be very pleased to hear that.' Susanne glanced across the room. The archaeologist was now surrounded by a group of vociferous people venting their disappointment, asking for explanations, insisting upon having their money back.

'Do let's tell him,' Susanne said and went ahead, weaving her way through the crowd, feeling like a starry-eyed princess bearing glad tidings. 'Captain Saheed to the rescue,' she said, speaking with triumph and confidence as though the arrival of a new plane was already pre-ordained.

The group fell back. Saheed explained. A buzz of excitement rose. Peter's face gradually cleared.

'I must go now,' the visitor said. As he turned, his hand brushed Susanne's and she caught her breath. Then the tour operator pushed through the crowd offering fervent thanks and the Egyptian was cut off. She found herself facing Peter again.

'He's going to fix it,' the archaeologist said with satisfaction as they watched the visitor's receding back. 'You'll notice he didn't say,

71

"Don't thank me yet, I can't be sure." I've a feeling he's going to fix it, all right.' He looked hard at Susanne. 'You seem to have been bowled over.'

'You too,' she retorted.

'You're not really going to go riding with him? You wouldn't go out in the desert with a man you've known about a minute and a half?'

'He probably won't follow it up,' she replied, eyes shining, knowing he would. 'But if he does, yes I will. I've got a pair of jeans with me.'

'I should think the last thing you should be worried about, in the circumstances, is what you'll be wearing. Here, let me fill your glass.'

Over in the corner of the bar the Colonel was saying to Vita, 'It would seem your daughter has taken young Saheed's fancy.'

Vita's lips tightened. 'I hope not.'

'You say that with feeling.'

'She's rather vulnerable at the moment. She's just emerged from . . . well, never mind.' Vita added lightly, 'Perhaps a diversion is what she needs.'

'I should warn her,' he replied, smiling, 'that I don't think the Saheed men could be described as diversions. I was stationed in Cairo when I was in my twenties. I knew his father slightly. Even in those days, young as he was, not much older than I was, he was a formidable man. I remember he was thought to be having an affair with a young

72

Englishwoman—no, Irish. County Irish. She was working in the British Consulate. I often wondered what became of her. The father was devastatingly handsome. And very much a ladies' man.'

'His son has inherited his looks, then.'

'Only to a degree. The family resemblance is striking. But he does seem to have inherited the father's personality.' The Colonel rubbed his chin thoughtfully.

That night when they retired Vita looked at her daughter, glowing as though lit by her own aura as she stood tall and slender in her thin cotton nightdress with her fair, shining hair falling over her shoulders. Vita felt troubled, remembering what Colonel Alison had said, that he wondered what had happened to the Irish girl who had worked at the Embassy in his time. She had never seen Susanne like this before.

'What a lovely day!' she was saying, gazing as though at some distant star. 'What a perfectly wonderful, wonderful day! This is another world, is it not? I can scarcely visualise green fields and big trees.' She was silent a moment, then breathed, 'Does England exist?'

Vita said briskly, 'Colonel Alison used to know that man's father. He seems to think the Saheed men are dangerous.'

'Oh yes,' Susanne replied dreamily. 'Oh yes, I think he's probably right.'

The archaeologist came into the dining-room when the tourists were seated at breakfast, tapped a spoon on a table and announced that the trip to Abu Simbel was after all on. 'We have Captain Saheed, the Egyptian who came into the bar last night, to thank for this,' he added. A murmur of appreciation ran through the dining-room followed by a burst of enthusiastic clapping. He made his way between the tables, paused beside Vita and placing his knuckles on the cloth bent over to look into Susanne's face. 'How about changing your mind?' he asked persuasively. 'There are vacant seats on the plane.'

She shook her head. 'I've had enough of planes for the moment. I want to go on the river in a *felucca.*'

He protested, 'We'll be doing that. It's scheduled.'

'I want to sail this morning.'

Vita surprised her by saying, 'I think, after all, I'll take advantage of one of the vacant seats.'

'Come on, Susanne,' urged Peter. 'Join your mother.'

'I think that's what she really wouldn't like me to do. We're not accustomed to sharing a tiny bedroom,' Susanne retorted. She turned to Vita, 'Isn't that right?'

Vita smiled. 'Delighted to give you some

74

space.'

'I may as well use my spending money seeing a little more of the sights,' Vita said when Peter had dragged himself away, disappointment showing in the hunching of his shoulders and his slow walk to the door.

Susanne leaned across the table and looked into her mother's eyes. 'So what really decided you? Is the colonel going?'

'Really, Susanne!'

'What's that word—bridling? I never saw anyone bridle before.'

'You're very perky this morning, I must say.' Vita folded her table napkin. 'The Colonel is good company and, as he points out, I may never come this way again.'

'True. Is he a widower?'

'Since you ask, yes. What has that to do with it?'

'Only that I can watch you for a change instead of you watching me. Have fun. But be careful. He may be dangerous.'

Vita laughed, too. 'All right. You've had the last word. I'm glad to see you so light-hearted.' She decided she shouldn't have taken the Colonel's warning seriously. Susanne could look after herself. Couldn't she? Vita's mind flashed to the evening she had come home from The Weavers, disappointed that she had not been able to ask Nigel to accompany her on this trip.

She rose from the table telling herself a

mother could not live a daughter's life for her. I shouldn't be here. If I'm going to worry about her then it's my own fault for allowing her to talk me into coming. She had better send a postcard to Gilbert and Felicity. Not that Gilbert deserved one, she thought, though good-humouredly. But for his interference . . .

Those going to Abu Simbel hurried off to collect their things then ashore to waiting taxis for the run to the airport. Susanne stood at the top of the steps to wave them away. There was a group, led by the guide Hassan, going off on the coach to visit an unfinished statue in a granite quarry. She saw them off, too, glad that she did not have to accompany them into the heat of the desert. An unfinished statue in a granite quarry, she said to herself, is the last thing I need to see this morning. There was half an hour to wait before the *feluccas* were due to pick up the residue of the party for their trip to see the botanical gardens on Kitchener Island.

She was less interested in the gardens than in the sailing. How lovely it would be to spend the entire day on the water. She sat down on a granite block watching the little horse-drawn carriages and busy pedlars offering their wares. A big black car rolled silently towards her. Her gaze moved casually over it. Then through the rolled-down window she saw the man at the wheel and the world went still.

He looked quite different now—softer,

76

somehow—than when she had met him dressed to kill for his important dinner the night before. He wore a short-sleeved shirt, the buttons open on his chest. One tanned arm lay along the lower frame of the window. She sat there, stunned, like a young animal in the headlights of a car, watching him as he jumped out. He came towards her with long strides. He was dressed in riding breeches, his legs encased in highly polished black boots.

He said, 'So, I have been very busy this morning, and here you are, perched on a stone like a beautiful bird wondering where to fly to next. I've come to make your decision for you. I have horses waiting. We're going riding in the desert.'

She jumped to her feet, stood on tiptoes, unable to believe what was happening. 'You said your horses were in Cairo.'

'Other people have horses that they are happy to lend to me. You said you were not going to Abu Simbel. Did you think I would fix the plane if you were going?' His lips parted over those startlingly white teeth. Those wonderful blue eyes were warm and glowing in his dark face. 'I have borrowed a couple of good Arab horses from the stables of a friend of mine. Now, are you ready to come?'

'Yes.' Susanne leaped down the steps, taking them two at a time, crossed the lower deck and ran up the companionway. She flung open the cabin door, tore off her thin cotton trousers

77

and blouse and pulled on a pair of jeans. She snatched at a T-shirt by Louis Féraud with an enormous flower on the front. Not very horsey. Never mind. 'Hat!' she muttered. 'Hat?' She couldn't imagine herself perched on a horse wearing a Valentino straw with a brim of epic width. She cast around for something to cover her head, fretting at the delay. She picked up a silk stole. In front of the mirror she wound it round her head, turban-wise, and knotted the ends behind. Then she hurtled back down to the lower deck.

Some of the passengers who were going on the *felucca* trip were standing around talking to the tour operator. 'We're due to go in five minutes, Miss Landseer,' Mr Logan said.

'Count me out. I'm going riding.' She sped up the steps. Saheed was already back behind the wheel. She jumped into the passenger seat. The car slid silkily away. 'You really are kind, Captain Saheed—'

'Omar, please.'

'Is that your name? Omar?' She turned it over her tongue, tasting the foreignness of it.

'And you are Susanne. I heard it last night. I have been calling you Susanne in my mind.'

She had a sense, as the car purred along, of moving down a road from which there might be no turning back. She thought she was blending with the excitement and the strangeness, going forward, leaving familiar things behind.

He said, 'You have a feel for my country. The way you have draped that shawl round your head, it is absolutely right.'

It felt right, for riding in the desert. 'I didn't bring my hard hat. I wasn't expecting to meet a man with a horse.'

He gave her a lazy smile. 'You will not need a hard hat.'

'No, I dare say the sand is soft, but I hope not to come a cropper, anyway.'

'I'm sure you won't.'

They passed donkeys, mules, a flock of goats; houses; sheds; and then suddenly, without warning the small town was behind them.

'This is the area irrigated by the waters of the Nile,' Omar said, braking then allowing the car to roll to a stop. Ahead lay fields of maize and cotton. There were water melons growing in rich, dark soil. Date palms. Lemon and orange trees. 'Wherever the Nile waters can be taken, the desert gives way,' he said. 'Do you know of the wonder of this river of ours?'

'Tell me.' She smiled at him.

He smiled back then looked out over the verdant land, 'It has been the life of the people for five thousand years or more. It provides water for drinking. It is our transport system. It brings silt for the crops.'

Susanne looked at her bare arm lying along the frame of the open window, reddening in the burning sun. Not a breath of wind stirred.

'Go on,' she said softly.

'You wish to know how the system works'

She nodded, wanting to hear him talk, wanting to know about him as well as his land.

'It starts working a very long way away from here,' he said, speaking softly as though recounting a well-loved fairy tale. 'Mighty winds laden with rain blow across the Indian ocean. They come in over our east coast and are forced up by the mountains, in Ethiopia, Eritrea, and the Sudan. When the winds can no longer bear the weight of the water they let it go and it falls as rain on the mountain slopes. From there it runs into the many tributaries of the Nile.'

She stole a look at him. He spoke dreamily, as a lover. A lover of the land. She watched his brown profile. Relaxed, Omar still wore that falcon look, but there was a dreaming centre now.

'The river flood rises above the banks carrying the soil from the mountains, turning it into silt as it rides, and after a while it is deposited on our valley farms. This cycle of wind, rain, rushing streams and flooding rivers has been repeated once a year for thousands of years,' Omar said. He turned to her, 'Do you wonder that our ancestors worshipped nature as a god? The sun, the moon, certain stars, and most importantly, for we could not exist without it, the wind.'

She smiled at him.

'The Greek, Herodotus, wrote about it in the fifth century B.C. He said, "All Egypt becomes a sea and only the towns remain above water, looking rather like the islands of the Aegean." Can you imagine that, Susanne? Boats sailing from town to town over this enormous lake?'

She couldn't. She thought of the vast tracts of desert they had flown over, the sand she could see from the river deck running away from the town. Endless sand, and the river confined within its banks.

'Of course, we now have the Aswan dam,' Omar concluded, suddenly practical. 'It is better for the *fellahin*, if perhaps not so picturesque. But we still celebrate a festival of spring. We call it *Shamm al-Nasim*. It means "smelling the zephyr", the spring wind. We have not forgotten our past,' he said.

She said, 'We have an archaeologist on board. But he has a different way of putting things.'

Omar shrugged. 'I could talk to you about engineering if that is what you want. My ancestors had to work out the rudiments of applied geometry in order to construct complex irrigation canals and ditches. With the Nile breaking its banks they had to re-draw boundary lines that were every year obscured by the flood waters. It was highly complex. Is that the way you wish to talk about Egypt, as an exercise in expanding your intellectual

81

horizons?' He sounded quizzical and faintly stern.

Susanne said softly, 'I prefer the winds and the gods.'

He did not reply, merely starting the car and moving on down the dirt road. They left the crops behind. Ahead of them now lay the desert, ridge after ridge of sand. Between them and the sand hills, tucked into a shallow dip, a little sand-coloured village lay. 'These homes of the people,' Omar said gesturing towards square, flat houses with square windows, 'are constructed of bricks made from sun-dried mud and straw. All houses in Egypt are made so.'

'It doesn't sound very permanent.'

He laughed over her comment. 'It is very permanent,' he said.

But he had said 'the homes of the people' and she thought, he does not live in one of them. Where does he live, and how? Omar ran the car down a dusty, sandy track lined with date palms. 'What do you do, Omar? For a living, I mean?'

'I act as aide to my father. And I ride, professionally. I buy and sell blood horses for clients. I am a good judge of horse flesh.'

'Here, in Egypt?'

'All over the world.'

'It sounds like a very pleasant life.'

'Life is what you make it, is it not?'

'Not entirely.' She was thinking of what her

father had done to Vita and herself. Of what Nigel had tried to do that had nearly enveloped her.

'You are talking about reversals, I think. They are not important. It is what you make of reversals that counts,' Omar said. She thought he sounded old and wise. Older than her in her Englishness. Old with Egyptian wisdom. 'Now, we leave the car here,' he said.

They slipped out of their seats and walked towards a roofless enclosure. Sand coloured walls about twelve feet high. Sun-dried bricks? 'You see,' he said as though reading her thoughts and outlined one of the bricks with a finger.

In front of them now, a small boy was playing in the sand. A mongrel dog lay stretched out in the sun beside him. As they approached the boy jumped up and ran inside. Immediately a large Arab in dusty headdress and long *galabiya* appeared in the opening. Only his bare brown feet showed beneath the gown. He smiled, showing stained and gapped teeth. Omar greeted him in his native tongue. He nodded then gestured that they should follow him.

'Hello,' said Susanne, though knowing he would not speak English. She smiled at him and he smiled back, offering his own greeting. *'Ahlan.'* They followed him into the compound.

There were two open stalls. In one, a

83

magnificent white stallion. Susanne's eyes widened. In the other a bay mare with a long black mane and tail. Omar said, 'The mare is yours. Her name is Wallah. It is Rose in English. The stallion is Pharaoh. What do you think of Rose?'

She was intrigued by the names. Old Egypt and the unexpected flower of England. She went forward, eyes alight with admiration. 'She's very pretty.'

'Have you ridden an Arab before?'

'No.'

'You'll find her different. Arab horses don't canter. They trot and gallop. You will soon get used to it,' Omar said. She took the reins and led the mare out, checked the girth, then tightened it while Omar looked on approvingly. She felt he was putting her to some sort of test. And why not, she thought. These were valuable horses. She gathered the reins in and stood with foot raised. He hoisted her into the saddle. She waited for him to mount.

'What happens to the car?' Omar had rolled up the windows but had not bothered to lock it.

'The servant will watch,' he replied in that easy way he had, as though accustomed to people giving up their entire time to him. She noted the word 'servant' with surprise and observed that he did not tell the man how long they would be away. Well, she conceded, she wasn't in England now where people had rights.

This is what you get with your dreams and your gods. Inequality, and . . . happiness? She looked at the old man and wondered if in fact he was old, or if the nature they all revered had wrought its excesses on him. He looked content. And after all, she thought, he doesn't have to get up and catch the seven-fifteen into the city, standing all the way. She felt light-headed. Who had said she wouldn't come to terms with Egypt in a fortnight and advised her not to try?

CHAPTER FIVE

The horses swished their tails, prancing. They crossed the sand and started up a stony path. After a while the stones gave way to fine sand. It was a white-hot day. The sun was a silver disk set starkly in an opal sky. They rode up to the summit of one of the low ridges. Ahead of them a golden valley ran away, its sloping sides lumpy with round, dark rocks, and beyond, vast tracts of desert, mile upon mile of undulating dunes. 'What marvellous country for riding!'

Omar nodded. 'But you must not ride here without a guide. You can very easily lose your way for all dunes look alike. When you get out of sight of the Nile you have no point of contact and it can be very frightening.'

She gazed up at the clear sky. 'How can you get lost when there is the sun to take your direction from?'

'When the sun is there. But you have heard of dust storms? And sandstorms?'

'Heaven forbid.'

He smiled, a flash of ivory white in his brown face. 'Allah sometimes plays little jokes. And, by the way, there are fox-holes to trip unwary riders. One must be watchful.'

'Foxes in the desert?'

'Oh yes. There are many animals.'

She gazed out across the smooth sand, feeling overwhelmed by the strangeness.

'There is something I must say to you,' he said. His face was solemn but his eyes danced. 'When you meet my father you will remember, please, that we did not ride unescorted into the desert. He would think you very, let us say, *emancipated*. He would think it better that we should have been chaperoned.'

Susanne bit back an incipient desire to laugh. Why should his father worry about the reputation of a tourist passing through? 'Are we going to meet him?'

'Yes.'

'Out here?' She was astonished.

'No. Not out here. Now, would you like to try out the lovely Rose? Shall we race?'

'Right.'

She was unprepared for the speed of her mare. She loosened the reins, touched her heels to the flank and Rose leaped forward, but Omar's stallion was too fast for her. He pounded ahead. A huge cloud of fine dust rose, then Omar tightened his reins and she was through it, riding alongside him with the dust clouding up behind them. They galloped neck and neck, sped round a sandy ridge into a valley, then on up a slope that took them out of it again. Here the animals began to flag.

'That's enough.'

She reined in, breathless and exhilarated. Together, the two horses walked soberly to the top of the rise.

'You ride very well,' said Omar, looking pleased. 'Sometimes people say they can ride, but when they see how fast the Arab horse is, they panic.'

'I didn't panic,' she said.

'No.' They smiled at each other. Below them now, tucked snugly into the landscape, lay another small village. There were sand streets and sand-coloured, box-shaped dwellings. Men in the ubiquitous *galabiya* and little red fezzes sat at tables outside their houses, playing some game.

'Backgammon,' Omar told her.

Children, naked and half-naked, stared at them. Four black-eyed tots came towards them riding a large-boned, amiable looking animal with horns like the handlebars of a bicycle.

'What on earth is that? A buffalo?'

Omar said it was a gamus. 'These children are very poor. They have no horses but they have a lot of fun with the gamus. You may often see one going round in circles pulling a water wheel with children riding on its back. A quiet kind of merry-go-round,' Omar said, smiling.

They went on up the slope behind the village and met the empty desert once again. From the top of a high ridge they looked out over a sea of shimmering sand dunes stretching away into the distance, then merging with the heat haze.

Susanne gazed on the emptiness with awe. Looking down on this country from the plane she had thought it dramatic, but from this angle it was awe-inspiring.

Omar said, 'We will give the horses a rest, and a little shade.'

'Shade?' she echoed, seeing nothing but sand. 'Here?'

He reined Pharoah round and headed into the next valley. Above them now lay an outcrop of rock. He turned east towards a steep little rise. The horses flexed their muscles, dug in their hooves and climbed the incline. It was very hot now. Their flanks were steaming as they zig-zagged up a hillside path riding nose-to-tail on the stony ground. A sharp turn, a steep incline and they were on a ledge, part sand, part rock with an overhang of flat sandstone. They rode into its shade.

'Jump off.' Omar leapt out of the saddle and Susanne followed suit. Swiftly, she unwound the shawl that covered her head and shoulders, ran her fingers through her hair, lifted it in the dry air, swinging her head so that the strands floated. 'Such heat!' she said.

'You can get used to anything.'

She felt he was telling her something. He smiled at her. 'Follow me.' They led the horses forward. Further along the promontory she could now see the yawning mouth of a cave. Omar deftly tied his reins to a metal ring set in the rock at the cave entrance then took Rose's reins and tied them also. He lightly slapped Pharoah's neck, caressed Rose's mane, then took Susanne's hand.

She went with him into the dimness. It was cool here. 'Oh, lovely!' she exclaimed and again tossed her hair, with one hand now because Omar was holding the other.

He turned, blocking her path, bringing her to a halt. He placed his palms at either side of her head, gently smoothing her hair down against her face. He examined her profile from different angles. 'A sculptured face,' he said. 'You do not need your beautiful hair.'

She seemed to be looking at herself from outside, seeing what he saw. She had not thought that she was beautiful before. The warmth he exuded enclosed her, trapping her senses.

She stood still within her entrapment, waiting to be kissed. In this new dimension she inhabited she was prepared to follow him to the ends of the earth. Then Omar's hands dropped to his sides. 'You are not ready,' he said. He was moving away, as though nothing at all had happened. 'Look,' he said.

Susanne shook herself out of the trance that was disappointment, a kind of shock, and something more potent.

He was pointing at pictures—murals—on the walls. A god with a falcon's head. Another god, this time with a crocodile's head. Hieroglyphics. She tried hard to concentrate.

'What is this place?' Her voice sounded strange.

'A tomb. Quite a modest one,' Omar said. 'There are many, many tombs or rather, caves that used to be tombs, in the desert. The bodies of the poor were buried in the sand, the rich in caves and tombs. When my brothers and I were small we occasionally dug up mummies when we were playing in the sand.'

She thought briefly back to her own country where she could visualise digging up a body in a field, calling the police, shouting murder. She moved back into this Arabian Nights world and felt oddly at peace.

'The dead have been taken away from this cave long ago,' Omar was saying. 'You may know that our ancestors used to be buried with their belongings. The Pharaohs believed that

90

when you entered another life you could take your possessions with you. But they had not taken into account the poverty of the people. When you are very poor you will do anything for riches. They dug up the bodies to rob them.' He gestured towards the back of the cave. 'It has happened here. There's nothing now but the pictures on the walls. Are they not beautiful?'

Soldiers, archers, boats. A man-faced bird hanging poised over a mummy.

'That is the winged Ba,' Omar said. 'It is a spirit symbolizing the physical survival of the dead. The winged Ba could ensure a dead man would return to his family and home. Meantime, he guards the body.' Omar spoke naturally, as though he shared these beliefs of his ancestors. She smiled at him.

They moved further along the wall towards the interior of the cave. A river scene. Narrow-prowed boats, a row of oarsmen, winging sails. Young warriors with sleek, muscular physiques. The colours were clear, the markings precise. The painting might have been done yesterday. Such colours! 'Surely they couldn't have lasted for thousands of years?' she breathed.

'They were made from a mixture of pigment and water with wax or glue as a binder,' Omar said. 'The pigments were minerals, which is why many of the colours are still fresh. Iron ore was used for brown, red and yellow.

Powdered malachite for green; gypsum for white. Even those murals on obelisks and walls that have been exposed to the sun have not faded. You will see many of these on your tour.'

'I wish you were coming with us,' she said impulsively.

'I will come.'

She glanced at him then glanced away and wandered further into the cave, looking at the hieroglyphics, at birds carved in the sandstone, warriors firing their arrows from elegant boats. More strange creatures with men's bodies and animals' heads. What had he meant? That he would join the party? How could he? They were now some distance into the cave. The light was growing dim.

'There's no point in going further without a torch,' Omar said. 'You have brought a torch with you?'

She nodded. 'We were advised to.'

'You'll need it. None of the tombs are lit.'

Again he took her face between his hands and in the gloom looked deeply into her eyes. Then he turned her round and walked with her back to the cave entrance, holding one of her hands against his heart. She could feel the beat of it, warmly, strongly. She thought he must be aware of hers; that he was absorbing her emotion through her palm. Emotion she could scarcely contain. He held her hand there until they came out into the daylight. The horses

lifted their heads and looked at them with
curiosity, drawing her out of the dream with
their gently stamping impatience and smell of
dried sweat. The stallion had relieved himself.
His long black member hung lazily from his
belly. The beautiful Rose raised her flowing
tail and farted. Omar laughed and slapped her
on the rump. Susanne jolted back into the real
world.

They undid the reins and mounted. 'Your
mother is a very elegant lady,' Omar said as
they rode back down the zig-zagging track.
'You must be proud of her.'

'Yes, I am.'

'It's good to see a mother and daughter
holidaying together. It's not usual in your
country, I think. Girls go with men, do they
not?'

'Yes, on the whole.' She thought of Nigel
who had sneered when her godfather said she
was taking Vita with her to Egypt, and of her
reaction. She buttoned the memory down, far
out of reach, feeling guilty at accepting Omar's
commendation, that she did not feel she
deserved.

'And your father?'

She sensed he was not going to approve of
what Darren had done. That the flippant
retort she sometimes used to cover the hurt,
'He ran off with a blonde,' would not do here,
close to the silent tomb where Omar had
gravely contemplated the wonders of his

ancestors. 'He doesn't live with us,' she temporised. 'He . . . er . . . left.'

Omar, showing himself after all as a man of the world, shrugged.

*   *   *

Phoenix appeared deserted. Susanne ran up to her cabin, wanting to be alone, hesitated at the door then turned aside, went to the rail and looked out across the brown waters of the Nile. The mighty Nile. Peter would know its length and width, Omar its grandeur. She wondered why she had thought of Peter, and then immediately knew that she was testing herself in this other dimension. Peter Quest was a symbol of solid, familiar ground. She needed to know if it was on solid ground that she belonged. A warm breeze drifted past.

She leaned over the rail, her thoughts returning to the ride back, to their neck-and-neck race over the hard sand, walking up the inclines, dashing down again. She had felt like a nomad in the wilderness, scarf flying out behind her, the mare's long mane streaming. The servant had been waiting among the date palms, sitting cross-legged on a mat.

'*Shukran*,' she said to him. Thank you. And '*Ma-el-salama*' which was good-bye. The man bowed with immense dignity.

'You have a flair for languages?' Omar asked in that way he had of going beyond the

94

immediate present.

'I got that out of the guide book. But yes, I think so. I speak French reasonably fluently, and a little Spanish. I cooked at a Spanish villa one summer.'

'You had to cook?'

She thought, he doesn't understand. His mother probably doesn't cook. Never did. There was a gap to bridge. 'English girls do it for fun, and of course to earn money.'

'Ah yes.' After all, he easily acknowledged that things were different abroad. She wondered what he would say if she told him she had back-packed half way round the world. She didn't tell him. She wasn't that girl any more. That girl had walked through India without feeling the essence of the East creeping into her blood. She had been English and sturdy and tough. She had spent nights out of doors in a sleeping bag, gazing at the stars twinkling in the sky, chatting to her friends about living with nature and what they were going to do when they returned to London. She had not taken those stars into her eyes. Had not felt herself drifting on a foreign breeze.

She held out her arms to the sun and lifted her face. Omar had said with regret that he would not see her this afternoon but he hoped very much to take her out to dinner tonight. 'It all depends on my father,' he said. 'If I cannot come, I will try to send you a message.'

'How?' She thought of faxes and telephones.

'There are thousands of little boys all over Egypt waiting for the moment when someone offers them a few *piastres* to take a message. And so, we help each other.'

His words lingered in her memory. *And so, we help each other.*

A cry startled her out of her dream. Three white-sailed *feluccas* were coming in. Their passengers waved. She waved back then went swiftly to her cabin to take a shower and change for lunch. She was not ready for her own countrymen. She felt their Englishness would upset the delicate balance she had in her mind and heart.

She chose her Prada jeans and Moschino blouse, sighing sharply over the labels as she tied the flowing tails of the blouse round her waist. As she approached the lower deck a messenger in red fez and *galabiya* came down the steps from the road, one arm extended, a tidy heap of colourful garments trailing over one arm.

'Kaftan,' he said, his face lighting up at sight of her. 'You give kaftans to passengers? All have names.'

Susanne agreed. She took them into the dining-room where half a dozen people had already seated themselves for lunch. A waiter came forward, took the garments from her and draped them over an empty table. 'Plenty of

96

room,' he said. 'Not many for lunch.' Susanne picked out the two she and Vita had ordered and carried them off to the cabin. When she returned the *felucca* party was seated. She sat down at a table by herself.

'Wouldn't you like some company?' a woman asked kindly from the next table. 'Do come and sit with us.'

'I'm really perfectly all right,' she said, then saw their faces close. Hastily summoning a smile, she went to join them.

They were agog for her news, their eyes bright with curiosity. 'Someone said you went riding with that Egyptian fellow who came aboard last night,' said the woman she knew as Mrs Lemon.

Susanne nodded. Smiled. Their questions were filtering the magic away. She looked down at the plate of chicken and rice the waiter was putting before her. 'This looks nice,' she said, endeavouring to change the subject.

But they wouldn't let her alone. She was their hostage. 'Someone said you keep racehorses,' said a man who introduced himself as Clem Barrow.

'Oh, really, the rumours that get about!' She spoke briskly, a little impatiently, meeting their bright, searching eyes. 'A racing man lives next door to my mother. When I'm in the country I help exercise his horses.'

'You live abroad?' The whole table was

warily agog.

'No. I mean the English country. We live in Suffolk.' That knowing woman was staring at her blouse. Their silence said she was prevaricating. Not being as friendly and open as they would like. They wanted her to share the details of a more glamorous existence than theirs. As a neighbour to a 'racing man' they would not see her living at Little Hammer, a tiny cottage let to them by a friend at a minimum rent. She wished Vita had not forbidden her to tell the truth. But, of course, she was right. Once you create envy you have to stay with it. For Vita's sake she must preserve their dignity.

'And this Egyptian feller? He owns racehorses?'

She told them she didn't really know Captain Saheed, or anything much about him.

'You were brave, weren't you, going riding in the desert with a strange foreigner?'

She felt their curiosity like needles in the tenderness of her memories. 'We are the foreigners,' she snapped. A terrible silence fell.

One of the men said kindly, 'He's very well-known, I understand. A man of substance. I'm sure Miss Landseer wasn't in any danger.'

'Susanne,' said Susanne and was gratified when they brightened.

'Well, Susanne, watch it,' advised a plump woman whose powdered face was marked with dark lines of sweat. She spoke with goodwill as she rose and headed for the kaftans. Susanne made her way thoughtfully on to the outer deck. As she passed through the door a voice behind her commented dryly, 'She's not likely to have ordered one of these. Too cheap, I'd say.'

I'll wear mine tonight, she said to herself, then remembered Omar hoped to collect her and take her out for dinner. If she was to match his impeccable navy-blue suit then she certainly would not want to wear a kaftan.

*   *   *

The afternoon dragged by. Granite, concrete, sand and water. Perhaps I am simply not a natural tourist, Susanne said to herself gazing at the imposing ediface that was the tomb of the late Aga Khan, hearing the noise around her as chatter, rather than words. The impressive and portly Hassan, who was guiding them, had a good deal to say but his words ran lightly over her consciousness. The dam was indeed a great engineering feat, as Peter had said. 'Behind it the Nile backs up to form a lake'—how many miles long? She was glad Peter had gone to Abu Simbel, relieved that those accompanying her weren't interested in whether she was improving her general knowledge, or not. She was like a child being forced to take lessons when she wanted to dream.

99

They re-crossed the Nile by *felucca* and arrived at *Phoenix* as the rest of the party came in from Abu Simbel. Peter, crossing the lower deck at a run, held out a hand to help her aboard. His Panama hat teetered on the back of his head. His nose had turned a rather alarming pink. He was flatteringly, embarrassingly pleased to see her.

'What it is to be young,' murmured a woman to Vita, nudging her.

'We all had our turn.' Vita was impatient with inanities, unaccustomed to them. She had been grateful for the company of Colonel Alison with his fund of stories about Egypt but she didn't want to pair up with him and give the party something else to talk about. She told herself there were bound to be people on board with whom she could find something in common. She liked women. She didn't have to have a man at her side. But these women had set her apart, made her more different than she was. She, too, had forfeited their friendship by bringing the wrong clothes.

Someone said the kaftans had arrived. 'Thank God,' she muttered, vowing to spend the rest of the trip in hers.

Peter climbed the staircase with Susanne to the middle deck where his cabin lay. 'So, how did you enjoy your day?'

'Great.'

'What did you think of the dam?'

'Impressive.'

'Did you see the tomb?'

'Yes, that was impressive, too.'

'You should have come to Abu Simbel. You should take every opportunity offered. You may never come this way again.'

'I'm sure you're right, but I did have a lovely day.'

'Ancient effigies are more interesting than modern tombs and dams.'

'I'm sure you're right,' she said again, thinking of the wonderful wall paintings in the cave.

'D'you know the height of this Rameses II that we went to see?'

'No, but I bet you can tell me.'

'Sixty-seven feet,' Peter said. 'Have you ever seen a statue sixty-seven feet high?'

'Not yet.' She went ahead to her own stairs that would take her to the top deck.

'Can I buy you a drink?' he called after her.

'No. I'll buy you one.' She waved to him and opened her cabin door.

Vita was standing before the long mirror holding the black and white striped kaftan against her front, looking amused. 'I don't think it's quite my thing, but I'm sure I'll be happy in it. Are you going to wear yours?'

Susanne flopped down on the bed. 'Mother . . .'

Vita went still.

Susanne laughed. 'Don't panic. I'm just telling you now, before someone else does—I

101

didn't go on the *feluccas*. I went riding in the desert with Omar Saheed, and I'm not wearing my kaftan because I may be going out to dinner with him tonight.'

Vita draped the long, shapeless garment across her bed. 'Omar,' she said, turning the name over on her tongue.

Susanne sat up and waved her arms theatrically. ' "Whoa there! I say, Captain Saheed, I'm having trouble with this mare." "Just keep a firm hold on the reins, Miss Landseer." ' She gave her mother a thoughtful look. 'This isn't E.M. Forster country, Mother.'

Vita took so long to answer that Susanne thought she wasn't going to. Then she said, 'I wish you wouldn't call me Mother, darling. It makes me nervous.'

Susanne watched her back as she disappeared into the tiny bathroom.

*   *   *

She wanted to look beautiful for Omar if he came. She chose the stunning Loris Azzaro silk, pale gold that was nearly the colour of her hair. So she was overdoing things. She didn't care what the passengers thought of her. Hadn't she already forfeited their friendship?

Peter, looking her up and down interestedly, said, 'I thought you bought one of those kaftans.'

'We didn't want to do a mother and

daughter act,' Susanne retorted lightly. 'Vita's wearing hers.'

'Why do you call her Vita?'

'Because that's her name.' She headed towards the bar. 'I promised you a drink. What do you want?'

He hurried after her. 'Oh, come on, I should be buying . . .'

'I always buy drinks for archaeologists. Come on yourself, what do you want?' She leaned an elbow on the bar and faced him, tapping her little beaded bag on the wood.

'Whisky, and watch the barman doesn't put his filthy Nile water in it. Not that I'm not highly suspicious of Cairo-bottled soda.' She felt his English needles sticking into the soft skin of Egypt, hurting.

Colonel Alison stepped between them. 'Hello, my dear. You're all aglow tonight. Egypt must suit you. I hear you went riding in the desert. That must have been exciting.'

She gave him a swift, glassy smile then turned to the barman. 'One whisky and soda. One gin and tonic, please. Yes,' she said to the Colonel. 'Yes, I did.'

'And how did you get on?' He was bluff and chatty. Seriously interested in where she had gone and what she had seen. He was kind. He didn't know what she had done that morning was hers, and Omar's. Not to be shared.

'I managed to keep my seat.' She smiled at the guide, Hassan, as he wandered past.

'Good for you. Two gin and tonics, please, Ahmed.' The barman pushed Susanne's order across. She handed Peter his glass, her eyes swivelling to avoid his.

'Thanks,' he said. 'Cheers.'

'Cheers.'

The Colonel turned his back, dealing with his order.

'You're a deep one,' said Peter ungraciously.

She didn't know what to say, short of being rude. She settled for, 'What makes you think you're my keeper?' and took her drink out on deck where she leaned on the rail. The bright orange sun was sinking fast, faster than any English sun could go. There was a moment of soft pink turning magically to gold then a flame of scarlet seared the western sky, consuming it, and blackness reigned. The night wind came in, cooling her hot skin.

She did not hear footsteps nor see anyone approaching. A voice said, 'I've only got your interests at heart. This chap, my God, you were taking a risk.'

She turned her head. Peter's face was no more than a smudge in the darkness. 'There's nothing to apologise for. I'm sorry you should think I'm not grown-up, quite sensible and a free agent.'

He muttered, 'I suppose money gives you that confidence.'

She bit back another sharp reply.

'Can we have dinner together?'

'I may be going out. I'm waiting for a message.'

Peter went silent again. She looked up towards the road. In the golden glow of the lamp hanging over the gang-plank she could see a small, black-haired boy making his way down. Clutched by irrational fear, she went to meet him.

He crossed to the deck, his sharp, shining black eyes darting. She went up to him. 'Hello. *Ahlan*. Have you a message for me?'

He gave her a wonderful smile, even white teeth shining. 'Mees Lansir?'

'Yes.' He held out an envelope. 'Thank you. *Shukran*.' She delved into her bag, took out some *piastres* and handed them to him.

He flashed her a delighted glance, then swung round and ran up the granite steps hell-for-leather as though fearful she would realise she had given him too much. On the road he merged with the straggle of beggars and purveyors of trinkets who hung around hopefully all day, watching the boat.

She tore the envelope open and took out a sheet of paper with the heading of the Cataract Hotel. 'Dear Susanne, It is not possible for me to get away tonight. I hope to be free tomorrow morning. But again I cannot count on it.' It was signed, Omar.

The disappointment was devastating. She tucked the paper into her bag, turned and there was Peter, watching her. She felt the intrusion of his curious eyes. Unnerved, she snapped, 'Just because we're the only people under fifty here, that's no reason why we have to hog each other's company.'

He looked taken aback. Then swiftly recovering he retorted good-naturedly, 'I don't mind hogging yours,' and she knew he knew what was in the note, that she had been let down, and he was glad.

'I think you should spread yourself around among the passengers,' she said, sliding past him. 'They'd probably like to ask you questions.'

'I have to have a bit of time off,' he protested. 'I've been answering questions all day.' She went on towards the dining room. He hurried to catch her up. 'Can we have dinner together?' When she did not immediately answer he added, 'I'll tell you something about me. You can trust me. If I say I'll turn up, I'll be there.'

CHAPTER SIX

The Colonel was seating himself at a table for four. Vita, in her black and white kaftan, was already settled in her chair opposite him. She looked up as they came in. Susanne spoke to the Colonel, 'May I join you and this local beauty? I say, isn't she handsome? A princess,

106

no doubt?'

'No,' said Vita modestly. 'Just an old water carrier. I lost my turban when I fell off the buffalo.'

Susanne pulled out a chair. 'Water buffalo. Or *gamus*.'

Vita frowned. 'You're getting very knowledgeable.'

'Sure. Why not?' She was aware of Peter hovering but she ignored him.

'May I sit with you?' he asked and the Colonel replied, 'Please do.'

*   *   *

'That was unkind,' said Vita as they were preparing for bed. 'You were so obvious, dear.'

'I meant to be.' She didn't want to say he had hurt her so she said, 'I'm trying to shake him off.'

'You should be grateful. Many a girl would be glad to have that nice young man paying them attention. I should think you'd had enough of unreliable men.'

'Some women are only attracted to unreliable men,' Susanne retorted. 'It's probably hereditary.'

Vita went in to the bathroom to clean her teeth.

*   *   *

Susanne was up early, standing at the rail looking out over the sand-coloured buildings of the town. A grey mist rose from the desert behind, brown overlaid with the pearl of morning. In the east the sky had gone from the palest eggshell-blue to a wonderful rose-pink. An elliptical sun emerged from the desert rim and burned its way slowly up over the horizon, flaming the sky above. She watched it grow wider until it became half a circle. From the town came the cry of the *muezzin* calling the faithful to their sunrise prayer. She could see the minaret, a tall tower sharp as a pencil, and a man wearing the ubiquitous *galabiya* standing in an open doorway, high above the town.

She followed his chant with the words Omar had given her:

> God is great!
> I testify there is no god but Allah;
> Come to prayer;
> Come to salvation.
> God is most great!
> There is no god but Allah.

No, he had said, he did not pray five times a day. He was not one of the faithful. He looked at religion with a critical eye, asked questions and made his own judgements.

She stood there for a long time absorbing

the wonder. Sounds emerged from below. A rattle of china. A raised voice. The splash of an object thrown into the water. The boat was coming to life. She went back to her cabin to dress.

Breakfast, some orders from Peter, some advice from Hassan. Hustle. Bustle. Susanne, with her big hat in one hand, stood leaning over the boat's rail watching the graceful scimitar-sailed *feluccas* plying back and forth across the river, dreaming. Already the heat of the day was upon them.

Vita came up beside her. 'I really don't think I'm a natural for package tours,' she complained. 'I have this delinquent desire to hire one of those little black carriages and let the driver take me where his fancy takes him.'

'I'm sure that would get you into no end of trouble.'

'Are you ready?'

'Ready for what?' There was a stillness in her mind as though the mystery of Egypt had taken her over and she only had to wait for the future to be revealed.

'For the trip to the granite quarry, of course, to see some half-finished statue. The one we missed yesterday.'

'Oh God! In this heat!'

'You must have felt a little heat on horseback in the desert yesterday.'

Susanne felt Vita was being irreverent. She too was out of countenance with the thought of tourism. 'Of a different kind,' she said.

'Same sun. Same sand.'

'Mother,' said Susanne, 'I hope we're not going to quarrel.'

'Of course not. Sorry. You must know I'm worried.'

'I think you know I'm grown up.'

Behind her the cheerful chatter of the tourists rose and fell. Susanne watched the *feluccas*. One of them, marvellously agile, was zig-zagging back and forth, its enormous sails filled with wind. Someone waved. Idly, Susanne waved back. The *felucca* turned about and came scampering towards the mooring. Regretting her impulsive act, Susanne was about to move inside when she recognised a familiar figure standing erect in the stern. She felt her heart stop beating.

'It's coming in.'

The passengers were crowding to the side of the boat. The waiters in their gold-trimmed robes and little white caps came smilingly to watch. The craft, deftly manoeuvred by a couple of long skirted, white clad boatmen, swung round and headed towards *Phoenix*.

Someone announced, 'It's that man who came aboard the other night!' A buzz of interest rose, going on to a crescendo. 'So it is! Who is he? He fixed the trip to Abu Simbel, didn't he?'

Omar looked younger this morning, dressed in white shorts and a blue and white striped shirt. Susanne gazed at him, absorbing his familiarity and his strangeness, his brown skin, that sleek, muscular physique of the athlete that appeared in the cave drawings. That high-held god's head.

The craft came alongside. She smiled at him, a smile from the heart. His eyes held hers. 'Are you coming for a sail?'

A murmur of excitement ran through the crowd. Mr Logan called, 'All aboard the coach.'

Vita's voice, 'Susanne . . .'

Someone gripped her arm. Peter said in a tight, angry voice, 'There are crocodiles in the river. Watch it.'

One of the crew was undoing the chain. He swung back a section of the railing. A boatman flung a rope. One of the waiters deftly caught it and pulled the craft close. Susanne reached out a hand. Omar took it and steadied her as she stepped into the *felucca*, knowing that this was what she had been waiting for since the great gaudy sun lifted above the horizon. The ropes were flung aboard, the vessel swung round. Its sail caught the breeze and they spun off across the water.

Omar was looking down at her as she sat amidships on a little bale of straw, laughing. 'Sorry about the public ordeal,' he said not looking sorry at all. Susanne thought, he is accustomed to being the cynosure of all eyes, and it's meat and drink to him. She pulled him

111

down beside her and slapped the back of his hand playfully. She could be easy with him because she had known him all her life. All their shared lives. She knew with an inner knowledge too deep for questioning that they had been together before.

'You're an exhibitionist,' she said softly.

'Oh yes. Why not? There is no fun to be had in hiding away. Life is for living.'

Yes, she thought, that's exactly what it is for. She was living now, in a glow. The glow enveloped them both. She felt the breeze sifting through her hair. It blew her thin shirt against her chest. She was aware of her breasts, of the shape of his thighs beneath the linen of his shorts.

Omar lifted her hat and put it on her head. 'You must not get sunstroke.' He examined it with his head on one side. 'It is a beautiful hat. Tourists come in hats for the garden. You are not a tourist. You are a woman of discrimination. Not part of the common herd.'

She lay back, smiling up at him. 'I don't think "common herd" is politically correct any more. Do you know what I mean by politically correct?'

'Yes. But how else can I say it? One does not compliment a woman for dressing well because she is rich.'

'I'm not rich, Omar.'

'No, of course not.' He accepted her denial with disconcerting negligence.

112

She wanted to say, I mean it, but that would be making too much of the matter so she changed the subject. 'I want a tan. That's why I wasn't wearing my hat.'

'We do not take chances with the sun. It is our friend, but it is also our enemy.'

She watched his dark profile while she told him how she had risen early to see this friend who was also an enemy come up out of the desert.

'Never have I accustomed myself to the beauty of our sunsets and sunrises,' Omar said. 'You will find this is so, too. After fifty years the beauty will still be growing in you. It sinks into the soul, enriching it.'

She loved the way he expressed himself. She shook her head, slowly. 'I haven't got fifty years to spare. Less than two weeks, now.'

'You have your whole lifetime. And more.'

No man in her life had ever talked to her like that. There was nothing proprietary about his manner towards her. She looked at his chiselled lips, saw again a reflection of the face of the gods and felt a sense of awe intermixed with unease.

'Today,' he said, 'we'll make up for last night. You know, because I've told you, that I'm not my own master when I'm acting as adjutant to my father. You understood about last night?'

'Yes. Of course, I was disappointed.'

'I would not have it otherwise. Today I'm

113

going to take you to The Cataract Hotel for lunch. He will be there. I want to introduce you to him.'

'Are you sure he wants to meet me?' She nearly said *me? A tourist passing through?* but that would have been shallow, and glib, after what he had said about her lifetime. She had a sense of teetering between two worlds, unable to accept his certainties, yet fleeing from hers.

'He has not yet been offered the opportunity to meet you, so no, I couldn't say I was sure he wanted to.'

She thought he was joking. She turned her bright face. Their eyes met. He was not smiling. She saw she had not taken account of his different way of putting things. She felt nervous of meeting his father. Felt she was stepping now on uncertain ground.

Above them on the rocky sandbanks the delicate fronds of palm trees drifted. *Feluccas* sped past laden with grain, with bales of straw, with timber. Every boat had half a dozen long-gowned men reclining lazily on the load. Children clung precariously to the top, dangerously to the sides. Smaller, more agile craft spun back and forth before the breeze. She gave herself up to dreaming.

Omar leaned down and spoke softly against her ear, 'You have an English saying, "A penny for your thoughts."'

'I have no thoughts,' she said. 'My mind was drifting. I scarcely know what has happened to me.'

He bent over her as though he was going to kiss her. Her heart stopped beating. She looked up at him through her lashes, waiting. It was like the cave over again. 'You have fallen in love,' Omar said. He looked into her eyes, examined the shape of her nose, her lips, her chin. She couldn't stand the waiting. Then one of the passing boatmen shouted and he raised his head.

'Does every girl you meet fall in love with you?'

'Not quite every girl. Perhaps nine out of ten. But I always fall in love with all of them.'

'Are you married?' Immediately, she wished she hadn't asked. She put it down to being emotionally out of her depth.

'Why should you ask that?' He seemed genuinely hurt. 'Would I act so with you if I were married?'

'I don't know. We're scarcely acquainted.'

'We have known each other from the beginning of time.'

She reached up and touched his face, tenderly. 'I love that idea. But you are very, very attractive, Omar. You must have many women in love with you.'

'The whole of Egypt, of course.' He had a way of conveying laughter without actually smiling. 'Tell me about yourself, Susanne.'

What was there to say that he would understand and approve? She thought with apprehension of her mother's business. Secondhand clothes, as Nigel said. She thought of her parents' situation. Was divorce acceptable here? She remembered they had lost Grange Place to the creditors. She didn't think bankruptcy was acceptable anywhere. Am I ashamed of my family? Of course not. But floating as she was between worlds she had become lost. England and the English, their criteria, had moved out of reach. She did not know how to talk about them.

'I have a great many brothers and sisters,' Omar said encouragingly.

'I have none. Only a mother, now.' She would deal with Darren if he asked.

'That colonel, he has his eyes on her.'

Susanne laughed. 'I expect so. They're of an age, and they're the only single people aboard except the archaeologist and me.'

'He is in love with you.'

'Pouff! He's only known me a few days.'

'Longer than I have known you, and I'm in love with you.'

'Yes,' she said softly. 'And I am in love with you.'

His fingers tightened on hers. They sailed back and forth across the Nile, in and out of the little green and rocky islands. They disembarked and wandered through the tropical gardens of Kitchener Island admiring exotic cactus and rare and wonderful creepers, taking a brief sabbatical from the sun, walking

116

in the damp and steamy shade. They re-joined the patient boatmen.

Patience, Susanne thought. If Egypt has a selfhood, it must be in its people's patience. The *fellahin*, the farmers, waited through the ages for the seasons to bring them bounty. The little black-eyed children play in the dust, waiting for tourists to hand them a few *piastres*. The man who looks after the horses waited on his little prayer mat until it suited Omar to come. He waited for us to return. And here, our boatman waits with smiling goodwill in that pitiless sun for us to finish wandering in the shade. They found him stretched out, half asleep, the rope held tautly between his toes. They went aboard and sailed upstream as far as the cataract.

'Now,' said Omar, 'we will go ashore for lunch.'

'How far is it? Can we walk?'

She thought he looked shocked, but then he smiled. 'In the heat of the day? This is not England. I have to look after you. There will be a car waiting.'

Indeed, there was. At the tiny landing stage a long black car was parked, its turbaned driver asleep at the wheel. Their footsteps must have wakened him. He sat up and slid out to open the door. 'This is not my car,' Omar said, 'so I may not drive it.' He looked impatient at the thought of being driven.

'Whose is it?'

117

'It belongs to the Government,' he said.

'But you drove yesterday.'

'That car belongs to a friend. It is not at my beck and call.'

But a Government car is, she thought with a touch of awe. He seemed too young. She wondered if his father had sent it, that father who did not know of her existence. Yet. Or merely if sons had more opportunity to play fast and loose with a father's perks here than at home. 'What shall I do with my hat?' she asked him. 'Leave it in the car?'

'No. Bring it with you. This afternoon we won't take the car. I propose to show you round in one of those horse-drawn carriages. Besides, I like your hat. Put it on for walking into the hotel.'

She recognised that he liked the woman on his arm to create a spectacle.

Obediently, she perched the hat on the top of her head. Omar readjusted it. She wondered if he was born with this attention to detail, or if he had acquired it over the course of many *affaires*. How could he not have had *affaires*, a man like him?

The entrance to the New Cataract Hotel was down a drive between blossom trees, green lawns and flower-beds. The bounty of the Nile. Contemplating this lush oasis, Susanne visualised the winds sweeping up over Ethiopia, Eritrea and the Sudan, bringing the water that now filled the dam. Exotic scents

118

drifted from the flowers. Purple, red and yellow bougainvillea. Delicate jasmine. Huge blowzy roses. A Judas tree. And then the imposing verandahed façade of the building.

They went in to a lobby. 'You would perhaps like to tidy yourself up?'

'Yes, please.' Her blouse and trousers had survived the *felucca* ride well, but her hair beneath the high-crowned hat was windblown. She went into the powder room, put her hat down on a small table, washed her face and combed her hair. She leant forward, holding some strands of it up between finger and thumb. Surely it was already a shade lighter? And her skin was faintly tanned. It looked good with the hat of cinnamon-coloured straw. She straightened her Ralph Lauren blouse, recognising its suitability for this hotel. Feeling absolutely right.

Omar was waiting for her. They walked past the boutiques selling souvenirs, silk kaftans, ivory elephants, jade ornaments, exotic necklaces. Here, in this exclusive setting, embroidered slippers such as Hassan wore were made of silk and stitched with gold thread. 'English hotels were never like this,' she said, awed by its glamour.

'You have been abroad before?'

She visualised the possibility of walking into a five-star hotel in Singapore in shorts and sandals with her pack on her back, and by-passed the question. 'My parents travelled on

119

business in the east. I've no doubt they're accustomed to this kind of thing.' Odd, she thought, how a whole world can pass you by if it doesn't concern you. She had never asked them where they stayed. 'Rich bitch,' she remembered saying lightly to Vita, noting the airline tickets lying on the desk were marked First Class. Then she remembered Vita saying, 'It all goes down as a business expense.' She wondered if they were about to lunch at the expense of the Egyptian Government.

They went into a lounge. There was a sprinkling of tourists and several groups of dark-suited Egyptian men. Omar led her to a table in the centre. 'Now you have made your entrance you may remove your hat,' he said. His directives, issued gently and smilingly, resulted in her unquestioning obedience. She took off her hat and placed it on the seat beside her. She felt it was he who had made the entrance. She had seen signs of recognition in the faces of the businessmen and more than that, an inferred ... what? Acceptance? Approval? Something like that. For her, only the faintest curiosity. That's it, she thought. They are accustomed to seeing him with women. Different women. And why not? He leads a public life, and he is not a boy.

Omar ordered drinks. She thought of the possibility of his being a Muslim. He had known the prayer the *muezzin* chanted from the minaret. She thought of his religion

120

prohibiting the consumption of alcohol. When the waiter came bearing a tray on which stood two glasses he gave her a mischievous look from under those thick lashes. 'I am westernised, you understand,' he said.

'Does your father drink?'

'We must make our own decisions.'

The loyal son.

'As a westernised Muslim I am exposed to many temptations. Tell me about your temptations, Susanne.' He leaned towards her, looking into her face, waiting.

She said, 'I'm not answerable to anybody but myself. My parents don't forbid anything, and nor does my religion, what there is of it. We're all answerable to our conscience.'

'I, too, am answerable to my conscience,' he replied gravely, 'but perhaps on another level.'

Her attention was attracted by a group of men who were coming into the lounge. Omar moved forward in his seat. 'There,' he said, 'is my father. I'll bring him over. Excuse me.' He jumped up and headed off between the little tables.

Susanne knew immediately which man was General Saheed. She recognised him by the way he stood for he held himself as Omar did. He led the little party towards the far corner of the room, walking, she thought, like a king leading his courtiers. She watched Omar accost him. The other men nodded at Omar and went ahead.

He spoke to his father at length. Youssel Saheed did not look her way. His movements showed impatience. A lifting of the head, a hand gesture, a half step forward. Then with an exclamation of impatience, without turning her way, he went to join his companions. Omar made his way back across the room, walking slowly, looking disappointed, but as he came closer he lifted his head and by the time he reached her he was serene again.

'My father is very busy today,' he said. 'Come, let us go in to lunch. Don't forget your hat.'

*   *   *

'There's a fashion parade tonight,' said Vita, 'open to all who've bought *galabiyas* or kaftans. Rupert—'

'Who?' Susanne had just come into the cabin. She knew there were stars in her eyes. She knew Vita had noticed. She didn't care.

'Rupert Alison. You must know—'

Susanne deliberately over-reacted, teasing. 'Not at all. I thought he was Colonel Alison. So it's Rupert now, is it?'

'And why not? With you off with your local god—'

'Local god!'

'Rupert and I agreed that all he needs is one of those smooth black wigs you see in the pictures of gods, and you could mistake him

122

for an ancient Pharoah.'

Susanne said lightly, 'That's not the way to put me off. I think of him as an ancient Pharoah.'

A moment of silence, then Vita took her black and white kaftan down from its hanger. 'So where did you get to this afternoon while we were visiting Elephant Island and Kitchener Island and the gardens?'

'You see,' said Susanne, speaking airily because she was walking on air, 'I didn't need to go with you because I had my own exclusive tour this morning. And then after lunch I was taken round Aswan in one of those wonderful buggies drawn by dreadful skinny horses. I do wish I could send them a shipload of oats. They remind me of the cats in Greece, all bones.'

She hurried into the bathroom because she didn't want Vita asking her what she had seen this afternoon. She hadn't seen anything. 'You absorb,' Omar had said, sitting by her side holding her hand within the privacy of the hood and its shade. Omar was a private man. A man for occasions. 'Don't look at the detail,' he said. 'There will be many things you would prefer not to see, but you cannot change them.'

They had seen a tiny donkey endeavouring to pull a vastly overloaded cart of hay. The driver was beating it mercilessly in an endeavour to move it on. Men in long white

123

gowns with dark faces, each wearing a red fez, had appeared like magic out of the crowd to join lustily in the beating. Their fiendish cruelty had lit a fire of anger in her.

'Why don't you jump down and stop them, Omar?' she had shrieked as the donkey sank to the ground, dying.

That was when he had said what he said, lifting her hat from her head and holding it over her face. She had been offended as well as upset for a while. He told her he understood. 'This is Egypt,' he said. 'One has to live with it.'

'I never could.' She was trembling.

'You could,' he said, pressing his opinion into her heart and brain. After a while she recovered. Where had the sticks come from, she wondered, concentrating on that pointless point, pushing the rest out of her mind. A dozen men rushing out of the crowd carrying sticks! Did they hide them under their galabiyas?

She showered and changed into her striped kaftan. 'I must say it's an easy garment to wear in the heat,' she commented, looking at herself in the mirror, lightheartedly swinging the loose body of it.

Vita had hers on, too. They were both grateful to be out of their designer clothes for one evening. The passengers gathered in the bar, self-conscious and jolly. 'They're fun, but when we are ever going to wear them at home,

124

I can't imagine.' You heard it on every side. Susanne found Peter leaning disconsolately on the bar.

He looked her up and down, grinning. 'I have to say that suits you.'

'I'm gratified. And yours suits you.' It didn't. It made him look long-necked and bony, all angles, an Englishman uncomfortable in fancy dress, not trying to come to terms with it.

'I'll be glad when we leave Aswan,' he said. 'I might get a chance to talk to you. I gather you're not going ashore for dinner.' He looked pointedly at her kaftan.

'You're quite right.'

'Have we seen the end of Mr Saheed, then?'

'He's having dinner with his father.'

'And you're having yours with your mother, I suppose,' he said sourly. 'What a pair you are.'

If she had known him better she would have called him a dog in the manger. Then she realised that would have been unkind. She understood his disappointment. The only girl of his age on the boat, by a quirk of fortune, had become unavailable. 'If you had bothered to ask me I would have said I'd be pleased to have dinner with you,' she said. 'Let me buy you a drink.' She spoke to the barman. 'Two gins, please.'

Peter pulled money out of his pocket and slapped it down on the counter. 'Right. I'll pay for these.'

She was glad to be able to raise his spirits. Across the room she saw the Colonel chatting animatedly with Vita. Everyone seemed happy, though mostly self-conscious, often giggly. They admired each other's fancy dress, exclaiming at the colours.

'I shall wear it as a nightdress when I get home.'

'D'you think it would be suitable for a barbecue?'

'I know I shall never wear mine. D'you think Oxfam would take it?'

Colonel Alison was dignified in his. He stood the way the Nubians stood, militarily erect. That was the way to wear the garment to its best advantage. She smiled across the room at him and he smiled back.

They wandered into the dining-room at the end of the queue and took a table for two. Susanne was aware of surreptitious glances, whispers. It didn't need much imagination to guess they were all agog with the knowledge that she had disappeared with the Egyptian this morning and now was accepting the attentions of the archaeologist. A goldfish in a bowl isn't the half of it, she thought.

Peter shook out his impeccably ironed table napkin and looked at her thoughtfully. 'Our Mr Abdou was asking some rather pertinent questions about you today.'

'Oh? What kind of questions?'

'You can imagine. You are a bit of a

126

mystery, aren't you? Two glossy rich women, mother and daughter, travelling together on a down-market package.'

Susanne reacted automatically. 'We are not rich,' she said very distinctly. 'I would be grateful if you'd take that fact on board. And I don't see why you should think us a mystery. My parents have recently been divorced. Vita was at a low ebb. And I've had trouble with my job. I came home while I was sorting myself out.' Nothing but the truth.

'Sorry about your mother,' Peter said. 'Sorry about your job. What kind of job was it?'

'Marketing.'

He gave her a puzzled look. 'Do you really need a job? I mean, how do you fit one in with those racehorses?'

She was bored with explaining the horses weren't hers. She leaned across the table, elbows akimbo, knuckles beneath her chin. 'What were these pertinent questions Mr Abdou was asking?'

'About your background. I said you kept racehorses and wore designer-label clothes. That's all I could tell him. It's all I know.'

She sat up erect in her chair saying in an exasperated voice, 'I do not keep racehorses. And an archaeologist wouldn't know a designer label from a hole in the ground. What on earth made you say that?'

He grinned. 'I keep my ears open.'

She looked quickly round to ensure she

wouldn't be overheard, then said in a low voice, 'I shouldn't think too many of these passengers would know a designer label when they saw one, either.'

'There's one who does. She used to work in Harvey Nichols and she's a great chatterer.' Peter looked smug.

Susanne heaved a sharp sigh. She said in a bleak voice, 'Didn't you ask Mr Abdou why he wanted to know about me?'

Peter fixed her with a stare. 'I thought it was pretty obvious. I thought he'd been asked to find out.'

She remembered that Abdou had been on the gangplank when Omar delivered her back to the boat. She recalled his accompanying Omar back to the carriage. They had walked up the steps slowly. She had watched them, both men with their heads down, deep in conversation. Why should Omar look into her background? 'Tell me about yourself,' he had said. That was all. Hardly a catechism. She had to admit she had been less than forthcoming. But all the same, he hadn't pressed her. Now she wondered. People in foreign countries had different ways of doing things.

'You're not drinking your wine,' she said, noting that the edge to her voice betrayed her apprehension. She raised her own glass and sipped. The wine was rich and silky on her tongue.

Peter looked into his glass, then lifted it to

128

his lips. 'This Captain Saheed is obviously important, but has he got any money, that's what you ought to be asking yourself, Susanne.'

She said, pretending to misunderstand him, 'Why should I care?'

Peter leaned forward across the table. 'Because I get the impression from these questions Abdou's asking that he's looking for a rich wife.'

The words 'Don't be silly,' rose automatically to her lips. She bit them back and said in what she hoped was a perfectly reasonable voice, 'You do seem rather to have money on the brain. I've told you I haven't got any so if you're sure of your facts and feel impelled to interfere you have my permission to tell Abdou to hand on the message that Captain Saheed is barking up the wrong tree.'

Peter looked hurt. At that moment one of the Nubian waiters came with a platter of chicken and rice. They sat in silence while he arranged the plates and the bowls of vegetables. Immediately he had gone Peter said, 'Let's forget this contentious subject, shall we?'

'With the greatest pleasure. If you hand your plate over I'll serve you.' She decided to put the matter out of her mind.

CHAPTER SEVEN

'So, what's happening today?' Vita asked next morning, standing in front of Susanne with a patient, waiting look and an air of expecting to be dismayed by the answer to her question.

'I've made my own arrangements,' she said.

'You're going riding with that man?'

'Let's not row over this, Mother. I'm not a child.'

'In terms of what you're faced with, maybe you are,' Vita said looking desperately worried. 'This isn't the Home Counties, my dear.'

Susanne recognised she should have faced up to her mother last night when her nerves had been smoothed by the dinner wine instead of pretending to be asleep when Vita came to bed. This morning, not only did she not want to talk, she couldn't. Omar was only an hour away. She felt his nearness, was concerned with her own vulnerability. She did not want to share these feelings that she scarcely understood; the nervousness and the certainty; the magic. Last night had been full of haunting dreams. She was afraid of the Englishness in Vita as she would be afraid of a knife cutting away at the newness before she could come to terms with it.

'I take it,' said Vita, sounding tired now and

rather desperate, 'that since you're wearing jeans you're going riding again.'

'Right first time.' It wasn't the kindest answer but it had the strength and rigidity to cut off further protest. Susanne opened the cabin door and went down to breakfast.

Later, she made no effort to check the excitement that leapt and danced in her as she ran up the steps from the gangplank to the road with the silk stole that was to protect her head from the sun hanging loosely over one arm. The clamouring children were waiting for her. They urged her with big, longing eyes to buy beads, ornaments, effigies of the Egyptian gods. She smiled at them and signed that they should make a path for her so that she might pass through them. *'Baksheesh! Baksheesh!'* they implored. Knowing she would be beseiged, she didn't dare toss a coin. She walked swiftly until she was out of sight of the riverboat. She was full of nervous anxiety. She didn't want the passengers to witness the precious moment when she met Omar.

He came down the road fast, driving his friend's car, and pulled up in a flurry of dust. She opened the door and slipped in beside him.

'You were having a morning walk?' He gave her an amused, questioning smile.

'I'm tired of the goldfish-in-the-bowl syndrome. The passengers' eyes stick out as though they're on stalks when they see me with

131

you. Do you get this sort of attention always?'

'Always,' he replied solemnly. 'At least I'm glad to hear you don't run off down the road because you're ashamed to be seen with me.'

She threw back her head and laughed, at ease with herself again, the anxiety driven away by his magical presence. His reality. His prompt arrival. Him. 'That's the most blatant false modesty I've ever heard,' she told him, eyes sparkling. He laughed with her. They drove by the fields of maize and cotton; past the date palms, the lemon and orange trees, and came to the enclosure where the old servant was patiently waiting.

'*Ahlan*,' Susanne greeted him and he bowed his head in acknowledgment. '*Ahlan.*'

Omar looked amused.

'I know all of four words now.'

'I'm very proud of you.'

He spoke to the man at length then they went into the little compound. The horses, already saddled, lifted their beautiful heads. Rose whinnied a greeting. Susanne kissed her on her velvety nose. 'I'll give you a leg up. We won't hurry,' Omar said. 'It's extra hot this morning. Do you feel the heat?'

She had thought she had imagined the heat. Surely one day in the desert was much like another? But when they rode out of the shade and the sun beat down on her face she knew it was hotter than yesterday. Ahead of them the desert was a blinding white furnace. 'We are, of course, an hour later,' Omar said. He reined in and Susanne pulled up beside him. 'It is too late,' he said with regret. 'This isn't fair to the horses.' He bent over and reassuringly rubbed his stallion's neck. 'We must find some shade.'

They followed the geometrical lines of the cultivated fields, walking in single file. There was no chance of a gallop. They rode for an hour until they came into a valley green with palms and lush vegetation. Omar drew rein then slid out of his saddle. Susanne followed suit.

He attached both pairs of reins to saplings. The horses immediately nosed down into the lush green grass that grew all round them. Susanne felt they had come to a crossroads and that the way ahead was beyond a decision that had to be made in her mind. A decision not to turn back. At the crossroads was the test. She felt herself trembling.

Omar took her hand and led her into some deeper shade. Around them now were taller trees overhanging, and on one side a sandstone rock. Before the rock was a spongy-looking mat of moss and grass and flowers. A drooping branch made a curtain on one side, and on the other trailing ferns that had grown out of the rock hung down so that one could see, with a surge of willing imagination, a little green room.

Omar put two fingers beneath her chin and lifted it. 'When the moment is right we see the

133

way ahead,' he said as though he, too, knew about the crossroads in her mind. That sculptured mouth brushed hers, exploring it. She felt his tongue between her lips, light and enquiring. It was as though the moment had been carried from that so poignant time in the cave the day before when he had said she was not ready. She was ready now. Ready to offer herself to him. He knew.

'Time after time we have been lovers,' he whispered the words, though there was only bountiful nature to hear them. 'Each time it is a renewal.'

She found it easy to believe how it would happen, down through the ages, in every incarnation a search for each other and a new beginning. She was carried away with the dream. She thought she was going through a rite that would take her with him, back into the world they had lost.

Swiftly, they divested themselves of their clothes and sank on to the soft green moss. Her tears were wet on her cheeks, or were they his tears? She felt a sense of deliverance from the past. She was going forward with him, losing her separateness. They experienced the binding of invisible threads; a oneness. Completion.

*   *   *

Omar, in a proprietary move that surprised

her, took Susanne's arm as they entered the hotel lounge, leading her towards the man who had already risen and was eyeing her critically. She walked as though her muscles were fluid, drifting rather than walking. She thought he must see, as everyone in the lounge must see, she was in a state of total love, given and received.

He took in everything about her. But not the love. Oh, he saw it all right. It slid across his outer eye from which it was discarded as unacceptable. He wanted her to know he did not approve of her being here, on the arm of his son.

Cocooned by Omar's love, Susanne remained untouched by his rejection.

Twenty-five years ago the General must have looked exactly like Omar. His hair was still as crisp and thick as his son's, but now it was greying at the temples. He had the same well-cut, firmly set mouth. Almost too firm, Susanne thought. And his figure was heavier, too. Good living had thickened it. He looked like a man who is accustomed not only to making decisions but to having his way. The same look Omar had.

'Please sit down,' he said when the introductions had been made. 'I will order something to drink. What will you have?' He did not smile. His words were more a demand than a courtesy.

'Orange juice, thank you.' She was thirsty.

135

'You have been riding again?' He addressed Omar directly. She assumed he had not expected her to be riding.

Omar nodded.

'It is too hot,' his father said curtly. 'You went in the desert?'

'No.'

Susanne was aware that the older man was waiting for details, and that his son was withholding them, not accepting his censure, not needing his approval. There was no tension between the two men. She sensed a demarcation line over which both knew better than to step. The waiter came and took their orders. She noted that Omar's father ordered whisky, not abiding by the rules.

He was watching her. His eyes were intrusive, seeing too much. She sought for something to say and came up with, 'It was very kind of you to sort out the trouble with the plane to Abu Simbel.'

He raised his heavy dark brows. 'I understand you did not go. There was a mistake?'

Omar said, 'I would not have asked the favour if Susanne had been going.'

His father smiled faintly. 'I see. My son bears watching, Miss Landseer. He's full of tricks.'

'I think she would like you to call her Susanne,' Omar said.

The General stared at his son, as though

waiting for an explanation. Omar stared back. Susanne floundered after something to say to break the discomfort of the silence, but the General spoke. 'That is a French name.' He said it critically, as though she had no right to a French name.

'Yes. But it's been adopted by the English.'

'You speak French?'

'Yes.'

'She did not speak French when she was named,' Omar said and suddenly they were all relaxed, and smiling.

She wanted to please him, this hard man who did not approve of her, so she said conversationally, 'I started going to France when I was ten. In England it's customary for children to make exchange visits with French children.'

'For some children.'

'Of course.' She was aware that he was remarking on her status.

'My business here will be over this evening.' Youssel Saheed spoke directly to Omar. 'We will fly back to Cairo in the morning. Perhaps even late tonight.'

'I shan't be going with you.'

The waiter came with the drinks. His father picked up his glass. 'I would like you to come,' he said.

'If you have a good reason, that's a different matter, but I have your diary. There's nothing that would necessitate my being with you.'

His father sipped his drink. 'We'll discuss it later.' He glanced at the watch on his wrist. 'My driver hasn't come. Perhaps you would find him.'

With innate politeness, Omar rose. Before he had gone more than a few yards his father said, 'You will understand, Miss Landseer—'

'Susanne.' She realised immediately that he saw her interjection as an impertinence. He did not wish to call her by her first name.

He took out a packet of cigarettes. His eyes were cast down as he selected one and lit it. He did not offer the packet to her. Then he continued as though she had not spoken, '— that though my son is a travelled and worldly man, no Egyptian is really accustomed to the liberated ways of western girls.'

So he knew they had been out riding together! Or guessed. Susanne felt the colour rise in her cheeks, felt hapless guilt looking out of her eyes. In that one sentence Youssel Saheed had reduced the beauty and wonder of the morning to a cheap encounter between two strangers.

His eyes came back to hers. He took a long draw at his cigarette and seemed to settle his feet more firmly on the floor, placing them slightly apart. 'My son is an extremely eligible man,' he said. 'There have always been women chasing after him. He likes women. He likes their company. And he likes to flirt with them. Last year there was an American. She was

138

beautiful, and very rich. My son is not rich, you know, Miss Landseer. Before Egypt became a republic my family had a great deal of land and many houses, but the new régime has changed all that. And of course it is right,' he conceded. 'There should not be very rich people when so many are without food.

'But that is not what we're talking about at the moment. This woman wanted Omar to go to America. She had a project for him. She wanted him to look after her racing stables. It was very tempting for him, and he was half in love with her.' General Saheed leaned forward, arms resting on those parted knees, and looked at Susanne with eyes like dark stones, 'She wanted him for his connections with people in high places. But he cannot be bought, you understand. He likes money, but he cannot be bought.'

Susanne felt her courage returning. 'I can't imagine what this story has to do with me. I'm not rich. I have nothing to offer him.'

Now the General was openly amused. Smiling. He had the same white, even teeth that Omar had. 'I was in love with an English girl myself. An Irish girl, to be quite precise. She said her family was poor. But as it turned out, they owned a castle in Ireland. Her father complained all the time about being poor.' Again that amused look. 'I understand you westerners. I understand what you are not saying. Of course your family don't work in the fields, up to their ankles in water for twelve hours a day, contracting bilharzia, like as not, and dying young as a poor man in Egypt does. There are degrees of poverty. But that a man can complain about being poor and live in a castle? This is not the Egyptian way of saying things.'

Susanne said, 'I think your Irishman who owned a castle would, in his terms, be poor because he couldn't afford to heat and renovate it.' She smiled at him. 'That's poverty of a kind. But I didn't say I was poor. I said I wasn't rich. I earn my living, as does my mother.'

'What does your mother do?'

He was over-stepping the mark. Susanne said indignantly, 'You have no right to question me like this.'

'So you have nothing to offer him,' Youssel Saheed nodded two or three times, looking down at his hands. 'We have plans for Omar.' She had a feeling he was about to say something of the utmost importance, perhaps the real matter for which he had come here today. Then he seemed to change his mind. He lifted his head and looked at her with worried eyes. The stony quality had gone. 'We are very close, my son and I,' he said. And then he added, 'Omar has never brought a western woman to meet me before.'

'The American?'

He shook his head.

'Your driver is waiting.'

At the familiar voice they both jumped. Omar was standing looking down at them with an amused expression on his face. His father rose and stubbed out his cigarette in the ashtray with fierce little jabbing movements. He stood erect, eye-to-eye with his son. 'I'll see you later.' Susanne recognised he was delivering an order. Then he turned to her. 'Good-bye, Miss Landseer.' She extended her hand but he ignored it.

'Good-bye General Saheed.' She watched him turn swiftly away. She felt no malice towards him, only sympathy. But beyond that sympathy, on another level, there was a touch of fear. Her eyes lingered on his erect back as he strode off across the room.

Omar sat down beside her, lifted her hand and looked into her eyes. 'Did he give you a bad time?'

She knew then that was what he had expected and bit back indignation. 'He did, rather. You took a mighty long time to find his driver.' She made a small movement to draw her hand away but his fingers held firm.

'I wanted you to get to know each other,' he said.

She recognised his sincerity. 'We didn't get to know each other at all,' she said. 'We had a sparring match. Your father doesn't want to know me.'

'He will. Some things take time.' He signed

141

to a waiter. 'I think you should have something stronger than orange juice.' He gave the order in Arabic then turned back to her. 'My father is a bit of a despot.'

She made a little gesture of acceptance. 'I gathered that.'

'But we have great respect for each other.'

She seemed to remember his having said that before, the part about respect. She felt edgy, thinking General Saheed had made it very clear he had no respect for her and her English ways. She felt unclean, as though she had allowed herself to be seduced by this fine, upstanding son of his who in the way of men, was expected to do what he liked with the kind of woman his father understood her to be. But more than that, he had jerked the magic carpet from beneath her feet. She saw herself now as an ordinary tourist, bumped up at that, passing herself off as the owner of clothes she could not afford. She shook her head, trying to shake the poison away.

The waiter returned with two gins. Omar carefully poured the tonic into hers, speared a slice of lemon, looked up, smiled into her eyes. His closeness was melting the protective crust she had swiftly grown to defend herself. She smiled back at him, felt the magic seeping towards her, sliding into the nooks and crannies of her mind. She felt again the silky texture of the magic carpet beneath her feet. 'Why did you want me to meet him?' she asked, thinking of the American who had tempted him but whom he had not introduced to his father.

'I wanted him to know that something has happened to me of which he may not approve. It is important for him to accustom himself to it. The other night, when I spotted you on the riverboat, I said to myself, "Stop! It is here. What you have been looking for is here."' He said thoughtfully, 'Somehow, I always knew I would recognise it when I saw it.'

'Even at sixty feet you recognised what you had been looking for?' She felt tearful, looking at his beautiful, lifted head, his dark and wonderful eyes.

'Sixty feet, or two hundred. Distance does not matter. I could tell.'

She was back where she had been. Where they had been together. She said, 'I wouldn't like to come between you and your father.'

'You will not.'

'You realise we don't know a thing about each other?'

'I am a man. You are a woman. What more is there to know?'

Over lunch in the big hotel dining-room, she repeated what Abdou had said, that his family was descended from royalty. 'Your king was driven abroad in the fifties. How does it happen that your family remains important now that Egypt is a republic?'

He laid his knife and fork down. His hands

fanned out briefly. 'My grandfather, who should have gone into exile with the King, persuaded the new powers-that-be to allow us to stay. After all, he was not so much a royalist as an Egyptian. He had a lot to offer the new Egypt. They confiscated our lands and our houses but,' Omar shrugged, 'why should a man have more than one house when there are people going without? You must know that human beings are very resilient. It would not be possible to get through life otherwise.'

She sensed another meaning behind his words. She dug her fork into the delicious fish, giving herself time. And after all, she did not come up with a suitable reply.

He answered for her. 'You will be surprised how resilient you are.'

She tried to look into the future to see when she was going to have to draw on this resilience but nothing presented itself.

Outside, a horse drawn carriage awaited them. Omar enjoyed her surprise. 'You didn't hear me order it?'

'I dare say I did, but in Arabic. It's easy for you to surprise me, me with my four words.'

'I shall expect you to know five Arabic words by tomorrow. But of course I will teach you the language. You'll not find it difficult,' Omar said. 'And I'll ensure the surprises keep coming.' He helped her aboard.

'And what is today's surprise?' she asked as they settled into the canopied seat, safe from the sun.

'A visit to the red-granite quarry which I believe you missed through coming riding with me.'

Her heart sank. Hadn't she been congratulating herself on missing this hot journey into a quarry to see a half-finished statue, ninety-two feet long as Peter said?

'I am taking you to look upon the Lord of Eternity,' Omar said. 'Osiris. Father of Horus, the falcon. The god-kings closely associated themselves with this falcon.'

Ah! That was a very different matter.

The driver whipped the horse. Omar spoke to him sharply. The man argued vociferously. Omar reached out for the whip and with bad grace the driver handed it over. Omar dropped it on the floor of the carriage and put his heel on it, signifying his contempt. The horse settled to clip-clopping along in a leisurely style. 'He is happy now,' Omar said with satisfaction. 'There is no hurry. Osiris has been waiting for us for two thousand years. He won't go away in the next ten minutes.'

'Tell me about him.'

'You don't know?' Omar pretended to be shocked. 'What is that archaeologist doing to earn his cruise?'

'I'm sure Peter has talked about him. In fact I know he has. He's very enthusiastic,' she said loyally. 'It's my fault that his facts and figures go in one of my ears and before they reach my mind, trickle out of the other. It's ungrateful of me, I know.'

'So, I will tell you about Osiris,' Omar said. 'It is fitting for us to visit him today since he is a god of the earth and vegetation. We came together, did we not, in the arms of the earth and sheltered by its plants.'

'Omar!' She felt engulfed by the poetry, the history, and his love.

'It was right. And natural. Too much of life is organised. To love in a man-made bed is not the same as blending your love with nature, beneath god-given trees. The bounty of Osiris. All your life and in other lives you will remember the soft green scents of the Nile valley where we came together again.'

When she came sufficiently out of the enchantment to speak she asked, 'What do you mean by the bounty of Osiris?'

'His death is symbolized in the annual drought. His miraculous rebirth was the periodic flooding of the Nile.' Omar smiled. 'Nothing happened in ancient Egypt that was not arranged by one god or another.' It occurred to her that he had a mischievous smile.

The horse was slowing down. The driver flung a query over his shoulder. Omar pointed out where he was to stop.

Susanne's first sight of the god Osiris, Lord of Eternity, was a shock. An abandoned stone statue, yet grand in its abandonment, the sand

and stones of the quarry its bedfellows. She gazed at it with awe.

'Why was it never finished?'

'Who knows?' Omar, hands in pockets, feet apart, looked broodingly down upon it. 'Perhaps it was meant this way. Perhaps it is meant to symbolise the fall of my country's once great civilisation. Whatever the reason for the sculptors laying down their tools, it's been irretrievably lost in the remote past.' His eyes had taken on that distant look with which she was becoming familiar. She thought he had gone off on his own magic carpet. They stood in contemplative silence, looking down.

He half turned towards her. 'You know your poet, Shelley? Percy Bysshe Shelley?'

'You have had an English education!' she exclaimed in surprise.

'No. But I know your English poets. I believe Shelley was looking at the unfinished statue of Rameses II when he was inspired to write his Ozymandias poem,' Omar said, 'but it's equally true of Osiris.'

Ozymandias! Yes, she remembered it from school.

Omar's eyes were misty as he gazed out over the desert, murmuring in a voice so soft it seemed merely to caress her hearing,

'I met a traveller from an antique land
Who said: Two vast and trunkless legs of stone
Stand in the desert. Near them, on the sand,

147

Half sunk, a shattered visage lies, whose frown,
And wrinkled lip, and sneer of cold
   command,
Tell that its sculptor well those passions read
Which yet survive, stamped on these lifeless
   things,
The hand that mocked them and the heart
   that fed.
And on the pedestal these words appear:
"My name is Ozymandias, King of kings.
Look on my works, ye Mighty, and despair!"
Nothing beside remains. Round the decay
Of that colossal wreck, boundless and bare
The lone and level sands stretch far away.'

Susanne lifted her gaze to survey those sands
stretching away into a heat haze, far beyond
where the eye could see. She felt some part of
her going into the distance, weeping. Moving
close to Omar, she touched his hand,
grounding herself in his love.

'Who knows what despair was attendant
upon the decline of my people?' Omar said
broodingly.

She felt overwhelmed by it, as though she
had been a part of that decline herself.

CHAPTER EIGHT

'Come,' Omar said, 'it's too hot here. We must get back into the shade.' The driver was hunched in his seat, head lolling. Omar snapped out an order in Arabic. The man woke up and shook his reins. The poor, sad horse lifted his head, shook himself awake and raised a desultory hoof.

'I am going to take you to the *souk*. It will be cool there.'

They were silent for a while as they rode back, sitting a little apart so that the air could move between them. Susanne's fingers were splayed on the seat. Omar stroked them thoughtfully. 'You have strong hands. You need them for the horses you ride. Your father is a racing man?'

'The horses I ride belong to a neighbour.' Hadn't she told him that? 'My father's in business.' Darren and his bankruptcy, his inability to run a business of his own until his debts were cleared, seemed far away.

Omar gave the driver some coins. He reacted with indignation. Omar spoke a few sharp words then taking her arm walked away. The driver's whining complaints followed them.

'Do they always argue like that?'

'Always. But one must not pay them what

they ask or the price would rise and rise until no one could afford them, and they would be out of work.'

They went together up the dusty road and through the *souk*. It was cooler here within the roofed arcades though the hordes of people inevitably kept the temperature up. Omar showed her the interior of coffee houses, perfume shops, tiny emporiums stacked with bales of cotton. In the distance she saw a little cluster of people from the boat. They stared hard at Omar, then turned hastily away.

'I want to buy you a gift,' he said leading her towards the door of a jeweller's shop.

'Oh no. Please. Please, you mustn't do that.' Susanne held back but he moved her inexorably on, into the shop then right up to the counter. 'There's no one here,' she said, feeling relieved.

He leaned over the counter, looking down at the floor behind. A salesman, or perhaps the owner, was kneeling on a prayer mat, arms outstretched in front of him, his forehead resting on the floor. Omar backed away. 'We will look at his jewellery. He will attend to us when he is ready.'

'Why is he praying?'

'There's no need to whisper. His English will be minimal. He will know only enough to sell to the tourists. He is obeying the rules of the Koran which says that a Muslim must pray five times a day with his body pointing towards

150

Mecca, the Arabian city where Mohammed was born. He will pray at sunrise, at noon, at mid-afternoon, sunset and evening. So when you hear the *muezzin* calling the faithful to prayer from the top of the minaret, don't be surprised if you find people all round you dropping to their knees,' Omar said gravely. 'It is the custom of the country.'

'With one's head on the floor? Do you go down on your knees with your head on the floor?'

Omar, with a gesture that seemed to lift him elegantly above the unquestioning masses said, 'No. That is not to say I am right.'

'And if one is caught out in a dusty street, or a muddy field?'

He smiled at her. 'Did you notice the servant who guarded our horses was sitting on a rug when we returned? That is his prayer mat. He carries it everywhere.'

She smiled back at him. 'You are not carrying a prayer mat.'

'I don't accept everything I'm told. It may be that I'm not so happy this way as those who blindly accept the teachings, but I believe we must ask ourselves why we are here. And what we should do about it.'

She felt she was getting to know him with her brain, which was different from the knowing of her heart.

He began to examine some trays of jewellery that were displayed under glass. 'Tell

151

me what you think of this.' He pointed to a necklace, gold set with coloured stones. 'Those are the stones of the desert,' he said. 'Amethysts, turquoises and carnelians. You would wear this?'

She visualised herself in a low-cut black dress wearing this magnificent piece, feeling like a queen. She thrust the image away, protesting, 'I love it, but I can't accept. I really cannot.'

He raised one hand and pressed his fingers against her lips. 'From me, you can accept anything. You will wear it tonight when I take you to dinner.'

'You may have to go back to Cairo tonight.'

'No,' he said. 'I will not return to Cairo. I will pick you up at the riverboat at seven-thirty.'

A dark head rose from behind the counter and spoke gently to Omar in Arabic. In a mirror on the back wall Susanne caught a glimpse of the people from the boat as they walked slowly past the shop, some peeping and smiling, some ostentatiously looking the other way. She hastily lowered her eyes. The Arab opened the display case and brought out the necklace. He laid it on a little cushion of black velvet.

'He says there's a bracelet to match.'

'Oh no, please.'

'It is not so valuable,' Omar said, 'only desert stones. But as you see, it is very

152

beautiful.' He lifted the necklace and put it round her neck.

'No, Omar. Really, I can't accept it.'

He looked puzzled.

Her English voice said, 'I've only known you a few days, Omar.'

'You have known me for all time.'

Yes, that was the dream. But the gift was earthbound. On a different plane.

'You are not ready,' he said, as he had said in the cave when she thought he was going to kiss her. She could see he was disappointed with her for refusing to accept the dream.

He replaced the necklace in the tray, spoke to the Arab shopkeeper, took her arm and walked out.

She wanted to apologise. She wanted to say she would after all accept the jewellery, but he seemed to have cast the matter aside. 'Come,' he said, 'we will find a gharry and I will take you back to the boat.'

As Susanne came up to the top deck she saw Peter standing at the rail. His forehead was red, his eyebrows had faded to blonde. The fair skin of his neck and the 'V' of his chest that was showing through his open-necked shirt was burned to a bright pink. He came forward to meet her, hunch-shouldered and angry. 'So you're back,' he said ungraciously. 'You're not getting your money's worth out of this trip, you know. You missed two coach tours today.'

'I've been riding again.'

'Am I supposed to know?'

'I'm sorry.' She could have told him it was none of his business what she did or where she went but she didn't want to make an enemy of him.

'You can't have been riding all day,' he said.

'Well, no. It's far too hot. I've been riding and lunching and sightseeing and shopping. But I'm sure you know all about my movements, Peter. I saw several of the passengers in the bazaar when Captain Saheed was helping me choose some jewellery. And they saw me.'

'Come off it, Susanne. You've been with him for a couple of days. You don't call him Captain.'

'I call him Omar.'

'Of course.' He seemed satisfied with having forced that out of her.

'I don't want to quarrel with you, Peter.'

'Nor I with you. So what did you buy, rich lady?'

'Nothing, in the end.'

He raised one hand, finger pointing as though scribbling in the air. 'Headline. Rich girl with thoroughbred horses takes up with son of one-time Egyptian Olympic champion.'

Swiftly hiding her surprise she said, 'You're confirming what I said about the gossip.'

'Has your friend, Omar,' the name grated off his tongue, 'ridden in the Olympics? Or his

154

father?'

'I don't know. He doesn't boast.'

'I'll bet he boasts about his so-called royal connections. For what they're worth,' Peter said, 'considering his country has been a republic for nearly fifty years.'

Susanne was running out of her carefully nurtured patience. Besides, she felt now he had by his sneering forfeited any rights to her sympathy. 'He answered my questions, no more than that,' she said. It was ridiculous that Peter should adopt this watch-dog attitude towards her. She made a considered decision to put him in his place, but she spoke gently, without rancour. 'What I do is no concern of yours.'

'What an English girl does on a foreign tour is the concern of those who are looking on. Logan's worried about your disappearances even if your mother isn't. He's responsible to his tour company for the safety of the party.'

She was angry now at his criticism of Vita. 'Really, Peter, you're being ridiculous. I've been riding, not disappearing, and with a man of high repute. According to Abdou, everyone in Egypt knows the Saheed family. Abdou hadn't met him when he saw him on the riverbank looking at the boat, but he recognised him.'

'How?'

'I don't know. Newspaper pictures? Or maybe his father's pictures. They're alike.'

Peter reacted sharply. 'How do you know what his father looks like?'

Chagrined at the slip, she looked away.

'How do you know?' he persisted.

She sighed deeply and assuming a pained voice, replied, 'Because he was at the New Cataract Hotel where we had lunch. I saw him. I'm now going to change. I really don't want to quarrel with you, Peter,' she said again and swinging round started to walk towards her cabin.

'Don't go,' he said, 'I heard something that might interest you today.' She hesitated. 'I heard it from Hassan. Your friend Omar had a suitable girl picked out for him a long time ago. She's sitting around waiting patiently for him to find the time to marry her.'

Susanne stared at him. It was as though Egypt stood still, waiting. On the outer perimeter of her mind she noted the expression of triumph on Peter's face.

'It's been arranged since she was a child. That's the way they do things in eastern countries.'

'I'm sure if that's what he wants he'll get on with it,' she said, not recovering but somewhere among the confusion, the withering humiliation, finding a voice to speak with, never mind the words.

Peter's eyes hadn't left her face. 'It's rumoured he wants a rich westerner instead.'

She managed to hide the shock though her

head was reeling. She thought of what had happened in the desert this morning, as Omar said, no more than a natural renewal of their love. Or had she been seduced by a foreigner with a sophisticated line in wooing second to none? She looked up into Peter's worried English face and read there that he knew something had happened. Something perhaps that meant she was a little mad from the sun.

He said, 'You'd better get ready for my lecture. It's on in twenty minutes.'

She thought by his tone that what he saw in her eyes had unnerved him. She felt unnerved herself.

Because she was not yet ready to face Vita in the intimate confines of the tiny cabin, she went to the bow and stood at the rail while gazing blankly down into the brown waters of the Nile. Impressions crowded in. Disappointment and jealousy could make a man react quixotically. Peter had been so delighted to find a girl in his own age group on the cruise. She couldn't blame him for being angry. Angry enough to make up tales about Omar? No, she thought not. She had to believe what he said was true. That Omar was trying to avoid an arranged marriage. It was something that did make sense in this exotic world where she was otherwise out of her depth.

No wonder his father had been hostile towards her. Recollections jumbled through her mind. She remembered Omar's confidently bringing up the fact that her father was a race-horse owner. She was certain she had made it clear she exercised a neighbour's horses. She remembered too that he had scarcely listened to her answer. Because he had latched on to something he wanted to believe? Because, like his father, he had a woolly view of English understatement?

She thought about the jewellery he had wanted to buy for her. With a sense of shock she realised he had been very easily talked out of it.

But he loved her. She was overwhelmed by the violence of her emotions when she thought about that. Omar had loved her over and over again, for thousands of years. Since the god Osiris brought them together. Osiris, who was the father of Horus the falcon. The kings of Egypt, who were also Omar's ancestors, worshipped Horus the falcon. She saw in her mind's eye Omar's high-bridged nose, direct eyes and challenging air.

A bird of prey?

So, have Vita and I made fine fools of ourselves, she asked herself, leaning on the rail watching the afternoon fade. Both of us. We who are on a cruise that we cannot afford, creating a sensation in clothes we cannot afford? She felt her muscles tighten with tension, confusion, and even a little with shame. Yet part of her still clung tenaciously to the magic of Omar.

Or was it the magic of the tales he spun?

Nobody came up to the top deck. She stayed until she was so muddled in her mind that she could no longer think, then went with dragging footsteps to her cabin. Vita had not come in. As she turned from closing the door her eye caught sight of a flat, square package lying on the dressing table. She picked it up. On a label on the front her name was scrawled in black ink. Susanne Landseer.

She stared at it for a long moment while a knowing crept through her, taking over her heart and mind. Then she opened the little top drawer in the chest where she kept her small toiletries, took out a nail file and carefully slit the brown paper. Inside she found a white cardboard box. She lifted the lid, then the tissue. She was looking down on the necklace and bracelet Omar had wanted to buy her in the souk and which, she remembered now her brain had miraculously cleared, she had refused. There they lay, side-by-side, bright Egyptian gold set with those beautiful desert stones, amethysts, turquoises, carnelians.

There was the sound of the door opening. She swung round. Vita was standing in the doorway. Her face was flushed beneath the brim of her Philip Treacy hat, and strained. Her eyes brightened and sharpened. Susanne could see immediately that Vita had not expected to find her here. 'Hel-lo,' she said

159

with pleasure and relief. Then she saw the box in Susanne's hand. 'What have you bought?'

She held out the beautiful gift. She could not speak.

'You bought that! Heavens! Isn't it wonderful!' She peered closely. 'It looks as though it belongs on a god.' She looked anxiously up into Susanne's face. 'That must have made a hole in your travellers' cheques.'

'Omar bought it for me.'

'Oh, my dear,' said Vita, distressed.

She backed on to her bed. Her shoulder bag slid, unnoticed, to the floor. She looked up at her daughter. 'You shouldn't have accepted it. Really you shouldn't.'

'Well, I did.' A cavern yawned between them.

'Is it valuable?' Vita managed at last.

'I don't think so. It's not gold. Not solid gold, I mean. I'm sure it's not. They wouldn't sell solid gold in the bazaar—I mean *souk*—would they?'

Vita picked up the bracelet, examined it.

'If you look closely, you'll probably find those stones are flawed,' Susanne babbled, remembering what Peter had said. 'After all, as I said, sold in a *souk*. They're bound to be flawed. It's probably not at all expensive.'

Vita gave her a testing look. She rose, put the bracelet back and lifted the necklace. She held it against Susanne's throat, then turned her round to face the mirror. Susanne looked

160

into her own eyes and saw them change. Saw the necklace was no longer exotic and foreign—or was it that her own face was no longer English? She saw the mystery of the ancients in her eyes. She might have been a long-dead Egyptian queen.

They stood in silence. 'Oh well,' Vita said at last, looking tired. 'I'd better have a shower.' She turned towards the bathroom door, then back. The look she gave Susanne was long, thoughtful, and very disturbed. 'I must tell you, dear, and I hope it won't upset you, but we're getting into deep water. Mr Abdou is far from discreet. It's all round the boat that this man is searching for a rich wife.'

'Peter told me.'

Again that thoughtful look. 'In such circumstances, a necklace like that could be a sprat to catch a mackerel.'

'I've told him I'm not rich.' She clung to that fact, though knowing Omar hadn't believed her. And neither had his father believed her. They thought the English were into understatement on a large scale. Men who considered themselves poor lived in castles, Youssef Saheed had said.

Vita broke into her troubled thoughts, her voice sharp and at the same time despairing, 'I wish you'd never won that damn competition,' she said. 'We seem to have got ourselves into a fine pickle.'

Susanne put the necklace back in its box.

Put the box in a drawer out of sight. Out of sight but not out of mind. 'Do you think we should come clean?' she asked as she had asked before when matters appeared to be getting out of hand. 'Shall we tell them about the secondhand clothes and the prize for filling in a few answers to some pathetic questions that could have been dealt with by a bat?'

'No,' her mother replied as she had replied before. 'It's too late. We'll just have to hold our heads high and get through the next ten days as best we can.'

There was no longer time to shower and change. They hurried down for Peter's lecture. The saloon was packed. Everyone looked up. Stared. In their prickly self-awareness they were conscious of the fact that nobody called, 'There's a seat over here'. As outsiders they were left to fare as best they might.

It was Peter who came to their rescue. 'I think you'll find somewhere to sit over there,' he said pointing to the far corner of the room. They made their way between the chairs trying not to look self-conscious. There were indeed vacant chairs in the back row. They sat down.

'Tomorrow,' he said, 'we start our slow journey down the Nile. We go ashore at Komombo to see the Ptolemaic temple. You'll see the magnificent carved stone effigies of the gods Horus and Sobek. Horus has a falcon's head and Sobek a crocodile's head.

'Horus was the son of Isis. Fathered by Osiris, the lord of eternity,' Peter went on. 'He holds the symbol of life in his right hand. You'll see . . .'

'Wake up.' whispered Vita.

'I am awake. I'm thinking.' Listening to Peter's pedantic facts after Omar's poem-pictures was like drinking Thames water after champagne. Susanne closed off her hearing and went into a grey inner world where she considered the taste of Thames water.

It shouldn't be too difficult to rid herself of the image of a man she had known for such a short time. Scarcely knew at all. She had behaved like a cheap tart, he like a normal predatory male. She would put these few days' happenings down to experience and no harm done. Everyone should do something silly once in their youth. It wasn't her first indiscretion, but certainly her most potent. Most serious. Most stupid.

She glanced out of the big windows. Beyond the tall date palms on the river bank the scarlet Egyptian sun, so much brighter and bigger and grander than their English one, was sinking into a purple sky leaving a trail of primrose streaks behind. She caught her breath at its beauty. Its magnificent unreality. Faintly in the distance she heard the *muezzin* on his minaret calling the faithful to prayer.

God is most great!

I testify there is no god but Allah;

As his voice rose and fell she had a sensation
of floating, of being transported with it into
the unknown.

'Susanne!' hissed Vita.

She shook the strangeness away.

'The temple of Horus,' Peter was saying.
'Two hundred and thirty-seven B.C.'

When Omar came aboard later she would
be ready with the jewellery. She would give it
back to him politely but firmly, offering her
regrets that she could not dine with him
tonight. Tomorrow they would be gone, sailing
down river, and soon the dream would fade.
No doubt Omar would find his rich westerner
and make her very, very happy. He was a man,
she recognised, who would make any lucky
woman happy.

*   *   *

She chose a dinner dress with a high front and
low back; the kind that would not take a
necklace of any kind. A Cerruti label. She
didn't think about that. The problem of the
clothes had fallen into place. As Vita said, the
cruise would soon be over. They would never
see any of these people again. She re-wrapped
the little white box in which the jewellery had
been delivered, removed her name label, and
took it with her when she went to join the

gathering in the bar.

She had not intended to look across at the river bank but her eyes went obsessively there, searching among the beggar boys and the long, thin, anxious-faced souvenir sellers in their dirty white gowns. An elegant, dark-suited man wearing the look of a god or a king would not be difficult to pick out. She strained her eyes but he was not there. Neither was there a little black-haired message boy running down the steps, bright-faced in anticipation of *baksheesh*. She recognised that some part of her, some large and very important part of her, was unwilling to let go of the immediate past.

She went into the bar with head held erect and a smile on her face. She caught a glimpse of the smile in the mirror behind the bar, garish in its glassy unreality. She thought she looked like a mechanically propelled doll.

'Hi!' said Peter. 'I've got you a gin.' He frowned at her as he handed her a glass. 'So, what was my lecture about?'

'Is this an exam? I didn't realise we were to have exams. Cheers. Thanks for the drink.'

'Not an exam,' he said, looking at her hard. 'What was it about?'

'You know what it was about. You thought it up.'

'Oh, very witty. Ha, ha.'

'By the way, if you find your audience inattentive,' Susanne said, ignoring his sarcasm, 'all you have to do is change the time.

165

Hold the lectures after dark. I dare say there were other people in the room who couldn't concentrate when there was a magnificent sunset outside. And the palm trees and desert were only a couple of hundred yards away. It's not conducive to listening to a description of something one is going to see tomorrow.'

'I wasn't describing what you were going to see. I was telling you the history. The dates of the different dynasties etcetera.'

She flushed. 'Sorry.' They sipped their drinks. She was aware of being stared at. Of whispers. What were they saying? 'The archaeologist will do when the Egyptian doesn't come'? Or maybe, 'She's young. She's having fun.' Susanne hoped some of them were sufficiently kindly disposed to say that.

'Why do you keep glancing at the door?' Peter asked. The resentment in his tone told her he knew why. 'You're nervous as a cat.'

'No, I'm not nervous,' she said. She curled the fingers of her free hand into her palm and gripped them tightly. 'You misread the signals. I'm watching for my mother. I'm worried that Colonel Alison is going to lead her astray.' She adopted a worried frown. 'He is, after all, a stranger. I've heard a rumour he's got several wives at home, and that he's thinking of embarking on another marriage, if he finds the right gal. He thinks, mistakenly, of course, Vita's a good catch. But you know all about shipboard gossip. None of it may be true.'

166

Peter laughed appreciatively and squeezed her upper arm. 'It sounds as though you're not scarred for life.'

'By no means. Under this tender looking exterior I'm hard as nails.' The bravado ran out and she choked on the last word.

Peter stopped laughing. He was looking at her as though he knew she was crying inside but being a clumsy English boy he didn't know what to do about it. After a moment he turned away.

She smiled into the crowd entering the bar, smiled, too, towards those whom she could see through the door, leaning on the rail. She turned and smiled at the barman who hurried towards her thinking she wanted something. She smiled and smiled and smiled, holding her smile ready for when Omar should come and she had to give him the packet she held in her hand. He would be here at half-past seven.

Peter said, 'Do you want another drink? It's past eight. The dinner gong will be going in a minute.'

'No thanks,' she replied, still smiling. 'Shall we go down?'

'What's that you've got in your hand?'

'I meant to put it in my cabin. I'll nip up now.'

'I'll wait for you.'

She didn't look out on the shore either going up the steps or down. She knew Omar wasn't coming. Knew it with misery and

167

emptiness and despair. She knew also that had he come she would have gone with him.

CHAPTER NINE

They watched the slow movement of Egyptian life from the upper deck with the sun beating down and the breeze cool along the river. *Feluccas* like great elegant swans swept past them laden with cargo; small ones, jammed to the gunwales with standing passengers, slipped across from one side of the river to the other. Along the banks naked children played while their elegant mothers, tucking their long robes tidily within the curve of their bodies, bent over the brown waters doing the family washing.

They passed sand-coloured villages nestling among lush green palm trees. They saw the large-boned gamus walking patiently round in circles, yoked to its waterwheel; watched the buckets rising full of water. They saw trains of camels bearing outsize loads, stark against the pale sand-hills like cut-outs in a children's picture book. They watched *galabiya*-clad men leading them, and their women, heavily veiled, walking behind. It was hot out on deck but nobody complained. They all wanted to see the desert slide by.

Susanne was lying back in a deck-chair, the

long skirt of her kaftan hauled up to expose her legs to the sun. A shadow touched her and she looked up to see Peter standing close by, watching her. 'So you're going to get blonder and browner as we go down river while I'll get more beetrooty and flaky,' he said, looking wry.

'You should wear your hat,' she retorted.

'I keep losing it. I'm glad you're concerned enough to be bossy, anyway.'

'Sorry.' She was on edge; out of sorts. She had scarcely slept the night before. The cabin had been unbearably hot. Vita, in spite of the heat, was sound asleep. Susanne had crept out of bed, and being careful not to disturb her mother, had wrapped a warm stole round herself and gone out on deck. She had stood at the rail for hours, looking out over the darkened town with its golden pinprick lights, the cold piercing her inadequate clothing, the stars diamond-bright in a black sky.

She had welcomed the cold as a friend, needing to experience pain that would dull the sharp ache of Omar's going. Had the General, in the end, forced him to fly back to Cairo? Omar had shown an ability to fight, but were Egyptian fathers omnipotent? Omar was not only his son, he was an employee. But why had he not sent one of those little boys with a message? It was always possible to find a message boy in Egypt.

Had the General arranged for Mr Abdou to

169

hear the gossip that Omar was to marry an Egyptian girl? She couldn't believe it was Omar himself who had set it up as a way of telling her he had been merely having a bit of fun. He would know that English girls were considered to be easy conquests abroad. He had no doubt seen the film *Shirley Valentine*.

She thought wretchedly that he had paid for his fun with the necklace. If you allow yourself to be seduced by a stranger, if the stranger is a foreigner, as Peter would no doubt say, you can end up with a beautiful necklace, though she would no doubt find, if she cared to have it valued in London, it was of little value.

In every life he had searched and found her. 'It is a trick of the gods,' he had said, 'to separate those who belong together. It is our challenge to find each other.'

Gazing up at the brilliant stars in the black velvet sky she re-lived the dream that had been played out in the long fresh grasses beneath those trees that had been greened by the waters of the ancient river; swollen by the rains that swept up over the mountains of Ethiopia, Eritrea and the Sudan. She felt again the silken brush of Omar's bare skin on hers, the dizzying crush of his lips, his strong and gentle exploring hands. She heard him whisper over and over that they had been here before. And before that. And before that.

'Wake up,' said Vita shaking her arm, 'you'll get terribly sunburnt.'

She reached down, picked up her hat from the deck, placed it over her face, and retreated again into the loneliness of the night before.

As the sun began to edge over the rim of the desert Colonel Alison came to join her wearing a dressing-gown over his pyjamas and carrying a glass of golden liquid in his hand. Whisky, she guessed. They acknowledged each other's presence with a smile. The sun crept higher, blinding in its brilliance, lightening the sky. More night-attired passengers padded softly across the deck-boards in their slippers. No one spoke, and so the magic of the morning held. Only when the sun was a golden circle in the sky did they drift away. Susanne, too, went back into the dark, hot little cabin. Vita was still asleep. She lay down on her bed and waited for time to pass.

They sailed downstream and went ashore to visit Komombo, trudging over the hot sand beneath that burning sun. Susanne carried a notebook. She had brought it thinking she would make sketches and notes. In the event it remained empty. They went back to the boat and listened to another of Peter's lectures.

During the daylight hours they moved downstream at a leisurely pace. There was a great deal to see. Camels, little islands, *feluccas* ferrying passengers from one side of the river to the other. Most of them seemed to be dangerously overloaded. 'Life's cheap here,' Peter told the passengers, playing for laughs and getting them. 'If they tip over and get eaten by a crocodile they'll be born again before you can say Jack Robinson. Those of you who listen to my lectures will know they're heavily into reincarnation.' He cast a sly glance at Susanne.

One of the passengers loaned her a pair of field-glasses. Far in the distance, across the sand and in amongst the rocky hills, she now saw the black mouths of caves and experienced a jerk of the heart, remembering Omar's tenderness; remembering how he had lifted her chin and looked into her eyes then told her she was not ready. Now she saw the tenderness as part of his strategy. Was this his way of working up hunger in a woman? A sprat to catch a mackerel, as Vita had said.

She returned the binoculars to their owner then went and sat down in the blistering sun with her face shaded by her big hat, the hat that Omar had said showed her to be a woman of discrimination; the hat he had pressed on her head saying she did not need the crown of her beautiful hair; the hat he had used to shield her from the cruelty of the streets where men with nothing better to do beat little donkeys to death.

She thought about the cruelty of Egypt. She bent the hat brim down over her face, absorbing the sand colour of it—cinnamon she had decided when she chose it from Vita's stock—wiping out the cruelty, conjuring up

172

Omar's gentleness and his concern.

Luxor! They saw the ruins ahead as they came down river. The boat crept in and settled against the bank. Eager pedlars with out-thrust arms dangled necklaces at arm's length. Chattering sales talk filled the air with excitement. Skinny horses imprisoned between the shafts of black Victorian carriages trotted up the road tossing their heads defensively, helpless against the whiplash of drivers eager to be first in line when the passengers came ashore.

Vita was bristling with indignation. 'I do hate the cruelty,' she said to the Colonel. 'Those poor creatures can't go any faster, and anyway they shouldn't when they're between shafts. They might tip the carriage over. Why is that wretched man whipping them?'

'Sheer habit, I imagine,' he replied.

Her glance was angry as well as indignant. 'Do I take it you can get used to anything?'

'No. But if you live here you can't afford to be torn to pieces twice a day so you learn to turn a blind eye. Or tell yourself it's the will of Allah.'

'Oh God!' She put a hand to her forehead.

'It's not just the animals,' the Colonel said. 'People get their share. When I was out here last they hanged six Muslim militants.'

Her head came up sharply. '*Hanged* them! What for?'

'We only stopped hanging in England in the

173

sixties, you know,' he said.

'For murder, yes. What were these fellows hanged for?'

'For infiltrating the country from the Sudan with a stockpile of weapons.'

'We never hanged anyone for bringing weapons into the country. Did they try them?'

'Yes. That was the court's decision. The death sentence.'

'They're barbarous!'

He looked at her quizzically. 'In Egypt they don't wait for innocent civilians to be ambushed. They go to the source. And frankly,' he added, sounding soldierish and stern, 'if a member of my family was killed or mutilated in an attack where those weapons were used I'd regret that the terrorists hadn't been put to death before they had the chance to distribute their arms. It might anyway be preferable to rotting in an Egyptian gaol.' He looked round, saw Susanne gazing broodingly out over the ruins and remarked, 'Your daughter's very silent.'

'She's conscious of being observed all the time.'

'Sorry.' Recognising that Vita was on edge, he laid a hand over hers on the rail sympathetically.

'It'll be the same for us if you continue to hog my company, Rupert,' she said, withdrawing her hand.

'I'm on my own, you're on your own. We're

174

the only singles on board. It's to be expected that we'd get together, my dear.'

Abstractedly, Vita moved away, not liking his choice of words. He followed her at a discreet distance along the rail towards the bow of the boat. There was nobody else up there. 'You're a very attractive woman,' he said coming up beside her. 'I don't wish to diminish the compliment but, frankly, I haven't found much in common with the rest of the passengers.'

Vita recognised that she was being touchy. She thought of all those lavish business trips abroad where she had gone at Darren's side. She had never known what it was like to be a lone woman, exposed to curiosity and whispers. But there's no getting out of this situation, she told herself. She had better accept the unpalatable fact that the two Landseer women were a gift to the gossips. She heaved a great sigh for what had been lost. Life had indeed been easier as a wife than it was now as an elegant divorcée. Vita was not falsely modest. She recognised that even the elegance, in the circumstances, was a disadvantage.

'Would you come with me to the *son et lumière*?' the Colonel asked. 'I still have a few words of Arabic. I could chastise the driver if he whipped the horses.'

She could see him doing that. The military man. She managed to smile. 'Thank you.'

'And your daughter, too, if she'd care to, though I dare say young Peter'll want to take her under his wing.'

She opened her mouth to say Susanne might be glad of an opportunity to get away from Peter, then closed it again and headed towards the companionway telling herself that what Susanne did was none of her business.

Nonetheless, the thoughts remained to torment her. What did a girl of twenty-six know of life? Specifically, about philandering foreigners who were likely to be out for all they could get. Forget that Omar Saheed might be after money. He'd find out his mistake soon enough if he came to England and found them living in a tiny rented cottage approached by a farm track.

She thought of Nigel Danvers who had made her daughter so unhappy. Susanne was vulnerable. That was what was worrying her. A girl could do something very silly on the rebound.

Susanne was emerging from the shower with one towel wrapped round her head and another round her body. She gave her mother a bright smile that did not for an instant fool Vita.

'We had better wear something warm,' she said. 'We could freeze in the ruins after the sun goes down. Now, which of my magnificent outfits shall I put on, not that anyone's going to see who's sartorially elegant and who's not

176

in the black Egyptian night.'

'I'm for the Jasper Conran trouser suit,' said Vita wishing Susanne would stop overdoing it. The fake jollity only made her feel more depressed.

'Good idea. Why don't you leap under the shower while I change.' Susanne sat down on the bed in order to provide enough space for her mother to pass. 'There's not much room for both of us to get dressed at the same time.'

Vita went into the bathroom. When she emerged, feeling considerably brighter, Susanne was wearing the Tomasz Starzewski jacket and looking at herself critically in the mirror. 'Do you know, this, new, would set you back five hundred pounds.'

'Not me,' said Vita. 'Not now. There was a time ... oh, well.' She reached into a small drawer for clean underwear then took a trouser suit down from its hanger. It was beautiful. Momentarily, she allowed herself a twinge of nostalgia and appreciation. 'Such a lovely colour,' she said. 'You don't get reds like that outside of the couture world.'

'Why?'

'They make their own dyes.' She put the suit on. Looking at herself in the mirror, after all, she felt her nerve failing.

Susanne saw the change. 'Be brave,' she said lightly. 'Tell yourself it came from Marks and Spencer.'

Vita's mouth turned down. 'I don't find

177

myself that gullible.' She returned to her reflection. Her eyes ran over the elegant shoulder line, the deep and cleverly folded neck line. 'I just feel so stupid. Stupid!' she repeated despairingly. 'Why didn't we make enquiries about the cost of this tour? That would have given us an indication of who was going on it.'

'You'll be saved by the dark,' said Susanne again, making an effort to comfort her, pushing her own spirits up at the same time. 'Besides, the passengers should be getting their money's worth, as Peter would say, by staring at the ruins. That's what they came to see, not your Jasper Conran pants.' She adopted a light, carefree voice, 'How does your friend Rupert happen to be aboard? He doesn't strike me as a save-up-for-the-holiday-of-a-lifetime type. And neither does he fit into the close-to-the-land category.'

Vita said, 'He had two weeks off. He'd planned to stay with his daughter but her husband was transferred to New York and he found himself rather *de trop* while they rushed around packing and letting the house. So he looked for a tour. His travel bureau came up with this cancellation, just two days before the flight.'

'Ah! Why didn't we think of that? It sounds like a good wheeze.'

'Too late I'm afraid,' Vita said.

'He has the world rights?' It was a strain

being flippant but still she persisted, 'You know, if we let ourselves, we could enjoy being a mystery.' She picked up the damp towel and held it across her face like a yashmak, just below the eyes. 'The mysterious Landseer girls. Come on Vita, smile.'

'I can't,' said her mother, choking. 'I'm worried witless about you and this Egyptian.'

Susanne was taken aback at the depth of her mother's distress. 'There's no need. Truly.'

'What are you going to do with the necklace and bracelet?'

'I shall wear it, when the opportunity offers.'

There was a moment of silence that stretched to two. Vita said, 'You're invited to come with the Colonel and me to the *son-et-lumière*. He's going to hire one of those carriages.'

'Thanks.' She wanted to say she didn't want to play gooseberry, but she recognised that Vita's mood had gone beyond the stage where she could be cheered.

'Perhaps you want to go with Peter?'

'We could all go together, if you'd like that.'

'I think you should go with Peter,' Vita said, clutching at straws.

'All right.' She felt guilty about upsetting her mother. It wouldn't hurt her to go with Peter if that would provide a small respite from her worries.

Vita stayed on the top deck a moment longer, watching Susanne as she descended the

179

steps. The Colonel was coming up from the deck below.

'Let her go,' he said softly as he reached the top.

'I suppose it's my fault for allowing myself to be talked into coming with her,' Vita said. 'This is a truly ridiculous situation, Rupert, a mother looking on at a daughter's escapade. That's probably all it is, and none of my business.'

'Of course you're concerned,' he said kindly. 'It's understandable.'

She hadn't been so physically close to Susanne for years, nor had she ever felt so distanced. In the silence that Rupert allowed her her mind ran back to that night when Susanne broke off the newly patched friendship with Nigel Danvers. But the young woman who had returned from The Weavers was not the same person who had held the necklace of Egyptian gold up to the mirror. She felt she didn't know that one.

'Let's go out and enjoy ourselves,' said the Colonel taking her arm and steering her towards the steps.

Peter was waiting impatiently on the lower deck. He saw Susanne coming. 'I thought we'd take a taxi,' he said as she reached his side.

'We may as well.' There were no memories attached to taxis. Susanne climbed in beside him and they shot off down the road, much too fast, scattering small boys with a threatening blare of the horn.

'Where are the girls?' Susanne wondered.

'Learning the habit of staying at home, which is a woman's lot in Egypt.' She was aware of his watchful eyes in the darkness. He wanted a reaction from her.

'Oh, yes,' she said non-committally.

'They do as they're told. They get married when their parents decide it's time, to a man of the parents' choice, and when he wants to divorce them he only has to say "I divorce you," three times before booting them out.'

'You're a mine of information,' she said. 'Actually, there are a few women not locked up at home. They go down to the Nile to do their washing and lead the gamus's round the water-wheel.' All the same she was remembering the men in dark suits at the New Cataract Hotel. It was true that the only women in the lounge had been foreigners.

The taxi swerved violently to avoid an old man leading a donkey laden with straw. The front fender came in contact with the donkey's flank. The leg that had been struck sagged. The load teetered while the beast tried to regain his balance. The taxi driver shouted.

'I say, go a bit slower,' Peter protested.

The man nodded zealously and flung some Arabic words over his shoulder.

'My Arabic's pretty basic, but I think he's saying the donkey should have got out of the way. Careless bugger,' said Peter.

181

Susanne, somehow containing her distress, wanting to know if the beast had recovered, forced herself not to look out of the back window. 'This is Egypt,' Omar had said. Where you have to put your hat over your eyes if you cannot bear the cruelty. She felt she could not.

The taxi pulled up before the ruins. Peter paid the driver who reacted with wails of protest.

'They always try it on,' said Peter looking pained and Susanne remembered Omar saying one must not pay the drivers what they ask or the price would rise and rise until no one could afford them and they would be out of work.

Hassan, who had changed his wonderful embroidered slippers for sandals, gathered his charges together and led them into the complex of temples lying open to the velvet sky. Far above them the stars twinkled, bright as diamonds.

'This lot covers four to five hundred yards and took a thousand years to build,' Peter said, 'which is understandable when you think all the stonemasons had to chip away at the sandstone with were bits of granite. Our chaps today would make short work of it. There are a hundred and thirty-four pillars here. Impressive, don't you think?'

Susanne said she thought it was. She trailed along with the crowd wishing she could shake off Peter with his statistics, listening to the story from the loudspeakers, drowning in the

182

music. Hassan's soft voice rose and fell. Thutmose the first laid out this. Thutmose the third laid out that. Pharoahs after the eighteenth dynasty ... Rameses the second added this hall ... Pylons ... Courts ... Statues ... Shrines ...

Peter's voice kept breaking in. 'A hundred feet long ...'

Susanne thought of Omar who lived with the gods in his heart and furrowed his brow over the fate of his ancestors; whose brooding rendering of Ozymandias had all but drawn her soul out of her body. She felt his fingers closing over hers. She allowed her eyelids to drift down, luxuriating in his ghostly presence, thinking she could manifest him out of her dreams.

'So I found you.' His soft voice touched her ear.

'Omar!' she breathed. Her fingers curved round his. In the pale darkness she gazed up at him. His almond-shaped blue eyes gazed back at her. For a moment she thought she was in Paradise.

Before her the pillars rose like giant tree trunks in a forest lit by an amazing light. He pointed out to her carvings in the stone that were scenes depicting the King worshipping Ammon, god of Thebes, sometimes a human, sometimes a ram, often a goose. He showed her how the shadow patterns were thrown by graceful columns, shadows as beautiful as the columns themselves. And all around them the music swelled, rising to triumphant crescendos, fading into the dark zones outside of the light.

The arm he slid through hers was steel hard. He drew her close against his side, possessive and possessing. 'Did you think I wouldn't come again?' he whispered in her ear.

'No,' she replied. 'I thought you must come. I willed it.' Was he listening to the wild beating of her heart?

'I would find you wherever you were.'

Yes, for he had tied her to him by a cobweb thread that would twist and turn and stretch and shrink and never break. They drifted together. The ancient carvings on the great columns stirred to life. Straight-backed warriors, holding their weapons aloft, marched ahead of them to war. Animals strode in single file.

The lights faded and the ruins grew deeply mysterious then light flooded in once more from above and Susanne caught her breath as an obelisk came out of the darkness, soaring magnificently ahead of them with the music swirling round it.

She slid back into that other world, hundreds of years B.C. She was in the narrow boat etched in the stone on the obelisk, moving up the Nile. The warrior standing looking down at her was Omar, slender in his body armour, grand in the black king's wig.

They walked through the temple of Amun, through its great hall. The stone glinted in the powerful lights. More towering obelisks. Susanne drew their mysterious shadows around her. And then it seemed that they were moving along by still water. 'Where are we?'

'At the sacred lake,' whispered Omar. 'This is where the sacred boats sailed on their way to the Nile.'

Dreaming, she felt she had been in a sacred boat.

'So there you are!'

The dream broke. 'I thought I'd lost you,' Peter said. Then he saw Omar. 'Oh! It's you.'

Omar, unfazed, offered him a light salute.

Peter said ungraciously, 'Good evening, Captain Saheed.'

The rest of the party had moved ahead and was being herded up to an open auditorium. They climbed to the back where they might be alone, looking out over the water, but Peter came to join them, seating himself on the other side of Susanne.

'I've brought you a rug,' said Omar and proceeded to fold it and spread it across the stone seat. 'There's plenty of room for three.' He gave no sign of resentment at Peter's intrusion. He was the perfect host, courteously entertaining a guest.

They sat in silence, watching the play of lights on the ruins and the water, listening to the voice coming over the loud speaker. Sitting

185

between the two men, Susanne was aware only of Omar's closeness, the desert scent of him, his belonging, his history, his past. His hand covered hers on the rug. She felt again the tug of that cobweb thread. She felt it was sealing them together into a cocoon, safe from the world.

The lights faded. The party began shuffling round in the darkness, preparing to depart. The air was cold, the ruins closing in on themselves for the night.

Omar said, 'I'm staying at the Winter Palace Hotel. Let's go back there now. And of course,' he nodded courteously towards Peter, 'I would like your friend to come, too.'

Susanne waited for Peter to refuse. He cleared his throat and said in an over-loud voice, 'Thanks very much,' then speaking directly to Susanne, 'You'd like to see inside the Winter Palace, wouldn't you? It's a relic of the Victorian era. It's quite a place.'

He's not so naive after all, Susanne thought. How clever of him to string them together as a couple of tourists being shown round by a guide. If Omar was aware he made no sign. 'I'd better tell Vita,' she said, 'or she'll wonder what on earth has happened to me.'

They found her with the Colonel waiting for a carriage. She said sharply, 'I think you should bring him back to the boat.'

Susanne bit back an equally sharp retort and managed to say casually, 'Peter wants to see the Winter Palace.'

'That's not why you're going,' Vita said.

Susanne was taken aback. 'I don't want to upset you,' she said, 'but why shouldn't I go?'

'If you don't want to upset me, then come back to the boat with us.' Vita glanced up to ensure Omar was not within earshot then said in a low voice, 'This man is an *Egyptian*.'

The Colonel, who had made no attempt to hide the fact that he was listening, took Vita by the arm. 'Come, my dear,' he said. 'Here's a carriage touting for our custom.'

She made as if to resist him then Susanne turned away and the fight went out of her. She allowed him to help her up. 'Sorry,' he said.

She turned on him. 'Oh my God! Did you see her eyes?'

'Yes, I saw.' He wondered if she meant the enchantment. 'Sometimes there's nothing you can do, my dear. You just have to sit back and wait until it's time to pick up the pieces.'

*　　　*　　　*

The pillared hall of the Winter Palace hotel, with its high ceilings and potted palms, was very grand. Omar paused at the desk to collect his key, spoke to the attendant at length, then turned back to them. 'I've ordered a little refreshment,' he said. 'Shall we take the stairs? My suite is on the first floor.'

'We can sit here, in the lounge,' said Peter

indicating a group of empty chairs.

Omar waved the suggestion away. 'Any tourist may come into the lounge. I offer you an opportunity to see the interior of the hotel.'

Peter turned to Susanne, frowning. 'I don't . . .'

Swiftly turning her head away, smiling at Omar, she said, 'I'd love to go upstairs.'

'I thought . . .' began Peter, then stopped for neither of them were listening. They had moved off together and had already reached the bottom step.

Omar's suite was enormous. Comfortably furnished, too. There were tall-backed armchairs, a Victorian desk, a good carpet. He led them out to a broad, open verandah where there were cushioned chairs and a table. 'You will be comfortable here,' Omar said. His consideration was a part of him. He wore it like an enveloping cloak. 'Excuse me a moment.' He went back into the room. Susanne went to stand at the rail and looked down into the garden. The night was full of drifting scents.

'He doesn't seem to be short of a bob or two,' muttered Peter at her side. 'What's he want a rich wife for?'

Without looking at him she replied, 'I dare say it's just one of those rumours.'

'I'm quite sure it's not.'

A waiter came bearing coffee, biscuits and tiny cups on a tray. Another one, following behind, brought a bottle of whisky, some ginger ale and glasses.

'This is very fine Scotch,' said Omar breaking the seal. 'I hope you'll agree with me.'

'I hardly expected anything else.' Peter's lightly veiled sarcasm put Susanne on edge. She allowed her eyelids to flutter down while Omar poured the whisky, a small one for her, a double for Peter.

The waiter poured the coffee into the three cups, then retreated.

'So, what brings you to Luxor?' Peter asked.

'Do sit down.' Omar gestured towards a chair. 'I came to see Susanne.'

Peter placed his glass on the table then sat down, looking uneasy, and stared at the floor. Susanne felt sorry for him. She knew in her heart Omar wasn't teasing. Or taunting. He was simply speaking the truth. Peter picked up his glass and stared into it, his face devoid of expression, then took a sip. Omar asked him about his work. Peter replied grudgingly at first, then gradually the atmosphere between them grew more easy. Omar offered Peter his card, at the same time inviting him to get in touch should he come to Egypt on an archaeological dig.

'Thanks.' Peter stared hard at the card then pocketed it.

Susanne sat back in her chair, listening to the insects droning in the garden below, smelling the perfume that drifted up on to the balcony, making no effort to follow the conversation of the men. A long time later it seemed, though it may not have been more than twenty minutes, they heard a knock at the door. Omar called out in Arabic. The man who had brought the coffee came and stood in front of Omar, speaking to him at length. Omar, registering surprise, questioned him. The Arab again replied at length. Omar turned to Peter. 'It appears,' he said, 'that you're wanted back at the boat.'

A look of amused disbelief passed over Peter's face and he said with elaborate sarcasm, 'Nobody knows I'm here.'

'Someone must know.'

Susanne broke in, 'My mother knows where we are.'

'It's about tomorrow,' said Omar. 'You are to go to the Valley of the Kings?'

Peter nodded warily.

'There's some problem about the *feluccas* that are to transport you across the Nile.'

'But this is a matter for the guides,' Peter protested, making no effort to rise out of his chair.

Omar turned back to the waiting messenger. They spoke at length then he turned again to Peter. 'The guides have been trying to sort it out but they have not been successful. They say they need to have you there. Are you not responsible for the smooth running of the

190

trip?'

Peter threw his host a look of veiled dislike, raised his glass to his lips, emptied it and rose. Looking down at Susanne he said, 'We'd better go, then.'

Omar was already at his side, one hand on his shoulder, ushering him on his way. Peter made a token effort to swing round then gave up. 'You'll come again,' Omar was saying warmly. 'This has been a very short visit. I'd like you to have lunch with me, if you can spare the time. And don't worry about Susanne. I'll escort her back. I'll take the greatest care of her.'

Susanne's eyes followed them through the doorway as the two men crossed the room, watching their very different backs, the one so firm and militarily straight, the other long and thin. She felt a certain sympathy for Peter, but all the same she had a wild desire to laugh.

The door closed and Omar came back. He sat down in the chair beside hers and took her hand.

'When he finds out it's a trick,' she said, gently smoothing his knuckles with the tips of her fingers, 'and there's no trouble with the *feluccas*, he'll be back in a flash.'

'Such strong hands,' said Omar. And then, 'It will not be quite in a flash. My tricks are the best in the world. He will find there is indeed trouble with the *feluccas*. The owners have orders to argue about prices and times until eleven, then to give in. That will allow us an hour alone for it's barely ten, now.'

An hour in which to tell him she had heard he was looking for an heiress. That she did not by a long chalk fit into that category. That she was on a cruise she could not afford wearing clothes she could not afford. The truth slid away into the Egyptian night and she held up her face to him.

He kissed her softly, gently, deeply. He seemed to engulf her in the sensuality of his lips so that they became one as surely as they had been one back in the green rushes on the verdant banks of the Nile. She was potently aware of his bed not more than a few metres away. Aware, too, that he was not going to take her to it. There had been nothing carnal in his desire when he took her beneath the hot Egyptian sky. His loving had been a seal and a promise. Now that the promise was made the stolen hour was theirs.

CHAPTER TEN

They came back to the boat at precisely eleven o'clock. In the hooded carriage she touched Omar's hand. 'Don't get out.'

'But I must see you to the steps,' he protested.

'We are at the steps. Please, Omar.'

He gave his characteristic smile, now overlaid with seriousness. 'You're not ashamed of me?'

'Oh Omar! How could you say that! I'm ashamed of my travelling companions, the way they gawp. You must know what a stir you've created.'

'But always I create a stir. As I said, life—'

'—is for living,' she joined in and the words, spoken together, became a chant. They laughed softly together.

'I will see you tomorrow.'

She frowned. 'We're going to the Valley of the Kings. I must—'

'Of course you must. I will see you, all the same.'

He jumped to the ground and helped her down though she was perfectly capable of jumping. She went to the top of the steps walking on air, danced down them. Vita was sitting in the bow with the Colonel, holding a drink in her hand.

'There you are,' said the Colonel looking at his watch, 'It's only eleven-o-three and here she is, all in one piece.'

There was no mistaking the happiness. Susanne brimmed with it. It was in the way she danced down the steps, in the way she smiled up into Peter's face when he rushed to meet her, though the smile was not for him. Even at this distance Vita and Rupert could see that.

Peter was saying, 'There was trouble all

right.'

Susanne looked solemn. 'You sound surprised. Omar told you there was trouble.'

'Yes, but I didn't believe him.'

'And you were wrong.' She screwed up her face at him, laughing.

'I'm glad you got back safely,' he said stiffly.

She headed for the steps that ran to the upper deck. Vita made to rise.

'Let go,' said the Colonel quietly.

She sat down again with a bump, knowing she was being rebuked.

'I'm going to get another drink,' he said, rising and picking up their glasses. 'And I think you should stay here with me for half-an-hour. Let her settle.'

*   *   *

The bright little *feluccas* slid in against the riverboat and took the tourists aboard. They were going to the Valley of the Kings. Susanne wore jeans, a thin cotton blouse and trainers. Peter had warned them there would be some distance to walk over the hot sand. A little climbing. A lot of dust. Humming quietly to herself, Susanne slid her fingers through the water and was sharply rebuked by Hassan. Bilharzia. Crocodiles. You did not tease the Nile. The broad sails of the little boats caught the breeze and they slid effortlessly across the water to what appeared to be a little village of

194

mud huts on the other side.

There was no pier, only some rough stone steps that were alive with swarming children all holding out their hands, all crying, *baksheesh, baksheesh.*

'Don't give them anything,' Peter said, 'or we'll never get rid of them.' Some people obeyed. Some did not. Peter was right. They descended with the speed of piranhas on those who gave, snatching at their clothes, gripping their arms with tenacious little brown fingers. The beleaguered tourists clambered thankfully aboard the waiting buses vowing they had learned their lesson. You cannot afford to be generous where generosity is so badly needed.

The road followed a canal that ran between one of those geometrically square fields of maize. 'My ancestors,' Omar had said, 'had to learn the rudiments of geometry in order to re-draw the boundary lines obscured yearly during the flood.' As their bus rattled along a rough road the tourists looked out on fields of cotton, sugar cane, and in the lower fields that were heavily watered, rice. They passed mud huts with roofs of woven corn and sugar cane stalks. Peter kept them well informed. There were camels, donkeys, and occasionally that strange beast the gamus gazing at them through its long lashes, its head bent low as though weighed down by its enormous horns.

The sun beat on the roof of the bus. Passengers fanned themselves with their hats.

195

Couldn't they open the windows? No, said Peter. The heat is less uncomfortable than the dust. 'You would be very sorry if I let that in.'

Ahead, ragged pink cliffs stood like sentinels, awe-inspiring against a cobalt sky. Up here, away from the water, it was going to be a very, very hot day. At least on the Nile there was sometimes a breeze. The stones on the ground reflected the heat up into their faces. They went down a track and found themselves hemmed in by precipitious limestone walls. The valley ahead looked utterly desolate. There was not a blade of grass or indeed any living thing in sight.

'We're going to the head of the valley where the most important tombs are to be found,' Hassan said, and Peter added, 'Including the most famous of them all, that of Tutankhamen. King Tut,' he said, showing familiarity with the god. 'Although, as you will know, the treasures from his tomb are now in the museum in Cairo.'

Susanne stood gazing at the walls of the ravine, pitted and perforated by caves, remembering how she had gone with Omar into a cave, and how he had not kissed her. Peter and Hassan led the way and the crowd moved off down the stony, dusty path ahead.

In the distance she heard the sound of a car engine and she swung round, breath held, eyes shining, somehow knowing. An ancient Bentley, covered in dust but keeping its former air of grandeur, came up over the hill behind and purred to a stop. Omar slid out from behind the wheel. This morning he was wearing shorts and a short-sleeved shirt open at the neck. His legs were very brown, his hair crisp and ebony dark in the brilliant sunlight. He came towards her, holding out his hands.

She went to meet him, her eyes misty. They stood for a moment drinking each other in, then he said, 'I have come to ensure that you see my country as I see it. And to make certain that you wear your hat.'

She obediently put her big hat on her head, smiling at him. 'Of course, you do not need me, though. Your guide and your archaeologist have all the information.'

'I do need you, Omar,' she replied, remembering how, with his feeling for the past, he had instilled magic into the *son-et-lumière* at Luxor. He would not refer disrespectfully to the great god-king, Tutankhamen, as King Tut.

'Hurry up there,' called a voice from the front and they went together along the rough path.

Omar pointed to a small wooden building not more than a hundred yards away. 'We'll be able to get cool drinks there. But anyway, it will be cool enough in the tomb. You have your torch?'

'Yes.' She pulled it out of her haversack. Ahead the tourists were disappearing into the

197

side of the hill. They followed and found themselves in a cave-like entrance with a corridor running off it, sloping downwards. It was cool in here where the sun never penetrated, and eerily quiet. The passageway was faintly lit by stark electric light bulbs that were set at intervals in the walls. Dust rose in puffy clouds, fine as face-powder.

Omar took a piece of gauze out of his pocket and handed it to her. 'There is an elastic thread. Put the cotton over your nose and hook the elastic round your ears. It's the same kind of thing that's worn in hospitals. Excuse me while I find your mother.' He slipped away.

Susanne fitted the mask on. A moment later he was back. 'The Colonel had given her a big handkerchief,' he said, 'but it's not the same. That Colonel is very attentive. Do you approve?'

'Very much. But . . .'

'But?' he queried.

She said cautiously, 'My parents have only recently been divorced.' It seemed a suitable moment to offer this piece of information, out of context and submerged within the greater drama of an ancient tomb. 'I always hope they might get back together one day.'

Omar merely nodded. Flashing his torch on the walls, he surprised her by saying, 'Tutankhamen was a comparatively unimportant king. He was only ten years old when he became king and nineteen when he died. There wasn't much time for him to become a great warrior, or a leader of men.'

'Yet he is the most famous of the lot?'

Omar shrugged. 'Only because the tomb is a comparatively recent discovery. And of course, to you English it is important, because it was opened by an Englishman. We must listen to your archaeologist.'

Peter was saying, 'You will all know of the curse on this tomb. The ancient Egyptians predicted that those who opened it would die. In fact, Lord Carnarvon, the British scientist who was in charge of the operation, did die shortly after the opening, and several of his assistants followed suit too soon afterwards for comfort.'

Omar whispered, 'Thieves broke in and ransacked the ante-chamber ten years after the king's death, but they didn't reach the tomb.'

'Perhaps they were afraid.'

'It's very probable.'

'What was there to take from the ante-chamber?'

'The possessions that he was meant to take with him into the after-life. His furniture, no doubt. Spears for hunting. Boats for sailing on the Nile. The usual things.'

The usual things! As though there was anything usual about this experience. There were wonderful wall pictures to see.

199

Hieroglyphics, and more of those remarkable coloured pictures of gods and goddesses. Susanne followed the line of the wall, shining her torch on each individual figure, gazing with awe, admiring the beauty and precision of the work.

Omar said, 'In fact, Howard Carter, the archaeologist who was present at the opening of this tomb, did survive. It is said that he was protected by a sheik from a nearby village who gave him a talisman inscribed with verses from the Koran. There were also certain magical symbols on it. This talisman had been used at a Dervish meeting where higher forces had been invoked. Spells were used. The sheik warned Mr Carter to carry it when he sensed the presence of hostile forces.' Omar's face was grave. 'This, it is thought, was why Carter survived.'

There was a concerted gasp. Susanne swung her torch round and saw that a crowd had gathered behind them and were listening to Omar's story.

Peter's voice came out of the darkness. 'What's going on?' He swung his torch and saw that his tourists had encircled Omar and were listening to him. 'Perhaps I should take the day off,' he said sarcastically. 'We seem to have an expert here.'

Susanne felt her hand gripped in Omar's hand in the darkness. Deftly, he slipped to the edge of the crowd, leading her, and took her a

200

little way back in the direction of the entrance. 'That was unfortunate,' he said. 'I'm going to leave you to your eminent archaeologist. Follow him. I'll sip a drink and wait for you in the kiosk.'

Susanne hurried back towards the entrance at his side. 'I don't see why—' she began but he signed to her not to protest then turned and clasped both of her upper arms, his face close to hers in the gloom,

'It is too easy for me to encroach on his territory. He is a very learned scholar—' At that she shot him a suspicious look but his face was solemn enough '—and you have paid to hear him. The stories I can tell you are not in his books. But there is plenty of time for those.' He let his hands fall and began to stride towards the entrance.

She ran after him. 'Let me stay with you.'

'Go,' he said, pausing and turning again. 'See it all in the English way.' And then he repeated what he had just said, 'There is plenty of time.' They came out into the open. The heat-burdened desert air met them, and the sun. He left her then, as though he knew that was the only way to get her to follow the party. She watched him go off across the stones and rubble, back straight and head high, making for the kiosk. She turned and saw the rest of the party coming out of the cave. Still she did not move until they were trailing off up the stony path. She felt distanced from them.

Peter came striding back through the crowd, calling impatiently, 'Are you coming?'

She shook the magic away and hurried up the slope, slipping on the loose stones. 'Yes, I'm coming.'

He fell into step beside her. 'It's a damned impertinence, his coming here.'

She understood he would see Omar's arrival as an impertinence. Perhaps it was. She ran ahead of him along the track. Those at the head of the party had paused beside a ladder that was leaning against an upright sandstone wall. Hassan said, 'You are going to have to climb up this ladder now, all those who wish to go into the cave. But if you don't feel safe, don't climb. There must not be any accidents.'

They gathered around the foot of the ladder, assessing its height. Susanne sought Vita in the crowd. 'Will you have trouble with this?'

'Certainly not.' Vita looked irritated, but perhaps that was less because Susanne had called her athleticism into question than because of Omar's appearance.

Susanne grinned, tucked her torch into her belt, put her hands on a rung at shoulder height, and scrambled up. In the cave above she went off into the darkness by herself, lighting the wall-paintings with her torch, moving slowly from one room to another. Dreaming. Behind her voices rose and fell. Hassan's solemn tones. Peter's voice, listing

202

archaeological facts. She shut the clamour out, wanting to absorb Egypt's history through her pores.

There were astonishingly vivid paintings on the walls and ceilings; royal portraits; sacred barques transporting mummies on their journey down the Nile; writhing serpents; winged pharoahs. So strange. So magical. She saw Omar's features in the proud faces of the kings; saw Omar's erect bearing in the way they walked. Peter's voice followed her, staying outside of her dreams.

She stood alone in the darkness as the oncoming torches lit up the wall paintings in their turn. They shone on scarab-beetles; on symbolical bats; on successive scenes showing the occupations of the deceased man along with his journey into the other world.

'That's it,' said Peter briskly and she started forward involuntarily towards the ladder, feeling the tug of that invisible cord. 'We'll go and get some cool drinks now,' Peter said, giving permission.

She took her hat in her hands and scurried back down the ladder. The air outside wrapped itself round her, furnace hot. She stood on the rough stones, straining her eyes to see Omar. Was that him on the verandah of the kiosk, waiting for her?

She set off down the track, leaping from one flat surface to another with a dancing stride. She felt she was flying on wings into the future.

She came up the little rise to the kiosk starry-eyed, with her face burning.

He had bought her a lemon drink. He rose as she came up the steps and handed it to her, shaking his head, a little smile hovering at the corners of his mouth. He said, 'Drink this and then I will take you away before your archaeologist comes and shows his displeasure. You are misbehaving. You are a worry to your worthy guide. It is not good.'

'No. You are right,' she agreed. She took the glass, thanked him prettily and and gulped the lemon drink down. 'That's wonderful.'

'You would drink another?'

'There isn't time.' She looked at him over the rim of the glass. 'Where are we going?'

'Where? I can take you on a personal tour to all the places you expected to see,' he said. 'Deir el-Bahari, the temples of Rameses. The Colossi of Memnon. Isn't that your schedule?'

'How did you know?' She was surprised. Delighted.

He gave her a secret smile. 'I make it my business to find out what I need to know. I need to know where you are. On the other hand,' and now he was not teasing, his face had become animated and his eyes were dancing, 'I can introduce you to the desert. My desert,' he said softly.

'Oh yes. Yes please.' She knew her eyes were shining. She was shining inside.

'Come, Susanne.' He took her empty glass

and placed it on the table. 'We have no need to make our excuses. They'll all see us go.'

Out of the corner of her eye Susanne saw the crowd moving in single file down the path from the tomb. She wanted to run to some far distant hiding place where they would never find her.

'We can ask forgiveness later,' Omar said, 'when we have had our day.'

It was audacious of him. Equally audacious of her. She was transported by their audacity. They ran to the car, side by side and hand in hand. He opened the passenger door and she slid into the seat then bounced out again, off the burning leather. 'Ow! It's hot!'

'You were too quick.' Omar reached over to the back seat and produced a woven mat which he proceeded to spread across the leather. 'You'll find that's better.'

'Even the mat's hot,' she retorted, laughing.

'It is a hot country,' Omar replied. 'Everything gets hot, but only in the daytime. He turned on the ignition, put the car into gear and they bumped off up the dusty road. Ahead lay limitless miles of desert, rocky outcrops, golden sun-washed ridges, shadowed valleys.

'Have you borrowed this impressive car?' she asked, becoming aware as they drove of the comfort of the deep leather seats; of the polished chrome.

'I have many friends,' he replied laconically.

She was awed by his ability to make things happen the way he chose. She wondered if he was as free with his own car as his friends were with theirs. Or was everyone anxious to do a favour for the son of Youssel Saheed?

* * *

They did after all follow the itinerary laid down in the tour's brochure, but they kept one step ahead of the crowd. 'You have paid for this,' he reminded her, though she had not. 'I must see that you get your money's worth.'

Was this the moment to tell him the truth? She allowed the moment to slide by.

He was wonderful company. He told her funny stories about his country and his countrymen. He teased her and joked with her. He left the gods and the ancient Pharoahs behind. He re-invented himself as a twentieth century lover.

He kissed her beneath the burning Egyptian sun, standing on the stones before the great twin statues of Amenophis III while the king gazed sightlessly out across the desert. 'He cannot see us,' Omar said, smiling, teasing her as he held her close. 'Our love is private.'

She felt she wanted to stay here, alone with him, forever, but they had to go otherwise the party would catch up with them.

From the Colossi of Memnon they headed towards the Nile. 'Now,' said Omar as they sped along the dusty track, in and out of the great boulders, down into mini ravines and out again, 'would you like to return to the boat?'

'I thought you were going to introduce me to your desert.'

'I could show you some Bedouin encampments. Would you like that?' And before Susanne could answer he added with a certain pride, 'I am descended from the Bedouin.'

'Bedouin! But they're nomadic tribes!' she exclaimed and a picture flashed across her mind of Omar in his impeccable navy blue suit.

He replied, 'My ancestors were nomads. You are astonished. Why is that so surprising?'

She blinked. 'But you are related to the King!'

'Our late King,' he corrected her. 'It is a very long time since we have had a king. But yes, he was of nomad stock.' With his free hand Omar touched hers. 'It is too surprising for you to understand. I recognise that. But you will absorb it all, in time.' He spoke with the utmost confidence and she felt she would.

They drove down a long hill. Through the white glare of distance, when they saw the beginnings of cropland they turned west where the sandhills lay in undulating, purple-shadowed folds.

'Where are we going?'

'You wanted to see the real Egypt. I am showing it to you.'

They were a world away, now, from the tourist bus and her chattering countrymen. The car ran along a rutted track with sandstone cliffs rising on either side. Susanne gazed dreamily out over the landscape, wrapped in the dream they were creating together as they went farther and farther into the desert. She forgot Deir el-Bahari, the temple of Rameses and the Colossi of Memnon that they had so recently visited. She forgot everything but the wonder of being far from civilization with this descendant of a nomadic tribe. This descendant of kings.

When she saw a rosy mist forming on the horizon she thought it was part of the dream. She watched it change into a woolly pall, like smoke loitering, waiting for the wind to come and stir it. Above, the great vermilion sun burned in the sky. She imagined the smoky horizon was a part of the dream.

But it was moving towards them, lengthening out slowly and steadily, rolling up to wind itself round promontories, unwinding, curving down. She watched it change shape, rise again, almost vertically, hover as though holding its breath. And then with appalling suddenness all the sand and sandstone of the landscape seemed to join it and turn their way, the whole edifice, coming at them like a monstrous ochre wave, enveloping them in a sunset darkness wild with hot wind.

She had heard Omar's cry of alarm but it

208

was unreal, merging with the noise outside. He had stopped the car. 'Roll up the window!' he cried. 'Quick!' at the same time raising his own.

'What's happening?' Susanne cried. The sky was full of sand, the light was going. A lifeless red disk that had been the sun hung above them in the sky.

'It's only a sandstorm,' said Omar calmly, brushing the invading sand from his shoulders. 'It will pass by.'

Only a sandstorm! She thought she would choke in the airless oven in which they were now trapped. Her fingers went automatically to the door handle.

'Don't!' said Omar sharply, recognising her mindless bid for air. Ochre-coloured worms of sand seeped through the windows between the bodywork and the glass. 'How long will it last?' she asked apprehensively.

'Not long. It is an experience for you.' Omar leaned back against the leather seat, extending his hand, tapping her knuckles with a fingertip. 'I said I wish you to know my country. And you wished to do so. So, I have waved my magic wand.' Dramatically, he raised an arm in the air, indicating power.

'I think I'd rather be broken in a little more gently.' She tried to laugh and failed.

'It is nothing,' said Omar sounding surprised at her nervousness. He took her hand and gripped the fingers tightly. 'These little

209

disturbances come up suddenly on a freak wind. They invariably turn in on themselves and die locally. It is nothing,' he said again.

She tried hard to absorb Omar's calm. There was nothing to be seen through the windows that were blocked with sand. She pulled the collar of her thin shirt away from her neck thinking, I'll bet Ungaro never expected his blouse to feature in a sandstorm. But maybe he did. Harrods were full of Arab women shopping. Did those who shopped in Harrods sometimes end up like this, in an old Bentley buried in sand? She felt disorientated. Omar switched on the windscreen wipers. They moved desultorily creating a tiny slit of clear glass, building up great wedges of sand at the side. He switched them off again.

'There's nothing to do but sit it out,' he said calmly. He slid an arm along the back of the seat. 'We could make love if it wasn't so hot.'

There was no teasing in his voice. She stole a look at him. He was not smiling. Was he hiding his own very real worry from her? His features had become insubstantial in the near darkness. Again she looked at the windows, seeing nothing. The track would inevitably be obliterated. How far had they come from the river? She stole another look at him. If he was frightened, he was making a very good job of hiding it from her.

'Tell me truly,' she said, 'have you been in a sandstorm before?'

'Lots of times. Oh yes,' he said, amused that she might think otherwise, 'lots of times.'

She didn't know whether to believe him or not. 'In a car?'

'Not in a car. No. But in caves. When we were children. It is one of the excitements of Egypt for small boys.'

She felt another tremor of alarm because he had not had this experience before. Talk. Talk to take your mind off the fear.

'You have brothers and sisters?'

'I have three brothers,' he replied.

'What do they do?'

'They are scattered in diplomatic posts round the world. My two sisters are married and living in Cairo.'

'I've been told that in the east marriages are arranged by the parents. Did your father arrange your sisters' marriages?'

'Of course,' he replied as though there was no other way.

She stared at him, though she could scarcely see him now in the darkness that had flooded the interior of the car, trying to come to terms with what he had said, that there was no way for a man to love a woman other than with his father's consent. She thought of General Saheed who had, in English terms, warned her off.

Suddenly Omar sat forward, alert. 'Did you hear that?'

A sound. Yes. It came again, a muffled cry.

Something struck the windscreen and Susanne jumped. A hand came into view, brushing the sand away. Bloodshot eyes peered in. Omar rolled his window down and the man moved towards it. There was the flash of a blade. Susanne gave an involuntary shriek of alarm and Omar touched her knee with a reassuring hand. 'The *fellahin* all carry knives. Don't worry.' He brought the window down a little further, shaking his head against the sand that drove in. The man's cowled head filled the aperture. His face was caked with sand and criss-crossed by rivulets of tears. He was babbling incoherently, gesturing wildly.

Omar spoke to him calmly then turned back to speak to her. 'I'll have to get out and help him. He's lost his children and he's crazy with fear. Demented, as you see. Omar took a pair of glasses from the glove box, put them on then pulled out of his pocket one of the little gauze masks he had given her in the tomb.

Susanne took her own mask out of her pocket and slipped on her dark glasses. 'I'm coming with you,' she said. Anything rather than stay here alone.

'No,' said Omar. 'You must stay in the car. The storm won't last long.' He put a shoulder against his door and forced it open.

'I'm coming with you,' she repeated and wrenched open her own door, pushing it against the wall of sand that had built up outside, then hurling herself through the narrow opening against the sand that was streaming into the car. She tried to push the door closed but it was blocked open now. It was a relief to be outside in the open. At least there was a little light.

The Arab father was waving his arms and wailing. Omar took him firmly by the arm, speaking sympathetically but sternly. The man nodded, turned, and began to walk along what had been the road. All around them the sand glowed russet red, taking its colour from the strange ball in the sky that had been the sun. The sand stung their faces. The wind rolled it into ridges and terraces.

The adventure took on an unreal quality. Susanne had the impression of being on a sinister journey that would have no end. They stayed together, stumbling into unseen boulders, tripping on hidden stones. Omar took her hand in his and held it tightly. 'You are not frightened?'

'No.' It surprised her that now she was out in the elements she was not afraid.

They became moving statues of sand. It piled up on their necks and in their elbows. It covered their sunglasses. Again and again they wiped them and the sand returned, blacking out their view. They walked on and on. Susanne lost all sense of time and space. They stumbled into a dry river bed, and made their way along it. How many hours had they been walking? What distance had they come? In what direction?

Then suddenly there was a triumphant shout from Omar. 'Look! It's clearing!'

Frantically, she again rubbed the sand from her glasses. The wind whipped up, driving the stinging sand into her face but also sending it on. As she blinked it out of her eyes she saw the sun again, saw it changing, saw the dull red slowly lighten and the familiar vermilion creeping in. Then all at once the wind dropped. Miraculously, the air began to clear. She shook her head and sand fell from her hair like rain.

'Just as fast as it comes, it goes,' said Omar looking round. 'We'll find the children now.' He spoke in Arabic to the Bedouin who was shaking his enveloping robe and blinking the sand out of his eyes. The man nodded. 'We've been going round in circles,' Omar said to Susanne, 'but better that than do nothing.' She understood it was necessary for this man to search even though the chances of finding his children were negligible. 'It would have been a miracle if we'd found them during the storm, but we'll find them now,' Omar said. 'They will have found a cave. Always, children find caves,' he added. Susanne wished she shared his confidence. Hoped the father did.

They hurried back down the dry river bed. A *wadi* Omar called it. They took turns shouting, *Ahlan*, the Egyptian *Hello*. The father called the children's names. He was calmer now, but still very distressed. Omar talked to him, comforting him. Susanne had lost all sense of direction. Her skin was burning, she was exhausted, and secretly frightened that Omar had lost his way. She imagined he would pretend all was well in order to keep their spirits up. She was afraid, too, that the children might have been buried in the sand. What would happen when the daylight went as it did so suddenly in the desert? She stole a look at Omar's face. He still wore a confident expression and he walked with great confidence, too. Then, as though he sensed her anguish he turned suddenly and said gently, with infinite compassion, 'Have faith.'

She was deeply touched.

'You think we are lost, don't you?' His sand-caked face creased into a smile. She shook her head, turning away, not wanting him to know how frightened she was. 'No. No, really.'

Omar took her hand in his. 'The Bedouin do not lose their way in the desert,' he said. 'You have two Bedouin to look after you now.'

'I'm worried about the children.'

'Please not to worry about them, either. Near here there are some caves. I think that is where we will find them. There are many caves just beyond that small ridge in front.'

They climbed up over some rough outcrops of sandstone, and there in front of them were the familiar dark holes in the hillside that she

215

now knew to be caves. Susanne held her breath as the Bedouin put a hand to either side of his mouth and uttered a long, eerie cry. They waited, their eyes darting from one cave mouth to another. The man called again and again they waited. Then two little figures dressed in the long robes of the Bedouin appeared on a ledge and began to run down the slope. Their father uttered a hoarse shout and ran to meet them, his robes swirling round him.

With tears on her cheeks Susanne looked up at Omar. He was a stick of sand with blue eyes and smiling white teeth. 'I wish I had a camera,' he said. 'You are a truly enchanting sight.'

'You, too.' She wiped the tears away. 'I can't believe it's over.' She gazed up at the sky that was now an extraordinary shade of blue. Not cornflower, or sapphire. Sky-blue, she thought in wonder for it was the sky. Sky-blue. She dwelt on the ordinariness of the word.

'It is over,' Omar said. 'As I told you these storms go as quickly as they come.'

'Yes, you were right.' Susanne nodded, still emotional.

The Bedouin came back to them with a child on either side, holding their hands. Their robes were free of sand. They smiled and chattered as they hurried along, seeming not a whit worse for their adventure.

'Why should they not be cheerful?' Omar

asked, shrugging her surprise aside. 'They are Bedouin children. The desert caves are their heritage. They would know they were safe.'

As Omar had known.

Together, they made their way back to try to find the car. It was there, less of a vehicle than a mound.

Susanne gazed at it in consternation. 'How on earth will we get that out?'

'Easily,' said Omar as though digging a car out of the sand was something he did every day after tea. Then turning to the Bedouin conferred at length with him. The man hurried away still clutching his children by the hand.

'He's going to get help,' said Omar with the air of a man who has every right to expect people to help him. 'Let us sit down while we wait.'

CHAPTER ELEVEN

They chose a little sandstone promontory, not comfortable, but it was good to take the weight off their feet. Omar gave her a quizzical look. 'Somehow, lunch has been missed.'

Lunch? She hadn't given food a thought. She looked up at the sun, moving towards the horizon. 'It will soon be dinner-time,' she said.

'Not for a while. We must get back before dark. You know how cold the desert gets when the sun has gone. I cannot have you catching a chill.'

Cold! She looked down at her arms, burning in the heat of the sun's rays, and smiled because she could not remember being cold. Found it impossible to imagine ever feeling cold again. Her throat was parched, her skin beneath the thin blouse dry as the sand. 'One doesn't sweat in Egypt.'

'That's good, isn't it?' He grinned.

She grinned back. 'I could do with a drink.'

'I'm sorry about the drink. That I cannot produce. But help will come soon. When we get back to civilization I promise you the biggest . . .' he raised his eyes to hers. 'What? What is your heart's desire at this moment?'

'I think a beer. A pale ale. Something I never drink except in a heatwave. It's very thirst-quenching. May I have the biggest pale ale you can find?'

'What an ambition! You may not like the Egyptian beer. However . . .' Omar took off his shirt and shook it, then used it to wipe the sand from his body.

Watching him dreamily she thought that if someone had told her a week ago she would be sitting on a stone beside a bogged car in the desert with a high-born Bedouin she would have thought they had gone out of their minds. She closed her eyes and tried to make her own mind a blank for the truth, and the impossibility of that truth, was awesome. The

218

silence of the desert crept in through her pores. After a while she became aware of Omar as part of that silence. Omar who was the core of what was happening and yet could not happen.

Transported into a dream she thought, I love him, I belong with him, I have given myself to him, all I have, which is all of me, and yet I do not know him, and nor do I know anything about him, except what he has told me and that is not very much. Vita will say such an attachment has been built on emotion, and is therefore not an attachment at all. She will think it is unreal. Quixotic, perhaps. Is it quixotic to love with all your being a man whom you have known only a few days? But everything around me, everything that has happened to me since we met—everything has been unreal. And yet it continues to exist.

Yes, Vita would be right to say he is a stranger, but that is on one level, the normal English level where we live. Yet I believe what he says, that we have known each other in many lifetimes. That we are not strangers.

'Rubbish!'

She started. Was that Vita's voice in her head?

'What are you dreaming about?' said a soft voice close to her ear.

She opened her eyes, still frowning. 'My imagination was running away with me. Oh, Omar . . .' Her voice trailed away.

'You do not need to tell me,' Omar said. 'You are of course thinking of the situation. I can tell by the frown. Your mother. Your friends. What they will think. What will your world think when they find you have been captured by this man of the desert. A beautiful girl like you, with the world at your feet, what are you thinking of to get involved with an Egyptian?'

'I have not got the world at my feet,' she replied gravely.

'But why not?' He affected to be astonished. 'You are rich and beautiful—'

She broke in with a rush of words, not looking at him, looking out over the strange undulating landscape with its rocks and crevasses and ridges of blown sand, 'I am not rich, Omar,' she said. 'Please believe me. I work for a living, and so does my mother.' She turned and, trembling, looked directly at him, 'Do you realise you haven't asked me anything about myself, or my life in England. Why?'

He shrugged. 'Of course I am interested, but it is not important. What is important is what is happening now.'

She said, the words spilling out of her, 'Perhaps this is the moment to talk. I have heard you are looking for a—' she broke off, swallowed the words 'rich western wife' and substituted, 'I have heard your father has chosen a bride for you.'

'Of course, all Eygptian fathers do that.' He

220

was amused.

'Have you told him ...' Again she swallowed, unable to go on.

'That I wish to marry you? Not yet. There is plenty of time.'

'I wanted to say, have you told him you do not wish to marry this girl he has chosen?'

'My father and I understand each other,' Omar said, and as though that was in his opinion a perfectly satisfactory answer and therefore the end of the discussion he lifted her hand and kissed it.

'You wish to marry a westerner.' She could not bring herself to say the word 'rich'.

'I wish to marry for love.'

'If you knew that I can bring nothing to this marriage except myself . . .'

He looked quizzical. 'What should I want but yourself, my darling?'

'In some countries the husband's family expect a dowry. We don't have dowries in England, and besides, I could not supply one.'

He appeared puzzled. 'Why are you—' He broke off as a shout rent the air. They both swung round, startled. An army of men was coming over the rise, all chattering excitedly, all burdened with some object, a shovel, a thick coil of rope, long poles. Some of them shared the weight of long pieces of timber. They looked businesslike, and at the same time full of excitement as though this was a great novelty to them, having to dig a car out

221

of the sand.

Omar spoke to her as he waved to the approaching crowd, 'Egypt is not short of labour, as you see.'

The moment had passed and was irretrievable. Susanne turned her attention to the motley gang of workmen, all dressed in the long, night-dress type *galabiya*, amazingly unhindered by the skirt. She watched fascinated as they surrounded the car, an undisciplined, rowdy mob, exclaiming, gesticulating, shouting advice to one another. Omar made no attempt to assist them and indeed they did not appear to expect him to. They worked amazingly fast. When they had cleared an open space round the car half a dozen young boys scrambled inside and proceeded to work enthusiastically on the interior, brushing the seats, sending cascades of sand out through the doors. Nobody seemed to be in charge. The air was peppered with orders and comments which everyone seemed to ignore. She said to Omar, laughing, 'I've never seen such a noisy bunch of workmen.'

'They're enjoying themselves.' He stood hands in pockets, a kingly figure by his stance even though he was covered in sand, as though it was his role in life to watch lesser men work for him. She watched him covertly, secretly marvelling at his equanimity and his detachment from the job as the sand was

222

cleared away and the track exposed. The long pieces of timber she had seen the men carrying were picked up and laid in front of the tyres. Ropes were attached to the front axle and eager, barefoot young men, seemingly unhampered by their long robes, positioned themselves with the ropes over their shoulders ready to pull.

'There's still a lot of sand inside,' Susanne said. 'What will the owner say?'

Omar shrugged. 'It happens all the time. People are experienced at brushing a car out. It will be immaculate when it is returned.'

She marvelled at the way he held power so easily and confidently. It was in the uprightness of his back, the firm and lifted set of his sculptured chin. She wondered if he had ever done anything menial in his life; if anything had ever been denied him. And then she remembered his father who would deny him his love.

She spoke in a rush to cover her emotion, 'You're taking this so calmly it's as though it's happened to you before.'

He laughed, teasing her. 'I have not had a beautiful English girl with me when I have been in a sandstorm before.'

She looked down at her sand-caked arms. 'What will they think when I turn up at the boat?'

'That you have been in a sandstorm. What else?'

223

The men began to clamour and sign to him to come. He jumped down from the rock and slid in behind the wheel.

The Bedouin who were not concerned with the ropes in front gathered behind the car, issuing advice in lively, challenging voices, scrabbling for position. Everyone wanted a space on which to place the flat of their hands so that they could do a share of the pushing. The car began to move. Omar called, 'Jump in. They'll tow us now, until the track's clear.'

She leapt down from the rock. Young men scrambled to open the passenger door. She slid into the seat that was hot and gritty with sand. Omar, beside her, smiled.

'I feel rather like the queen,' she said. And yet she felt oddly humble, too, to be sharing all this goodwill.

'Tonight,' he said confidently, 'you will look like a queen. You will dine with me wearing your necklace and bracelet. Promise?'

She thought of the half-spoken confession that had been interrupted by the arrival of the rescue gang and wondered if he had taken in what she had begun to tell him, or if in truth her lack of a dowry meant nothing to him. It was too late now. She had seemed to have the right moment at hand but it had been snatched from her.

'I promise,' she said.

They drove back to the little village where that morning the party had disembarked.

There was no sign of the tourists. An imposing man wearing Egyptian clothes and an impressive red fez with a black tassel was waiting to take delivery of the car. Susanne was reminded of the man who had charge of the horses Omar had borrowed at Aswan. He had waited also with the same air of consummate patience, as though time did not exist. This Egyptian showed no sign of surprise as he slipped into the sandy seat, only bending down to shovel with his hands some of the sand away from the brake pedal.

She said to Omar with a wry smile, 'You'd think he collects cars full of sand every day of the week.'

'This is Egypt,' said Omar and she recognised that he did not wish her to see with the eyes of a tourist.

A little flotilla of *feluccas* lay waiting, their bows digging in to the sandy banks. One boatman, the most enterprising, had managed to bring his vessel in lengthwise against the lower step. Omar stepped aboard. He might have been a king going aboard his private barque. Then he reached out a hand to help her. Though she could very easily have jumped, Susanne accepted his help with grace, knowing this was what he wanted her to do. She took a comb out of the pocket of her jeans and leaning over the side combed little showers of sand into the water.

'It will wash off,' said Omar carelessly.

'There is plenty of water in Egypt. Don't forget I will pick you up at seven and you will be wearing the necklace.'

'Oh yes.'

'Now, put that beautiful hat on your head. But your shoes, if you will take them off I will empty them over the side.'

There was sand between her toes. She rubbed it away with her cotton socks while Omar dealt with her trainers. When she looked up they were close enough to *Phoenix* to see that the day trippers with whom Susanne had started out had returned. The lower deck was filling up. She saw their curious, watching faces. Some of them pointed. None of them was smiling.

'Damn!'

Omar laughed and picking up her wrist, shook it. 'Of course they are interested,' he said. 'Why should they not be? Don't turn your head away. They will enjoy seeing your happiness.'

Susanne thought that with one or two exceptions they were judging her to be a loose woman who had picked up a foreigner. Never mind that he was descended from royalty, that his father was a man of consequence. *Shirley Valentine*, she thought again nervously, pulling the hat brim down on either side of her head in order to hide her face. That's who they're thinking of. She wished she could shout at them across the water that she and Omar had been through a hundred, a thousand lifetimes together. That they were bound to one another as surely as though they had been tied by a papyrus cord.

Omar exclaimed in consternation, 'Such an expression you are wearing!'

'Oh my goodness, I'm sorry. I'm so sorry. I get mentally disturbed when ... it's this goldfish-in-a-bowl syndrome, Omar.' She looked at him with pleading eyes. 'Couldn't you let me out further upstream? I could run down the street.'

'You are ashamed to be seen with me?'

'Of course not,' she babbled. 'You know I'm not. Quite the opposite.'

He acknowledged her distress, touching her wrist gently. 'So if you are proud, then lift up your head with pride and smile at them.'

She felt the stars come back into her eyes and turned to look at the boat. As they came inshore one of the tall Nubian waiters in his glamorous red gown came forward, parting the crowd. He undid the chain railing. Omar stood up, steadying her with one hand, the Nubian extended his and the *felucca* slid alongside. Susanne stepped aboard and in that same moment the little boat spun round, heading upstream.

Susanne smiled across the crowd. Some of them smiled back. Some merely stared. A voice remarked with ill-will, 'It looks as though she's had a roll in the sand.'

227

Several giggles. She flushed angrily but managed to say lightly, 'We were caught in a sandstorm.'

Someone laughed. A voice said maliciously, 'A likely story!'

Then a tall man was standing before her saying genially, 'This way, my dear,' and she recognised the Colonel. He took her arm and escorted her protectively across the deck to the companionway. 'Toss your shoes and clothes outside the cabin,' he said. 'The staff will clean them up. They're always anxious to please.'

As she stepped on to the iron rung she briefly turned her head to say, gratefully, 'Thanks,' hoping the anguish she felt was not showing in her face, then she ran up to the top deck, opened the door of her cabin and hurtled inside.

There was no sign of Vita. She dragged off the clothes that were sticking to her skin and tossed them out on the deck as the Colonel had advised, shaking her head over the way she was treating the Ungaro blouse. As Omar had said, there was plenty of water in Egypt. She shampooed her hair until it was squeaky clean. The sand seeped away, chased by the powerful jet of water. She emerged feeling astonishingly clean with a towel wrapped round her head, grimacing at the sand on the floor, stepping over it.

There was lemon soda in the little cupboard in the bathroom. She gulped one down straight

228

from the bottle, then another. Even after that she was still so dehydrated she felt scarcely satisfied. She slipped into a cotton shift and went out on deck to dry her hair. There was no one on the upper deck. Her clothes and shoes had been removed and the sand with them. She leaned over the rail combing her hair. A tiny breeze had sprung up. The sun was touching the horizon. Soon the light would have gone.

The Colonel came up carrying two cups of tea. She accepted one of them gratefully, telling him about the two bottles of lemon soda she had swallowed, scarcely tasting them.

'You'll feel better when you've had the tea. I brought them both for you.'

'You are kind.' She took the second cup. 'That was a bit of an ordeal coming aboard.'

'Your mother heard. She's upset. And upset about your disappearing. I thought I should warn you about that.'

So Vita was in hiding. 'Thanks,' she said. 'I am over twenty-one, you know.'

He smiled down at her in that benevolent way he had. 'I do know. But be kind to her. She's genuinely worried.'

It was on the tip of Susanne's tongue to say, *She has no need*, but she bit the words back, knowing they were inappropriate. 'I believe you knew Omar's father.'

'A long time ago. And not well. Mainly by repute.'

229

'What was his reputation?' She looked at him over the rim of her cup.

'He had immense charm.'

'I've met him,' she said. 'He didn't try to charm me.'

She couldn't tell if the Colonel was taken aback. He was good at hiding his feelings. He was silent for a moment then said, 'It might be better if you don't tell your mother that.' Then he took her empty cups and walked away.

She leaned out over the rail, not wanting to join the crowd, feeling grateful for the Colonel's protective intervention and for his concern for Vita. She decided to stay where she was until it was time to dress for dinner then wondered if, by bringing the tea up, he had been making it possible for her to stay away.

What was going to happen now? She was going to dinner with Omar wearing the wonderful jewellery. There was no way she could creep undetected off the boat. She leaned on the rail, experiencing a mixture of emotions. Excitement, apprehension, a nervous intolerance of her fellow passengers, perhaps equal to theirs of her. She told herself she must not blame them if they thought of Omar as a native she had picked up. For many of them, she knew, this was their first trip abroad.

There was a sensation as if the boat was moving. It swung away from the mooring. She gazed down into the water thinking of tides and eddies. Then she saw that the stern of the boat had broken free of the bank. With a cry of alarm she sped across the deck to the starboard side. Down below the crew were hauling in the ropes. Vita was coming slowly up the last few steps.

'What's going on?' Susanne asked shrilly.

'We're leaving.' Vita's face was expressionless.

'Why? Why are we leaving?'

'Peter says he's got transport problems again. There's another upset at our next stop.'

'How does he know everyone's aboard?'

'He's counted heads.'

'He didn't count mine.' Still that shrill voice. She seemed to have lost control.

'He knows you're here.'

Susanne gripped her hands tightly together. Had Peter discovered that Omar had tricked him over the *feluccas*? Was this his revenge?

'He decided it would be a waste of time to stay here for another night when we could see an extra temple by arriving at the next stop early in the morning. I must say,' Vita added in a clipped voice wholly unlike her own, 'I'm rather full up with temples and tombs. I could do with one less, not one more.'

'I was going to dinner with Omar,' Susanne said, her voice breaking, feeling a loss too deep for tears.

Vita appeared to soften. She put an arm

231

round Susanne's shoulders. 'Perhaps it's for the best, dear.'

Susanne brushed her arm away. 'It is not for the best,' she said distinctly, 'and I am not seventeen and I'm sick of people interfering in my life. You're right, Mother, I should not have brought you with me. I should have brought someone who was on my side.'

Vita turned and went in silence into the cabin. Feeling desperately ashamed yet too broken to apologise, Susanne followed her. She went to the wardrobe and took out a low-necked gown. By Lanvin, but who cared. She slipped into it, removed the necklace from its box, clasped it round her neck, then clipped the bracelet on to her wrist. She glanced at herself in the mirror then went out on deck to watch the sun going down. After a while there were footsteps behind her. She turned, claw-sharp in her mind, expecting Peter, but it was Colonel Alison.

He said, 'That's a very flattering necklace you're wearing, my dear.'

She lifted her head like a queen. 'Omar Saheed gave it to me.'

He nodded.

'You're free to tell anyone who asks. If anyone says, *How about that necklace that girl's wearing*? you have my permission to tell them Omar gave it to me.' She was immediately ashamed of the childish outburst.

A small smile touched his lips. 'I doubt if

anyone would ask me, and if they did I wouldn't consider it my business to tell them,' he replied mildly, then added, 'Peter is young and unsophisticated. Don't be too hard on him.'

'He's got a cheek. I scarcely know him.'

'Indeed.'

She waited for him to say she scarcely knew Omar. He did not and she realised how tightly strung she was. 'I'm glad you're making a fuss of Vita. She's had a hard time.'

He nodded. 'She told me a little about it. I've one or two well-off relations. She's given me her address to hand on to them.'

Susanne looked at him sharply. 'She told you about the . . . er . . . business?'

'Yes. Very enterprising of her.' He smiled. 'She must be doing very well or you wouldn't feel free to help yourselves to the stock.'

Some of the poison Nigel Danvers had put into her mind drained away. The voice of her conscience told her she should not have passed it on to her mother. 'Life's a pig,' she muttered and looked out over the town where Omar was dressing, preparing to come and pick her up, not knowing the riverboat had gone. She saw it through a haze of tears.

'Yes, but if you tie a ribbon round the pig's tail it's surprising how much better it looks.'

'A pig with a ribbon on its tail is still a pig,' she said. 'But I'm glad to know you. You're a great help.' She smiled at him with sadness.

'Excuse me, I've got some apologising to do.'

She went along the deck and opened the cabin door. Vita was standing in the middle of the room in her Valentino shift, brushing her hair. She looked sad. Susanne put her arms round her. 'Sorry you've got such a foul daughter,' she said. 'But you've got a jolly nice admirer out there waiting for you. And by the way,' she added, ruefully apologetic, 'I wouldn't have said that about not bringing you on the trip if you hadn't put the idea into my head. You have to be careful what you say in front of people who are easily led.'

Vita hugged her and wiped away a tear.

Down in the bar Peter was standing alone with a drink in his hand, watching the door. He looked startled when she came in. She was aware of his eyes on the necklace. She walked right past him and up to the bar. 'I'd like a gin and tonic, please.'

Peter swung round. 'Let me get it for you.'

'I'm quite capable of getting my own drinks,' she replied. 'I think its very irresponsible of you to change the schedule.'

'I'm trying to help people get the most out of their cruise.'

She looked hard at him until he dropped his eyes. His face went beetroot red. She held her gaze steadily until he looked up again. 'People with your colouring shouldn't tell lies,' she said.

'Can't we be friends?' He was begging.

'Sure. I saw you looking at my necklace. Omar gave it to me. I'm wearing it tonight because I expected to go ashore to have dinner with him. Sure, we can be friends if you just stop interfering in my life.'

'I'll be here to pick up the pieces,' he said. 'And believe me, Susanne,' he added fiercely, 'there will be pieces to pick up.'

'After all,' she said coldly, 'I will let you pay for my drink.'

*   *   *

They cruised slowly down the Nile. Omar was not at Denderah. Why not? He was cognisant of every detail of their itinerary. She visualised him coming to the river bank at Luxor at seven-thirty in the evening; his shock on seeing the berth vacated. She ached with loneliness.

They visited the temple of Hathor, and the ruins of ancient Tentyra. All the time Susanne kept looking over her shoulder. Why had he not come?

They went ashore and took taxis to Abydos to see the temple of King Seti I and the temple of Rameses II. Here, surely, Omar would catch up with them. He was not there either. They spent another day cruising, watching the strings of camels moving up river, waving to the crowds in their long Arab robes on the riverbank, watching the women beating their laundry on the stones. The days flowed by as

235

endlessly as the brown river and still no message came.

They arrived at Beni Hassan and travelled on little grey donkeys to the limestone cliffs above the east bank to visit the painted tombs of the Middle Kingdom. 'It's hard to believe that these wonderful pictures have survived since 1900 BC,' Peter told the party. Susanne thought it was hard to believe that so many days had passed and Omar had not appeared. She lay awake at night imagining that he thought she had not bothered to send him a message saying the *Phoenix* was sailing early. She imagined that he had met with an accident. She grew listless and disenchanted with the relentless sightseeing.

From Beni Suef and El Ayat there were good roads within reasonable reach of Cairo, but still Omar did not appear. The days grew increasingly, blindingly hot, the nights increasingly cold. Even the tomb of Mereruke where the mummified bulls had been buried— what was it, two thousand years BC?—failed to move her. She did not wear the necklace again. She was aware of whispering, and watching eyes.

They moved down river between the lush green banks where the waters of the Delta had made the desert into a tropical garden, then past the big apartment blocks and hotels to the pier literally in the middle of the city of Cairo. Susanne was up on deck as they steamed in, her eyes anxiously searching the shore. There were many men dressed in European clothes hurrying back and forth, but no one carrying himself like a king.

It was then she faced up to the fact that Omar had, after all, taken in her confession about the lack of dowry as they waited for the mob to come and dig the car out of the sand. He was an intelligent man, a man of the world, adept no doubt at covering a sense of dismay, or shock. Equally adept at acting out his part right up to the time he put her aboard the *Phoenix*. She had been a fool. It had been hubristic of her to ignore the rumours. Gossip was not manufactured out of the air. It travelled from mouth to mouth because people believed it. Because it made sense. Because it was invariably connected to fact. She understood that a sophisticated man like Omar, travelled and wise, would want a western wife rather than an young Egyptian girl straight from the bosom of her family. But a western woman without a dowry . . . Another matter altogether.

She remembered what the General had said to her: 'So you have nothing to offer him.' He would have told Omar he heard it from her own lips. He would point out that she had nothing to gain by telling him a lie. Was it because Omar needed to think that he had not turned up to take her to dinner at Aswan, nor sent one of Egypt's small boys with a message?

But then he had come to Luxor. And he had not broached the subject of letting her down. She, in her enchantment, had felt no need to ask.

'Susanne?' She turned to look into Vita's concerned face and smiled a brittle smile. 'So, it was an experience,' she said. 'Let's go down to lunch. I'm really excited about seeing Cairo, aren't you?'

CHAPTER TWELVE

They gathered in the saloon after lunch where they were briefed by the large, dignified guide, Hassan. 'This afternoon we will transfer to our hotel which is out by the pyramids at Giza, but first I will take you on a tour of the city. Be sure your cabins are clear for your baggage will be taken ahead. To begin, I will lead you into the *souk* where you will be able to complete your shopping.' He went on to explain that the Cairo *souk* was not at all like the comparatively safe one they had shopped in at Aswan. 'You must stay together,' he warned them, 'for if you get lost you may never be seen again.'

Someone giggled and the big man frowned. 'I was never more serious,' he said. 'I have lived in Cairo all my life, but even I could get lost in the *souk*. All the streets look alike. And there are caves and alleyways that do not have names. Besides,' he added with a twinkle, 'if they had, you would not be able to read the Egyptian words. So keep close to me. Do not let me out of your sight.'

They followed him aboard the coach and settled gingerly into the hot leather seats. The heat was oppressive. The engine ground noisily into gear and they were off, winding through a dense and chaotic selection of bullock carts, taxis, old bangers, buses so laden with passengers that clusters of men balanced on the steps, clinging dangerously to any piece of metalwork they could reach. Susanne thought she had never seen so many people in the whole of her life.

'It's like a football crowd,' Vita remarked, half laughing, half awe-struck. Men leaped in and out of taxis in their Arab robes, their little red fezzes, their turbans. Men wearing city suits jumped on buses that were already jam-packed, somehow insinuating themselves among the precariously balanced passengers. Men and black-clad women in yashmaks scurried up and down the streets and lanes and alleyways like ants. Susanne scoured the crowd looking for a straight-backed man with a king's blue eyes and crisp black hair. A man who was tall for an Egyptian, and anyway would stand out in any crowd.

The bus pulled up outside the *souk*. The passengers prepared to alight. Susanne continued to stare out of the window. Omar was probably tied up with business for his father. Omar had decided his little *affaire* was over. Omar was ill. She experienced a tremor of fear. Outside in the street the drivers of cars and taxis that were blocked by the stationary bus hooted impatiently.

'Miss Landseer, you are dreaming!'

She jumped up with a little moue of apology, hurried along the aisle and down the steps. A man in a light blue shirt and jeans leaped out of his car, and rushing up to the window of the car in front, thumped on the glass. She could only see the back of his head now. She gasped, and stood transfixed. Then he turned his head and it was not Omar.

'Come on, Susanne, don't hold us up. What are you looking at?' Peter was shaking her arm.

'Sorry.' She moved on, her heart like lead, and attached herself to the outer rim of the party. Hassan was herding them towards a lane running at right-angles to the street.

Vita came up beside her. 'I'd like to buy something for Felicity.'

'I'll get a present for Gilbert,' Susanne said remembering with gratitude how he had saved her from making a fool of herself.

They wandered through the alleyways, waiting while one member of the party after another examined desert stones, rings and kaftans. Hassan stood around casting a benevolent eye over them, alert for strays. Susanne lagged behind, glancing desultorily at the stalls, feeling depressed. What on earth could she find to buy here for her godfather? Then some little distance away she saw a stand covered with a display of boots and shoes. And there was a pair of black velvet slippers embroidered with gold. From this distance they looked very like the pair Hassan wore on the boat. She hesitated, wondering if they might look ridiculous in the clear light of England. No. Gilbert was an extrovert. He would think they were fun.

The stall was some yards behind them, situated on a corner from which one of the numerous alleys ran away. If she were to get the slippers she would have to break from the party. She looked round for Hassan and could not see him. Where was Peter? There was an upsurge of laughter from the people gathered round the kaftans. One of them was parading self-consciously in a golden robe. She felt certain they were not going to move on just yet. She glanced back at the slipper stall, hesitated, then again looked for Peter and Hassan. One of the women who was standing nearby happened to turn her way.

Susanne spoke to her. 'I'm going back, just a little way, to look at some slippers. If the rest of the party start to move on, would you mind telling them where I am?'

'We're all supposed to stay together,' said

the woman primly and Susanne recognised her as the one who had made the insulting remark about her as she came aboard *Phoenix* after being caught in the sandstorm. Oh hell! She looked round impatiently for Peter. Where on earth had he gone? Where was Hassan? They couldn't be far away. She decided to take a chance. 'Don't let them go without me,' she said, and giving her unfriendly acquaintance a tentative smile, she slipped back through the crowd.

The slippers were perfect. Black velvet with soft leather soles and on the toes an impressive design in red and gold embroidery. She glanced back in the direction from which she had come and saw with relief Peter's fair head lifted above the crowd. He would notice her absence even if the woman didn't hand on the message. The salesman behind the stall thrust out an eager hand, 'You wish the slippers?'

'Yes, please.' She took her wallet from her bag.

He was making flamboyant gestures, wrapping the slippers in little sheets of puce-coloured paper. 'Beautiful slippers? You think they are beautiful?'

'Yes,' she said. 'Would you mind hurrying?' Anxiously, she glanced again behind her over the heads of the crowd.

'Is present for husband?'

'Godfather,' she said impatiently. The party was still engrossed in the business of the gold

242

kaftan. The slippers were being slowly and very, very carefully wrapped.

'You from England? Or America?'

'England. How much are they?' She asked. She would have to pay the asking price. There was no time to haggle. Again, she glanced back over her shoulder. She was holding her wallet lightly in her palm.

A dark form slipped past her, a dark, thin hand shot out and her hand was empty. She screamed. Fast as a snake the overtly friendly salesman disappeared behind his wares. The crowd oozed round her, cutting her off. Squat women in long black robes, their faces hidden behind yashmaks, small men in shirt sleeves, large men in *galabiyas*, jostled her, ignoring her distress. It seemed to her that they must all be involved in the theft. She had no breath left to scream. She was helpless. At their mercy. She was being pushed in the opposite direction from where the party waited. She fought her way through them and broke free. But where was she now? She looked wildly round. Above her head was a mud archway, and beyond that a cave-like indent.

The crowd was behind her, the alley, dark and sinister, ahead. The thief must have gone down there. There was a flash of white a little way down where the darkness thickened. Involuntarily, she leapt forward, but there was no one there. She swung round.

'Peter!' she yelled, half hysterical with fright.

243

'Hassan!'

What was that? A sound of quick breathing, terrifyingly close at hand. Her heart palpitated with fright. She couldn't see the entrance. She must have turned a corner. Again, she heard that sinister breathing. She took a chance and dashed in the opposite direction, praying this was the way she had come and found herself on the edge of another crowd. But where were the stalls? She glanced up. There was no archway. She was lost. This was not the way she had come. She had strayed into another alleyway with another set of stalls.

'Peter!' she screamed. 'Hassan!'

She seemed to have lost all sense of direction. She turned round, then turned again. From beneath the archway a man in a dirty *galabiya* with filthy hands and feet came creeping towards her. In his outstretched hand he held her wallet. Her first instinct was to make a grab but as quickly she recognised he was using the wallet as bait. Forget the money. It was only important to get out of here. She made a dash forward, then back. She didn't know which way to run. He saw her hesitation and came at her fast as a cat. She felt his fingers close over her wrist and mad with fright she screamed, 'Omar!' The man jerked her in beneath the archway. 'Omar!' she shrieked in despair as though she could manifest him out of her need. 'Omar! Omar!'

The man was small and wiry, but he was

strong. He jerked her towards him. Her face was up against his robe. She could smell the dry, musty, dusty odour of it.

There was a rush of feet. A slim figure in blue sped past her. She felt her assailant's fingers loosen on her wrist. There was a flash of metal and to Susanne's horror she saw the Arab had drawn a knife from the folds of his gown. At the same moment the man in blue lifted one foot and with a powerful kick knocked him back against the wall. The knife spun from his hand and rattled across the stones. There was a spate of threatening Arabic. The thief, cringing and whining, tried to rise from the ground. Her rescuer gave him another kick.

Susanne looked into Omar's concerned face and thought this was one of those mirages people had in the desert. In a moment he would disappear and she would be at the mercy of the thief once again. She swung round and saw he was dragging himself to his feet.

As his abject countryman struggled upright the apparition who might be Omar grasped his shoulders and shook him violently. Whining for mercy, the man reached into his dirty white robes, drew the wallet out and handed it over, then ran.

Susanne stumbled up against the mirage that was Omar. He put a flesh and blood arm round her. 'How on earth did you get here?'

245

'I don't know.' Now that she knew he was real all the strength drained out of her, her knees shook and tears rolled down her cheeks.

'It is like this in the Cairo *souk*, I'm afraid,' Omar said. 'Impenetrable. You can't find your way out.' Still with an arm round her he hustled her through the crowds.

'Do you know where we are?'

'More or less. I've been coming here since I was a child and my sense of direction is good. We will get you back with the party, don't worry. They will be frantic.'

They were, indeed frantic. But they were silent, for they had listened to Hassan's warning and they, too, had been frightened. Vita put her arms round Susanne, momentarily unable to speak.

Omar said, 'I will take her away.'

'She had better stay with the party,' Peter said, his voice cold but with a trace of uncertainty.

'I'm not sure she's safe with the party.' Omar delivered his mild rebuke with a very direct look.

'We can't keep an eye on everyone all the time.' Susanne recognised that he was angry because he too had been badly scared. 'She's a loose cannon—' He broke off and Susanne saw in the expression of disdain on Omar's face what had silenced him.

'I'm very sorry,' she said shakily. Again, she was close to tears. She turned to her mother.

246

'If you don't mind, Vita, I'd like to get out. I don't like this *souk* very much.'

'But where will you go?' The Colonel, standing by Vita, was concerned.

'She will be safe with me,' Omar replied. 'I know your hotel and I am known there. You need not worry, she will be well looked after.'

Susanne kissed her mother on the cheek. 'Don't worry.'

'I can't help worrying, dear.'

'I'm sorry.' They were whispering, though the crowd had turned away.

'Vita, Omar saved my life. I'll tell you about it later. Believe me,' the words came out in a whisper with a little sob behind, 'I am very safe with him.'

The Colonel took Vita's arm and led her away.

Susanne was still shaking as Omar settled her into the passenger seat of his car.

'I can't believe it,' she said. 'How did you manage to get there—just at the right moment—when I needed you?'

Omar smiled, a laid-back, devastating smile that turned her knees to water. 'The gods look after lovers,' he said in a voice that told her he was surprised she didn't know. 'They have allowed us to find each other. They would not go to that trouble then allow it to go wrong.'

Feeling cherished, Susanne accepted the magic. Omar negotiated a path through the chaotic traffic, vying for space with bullock carts, buses, bicycles, miraculously avoiding darting pedestrians intent upon short cuts with suicidal disregard for safety.

'How did you know where we were?'

'As soon as I could get away I went to *Phoenix*.'

'Away from your father?'

Omar's mouth turned down, but there was a look of gentle triumph in his eyes. 'He has been keeping me on a tight rein. Your manager told me what time you left and where you had gone. It's the route tourists take. And so I knew I would find you. But what happened at Luxor?'

'Oh, Omar!' She remembered the anguish, and the pain. 'I was spirited away. Peter changed the plans.'

'Ah, it was Mr Peter, was it? It was a good try,' Omar conceded magnanimously. 'But I was very angry at the time.' He raised his voice so that she could hear him over the cacophony of klaxons brought into play by impatient drivers all vying for space. 'Very angry indeed. I came to the river bank, all dressed up as befits an escort for a princess. I had booked a table and ordered flowers. It was to have been an occasion,' he said and his face hardened. She thought she glimpsed in that moment a man who might be dangerous to cross. She remembered how he had summarily dealt with the thief who was carrying a knife.

'You, too, were angry?' he asked, looking at

248

her with questioning eyes as though he needed affirmation that she had shared his feelings.

'Very,' she said. 'I put on my best dress that evening for dinner anyway and the jewellery you gave me. People stared but I didn't care.'

'It was an act of defiance?'

'Yes.'

He reached out and touched her hand where it lay on her knee. 'I understand. As for me, good Muslim that I am, I went to my room with a bottle of whisky.'

'Oh, Omar.' She laughed weakly.

'Yes, that is what I thought next day when I wakened with a headache that was almost unbearable. Oh Omar! What have you done to yourself?'

'So what happened? What did they say? The passengers?'

'They don't say much any more. They just watch me. I think some of them actually felt sorry during the last few days when you didn't turn up. They could see how miserable I was when you didn't come to Beni Suef. And then again at El Ayat. I wasn't able to hide my feelings. I don't think I even tried very hard. I was too full of despair. Why did you not send a message?' she asked looking up at him wanly.

He surprised her by saying, 'One does not spar with Fate. One waits for the luck to change.'

Susanne sucked in her lower lip. Would reversals be easier to bear if one adopted a

249

fatalistic attitude to them? Or was Omar so accustomed to getting his own way in the end that he was able to sustain disappointments assuming them to be temporary? She glanced around the interior of the car, recognising for the first time that it was English, and far from new.

'Yes,' he said, reading her thoughts. 'This is my own car.'

She was surprised that he should choose a Vauxhall. She remembered the glamorous cars he had borrowed in Aswan and Luxor. She had expected him to have something much smarter. He seemed the sort of person who, even if hard up, would find enough for a nifty little sports car. Then she remembered what his father had said. He needed to marry for money. She must not think about that.

'You're wearing riding gear!' she exclaimed in surprise.

A short-sleeved blue shirt, riding trousers and very shiny black boots. 'I am already dressed to take you out in the desert on one of my Arab mares just as soon as you have changed into your smart equestrian attire.'

She laughed softly with him, seeing herself in her Louis Feraud T-shirt with the outsize flower on the front and the silk stole wound round her head.

They drove across a bridge and then through palm fringed streets. 'This is the suburb of Giza where your hotel lies,' Omar

250

said. Here the traffic was much lighter and they were able to put on speed. He turned the car in at wide, ornate gates and she saw ahead the long, low-lying building with its wide verandah that was their hotel, nestling among green palms and tall bushes displaying colourful, waxy blooms.

'How lovely!' She caught the glint of water and there was a beautiful swimming pool. It would appear that the cut-price package was doing them proud for their two final nights. She thought dryly that the borrowed clothes might not look out of place here.

Omar parked the car in the partial shade of a tall green tree and escorted her up the wide stone steps into the hotel. A man who wore the air of being in charge hurried forward and shook him by the hand. He introduced Susanne. 'Mr Fayed is the manager. He will look after you.'

The man bowed and assured her he would.

'She is coming riding with me. You will give her the key to her room,' said Omar in the way he had of making an order sound like a compliment. The manager hurried over to Reception and returned followed by a boy carrying a key.

'You will be quick,' said Omar.

'I will be very quick.'

They were still in conversation when she ran back downstairs dressed in her makeshift riding gear. They shook hands again and

251

hurried out to the car. 'Now we will visit my stables,' Omar said as he slipped in behind the wheel. 'They are not like your English stables. You may be disappointed. Certainly you will be surprised.'

'Everything here surprises me.' She hugged her knees, feeling exultant. 'Surprises are fun.'

He swung the car round and swept back down the drive.

They left the main road and drove along sandy lanes with shacks on either side and here and there a broken wall. Omar drove fast. After about a mile he swung round to face a high mud-brick wall into which were set a pair of wide iron gates. With one arm lying crooked on the steering wheel he laconically pressed the horn. Susanne's eyes followed his to a slit cut in the wall about six feet up. Almost immediately a pair of black eyes appeared, then as swiftly disappeared again.

'My groom, Moussa,' Omar said. The massive gates swung open.

His groom was a large man in flowing Arab robes and wearing a small, rather grubby turban. There was a good deal of black stubble on his face, probably a week's growth. He smiled broadly, exposing an incomplete set of enormous and rather grimy teeth. Omar greeted him warmly and was warmly greeted in return. There appeared to be great affection between the two men.

Moussa spoke to her courteously in his own

tongue. 'He is saying, "May your day be happy."'

'How kind of him.' Susanne smiled up at the big man thinking how very happy her day was, now that she and Omar were together again.

Across a dry mud courtyard that was peopled by a strutting cock, half a dozen ducks and a few hens, lay a low dwelling made from mud bricks and to the right a similar building which was evidently the stables. Susanne swiftly hid her surprise, but Omar had seen. His eyes held a glimmer of amusement. 'I warned you it is not at all like what you have in England,' he said. 'I have visited English stables such as you have.'

'I have no stables,' she replied, speaking swiftly, unable to keep a note of anxiety out of her voice. 'I told you, I ride a neighbour's horses. They are not mine.' But he was scarcely listening. He was gesturing to her that they should follow Moussa who was leading the way to the front door of the little house. They entered a sizeable room where a pretty woman was kneeling on the mud floor stirring some pungent smelling food. An iron pot hung from a trivet over a small open fire. Instead of rising to her feet as Susanne had expected, the woman squatted back on her heels and smiled up at Omar with childlike pleasure.

Moussa could have been any age between thirty and fifty, but his wife looked very young. A child bride, handed over by her father? She

253

would ask later. Or perhaps not. On the floor beside the young woman a grubby baby, dressed in a long gown not unlike the ubiquitous *galabiya*, played with two sticks. Omar, his eyes grown tender, picked the child up. He flung the sticks away and shrieked delightedly as Omar threw him into the air.

'Moussa is the Arabic form of Moses,' Omar said, putting the boy down and in an oddly courteous gesture, handing the sticks back to him. Moses! Susanne glanced at the father and had a disturbing vision of biblical figures gathered in just such a dwelling as this, all those years ago.

They went back into the yard. 'So, what do you think of my stables?' Omar asked.

She was astonished that a man who was said to own the best horses in Egypt should keep them in a dried mud yard. 'Very much of the country,' she replied, smiling.

Moussa led out a beautiful bay stallion with high arched head and rounded flanks. 'This is Mush, my favourite,' Omar said. The stallion was delighted to see his master. He nibbled at Omar's fingers and stamped his feet, impatient at the prospect of a ride. 'You shall have Hatshep,' Omar said. He took Mush's reins and the groom went back to get the mare. 'She has a soft mouth so you will be gentle with her. Give her her head if she wants to gallop. You will come to no harm.'

Hatshep was small and lightly built, the

254

colour of warm fudge. Her long, cream-coloured mane and tail had recently been brushed so that they gleamed like silk in the sunshine. Susanne was entranced.

Omar was watching her face. 'You like my Hatshep?'

'She is just the most beautiful creature!'

'She shall be yours,' said Omar with the casual benevolence of a king bestowing a precious gift on his princess. Susanne looked at him sharply but he had turned to take the saddle from Moussa and was settling it on the mare's back. She went eagerly to the opposite side, straightened the girth and handed it under the mare's belly then slid the crupper under her lovely tail and buckled the strap. Omar gave her a leg up. Hatshep turned her head and nudged her bottom with soft lips.

Omar laughed. 'She only does that to people she approves of.'

Susanne said breathlessly, 'I thought she was going to take a nip.'

'No my darling. She would never nip.' He went back to the stallion. Moussa legged him into his saddle. They reined round then rode out of the gates and crossing the car track headed into a narrow lane. At the bottom it turned sharply left, then rose. Ahead were covered stalls and a milling crowd of people. 'We have to ride through this bazaar,' Omar said. 'But don't worry, the horses are accustomed to crowds.'

Two stray dogs wandered across their path, then a skittish donkey headed out of the crowd pursued by its owner swinging a rope threateningly, shouting. Susanne turned away, not wanting to see the donkey caught and taking its inevitable punishment, remembering what Omar had said, 'This is Egypt'.

As they approached the bazaar the crowd parted to allow them through. Smiling faces gazed up at them. An important looking man stepped forward extending his hand and Omar bent down to shake it. The man spoke garrulously and at length. Omar listened, a thoughtful, sympathetic expression on his face.

Susanne reined in and looked round. There was an enormous amount of merchandise on display, pots and pans, plastic buckets, bolts of material, sweets. The man talking to Omar backed away and merged with the crowd. Another one hurried forward and reached up to shake Omar by the hand. And then another. Everyone, it seemed, knew him. The women were looking at her with startled curiosity. She thought, I am riding here because I am a foreigner. They accept that. But do they envy me? Not wanting to be too conspicuous, she drew the shawl across the lower part of her face.

Omar explained as they left the bazaar behind and headed across the sand, 'That man who was talking so earnestly to me wishes me to find a job for his son. He has been out of work for a long time through illness.'

This was a new view of Omar's life. 'Will you be able to get him a job?'

'Oh yes.' He spoke as though it was an everyday event, this finding jobs for the sons of his friends.

Ahead now lay the pyramids, and close at hand the sphinx with its man's head and lion's body crouched in the sand, looking with its inscrutable smile over the vast tracts of desert. Susanne caught her breath. 'Does anyone know who it is meant to be?'

'It's believed to be the head of Khafre, the King of Egypt at the time the statue was carved,' Omar replied. 'As time went on it was forgotten and of course it gradually became enveloped by sand. In the end there was only a small piece protruding to show that something was hidden there.'

'Enough to cast a bit of shade.'

Omar turned to look at her, brows raised, a smile playing at the corners of his mouth. 'You know the story?'

'Only from the guide books.'

'Then you must tell me what the guide books say. If I talk all the time you will think I am—what would you say—big-headed?'

'No,' she said gravely. 'Never. And besides, you have a way of telling that creates magic for me. There was a prince ...' She smiled at him, waited, and he went on, ' ... who was riding in the desert. He was only a boy. He paused to

257

sleep in that bit of shade. As he slept, the sphinx spoke to him. Can you imagine the sphinx speaking?'

'Yes,' she breathed. She was seeing the great creature in half profile now.

'"I am buried beneath the sand," the sphinx said. "If you will have it cleared away you will be king of Egypt." The prince did as he was asked and when everyone saw the man's head and the lion's body they fell back, awestruck.'

'And the boy was proclaimed King of Egypt?'

'Yes. I've never lost my awe for it,' said Omar. 'Such power and mystery it has.'

Power and mystery indeed, Susanne thought as they passed below the great statue. And such grandeur! She was overwhelmed by it.

Ahead of them now lay the pyramids, solid, bulky memorials enduring on their rocky plateau. Omar gave her a mischievous look. 'Now that Peter, our excellent archaeologist, is not with us, shall I tell you some facts that are not in the guide books?'

She laughed. 'I could bear it from you.'

'That pyramid,' he said, pointing, 'is Cheops. It is in the unique position of being in the exact centre of the world. Here is the natural zero of longitude for the entire globe. Its four sides front the four points of the compass.'

Susanne loosened her reins and sat back in the saddle. 'Built by the ancient Egyptians?'

He nodded.

'How amazingly clever. Ancient? What are we talking about?'

'Those who lived two thousand, three hundred years before Christ.'

She was thinking that Anglo Saxons were probably living in caves at that time and catching their food with spears and clubs. 'But I understood the pyramids were tombs.'

'So they are. The Great Pyramid was built by a Fourth Dynasty Pharaoh. The Egyptians of the time wanted a first-class and truly original tomb for their king. Would you say they did him proud?'

'Golly! I should say so. So he's under that great pile.'

'What is this "golly"?'

'Slang. Sorry.'

'You must not be sorry. You are teaching me colloquial English. I prefer that to the text book kind.'

Yes, she thought with an uprush of warmth and admiration, he would want to do everything properly. Better than other people.

'The Pharaoh is not under that "great pile" as you say. He is in the middle of it. There are passages leading to the tomb which is situated exactly in the centre.'

'Dead centre,' said Susanne looking at him mischievously. He frowned. 'You said you wanted to speak colloquial English.'

'Thank you.' Omar nodded gravely but

those incredible blue eyes were dancing. 'I am glad this ride has turned into an English lesson. We have a lot to teach each other. Shall we go back to the statistics of this pyramid?'

'Sorry.'

'The entrance is set at an angle so that it points towards a part of the heavens that would always be occupied by stars. The stars know what is expected of them,' said Omar. 'They come in turn to keep watch.'

She was again touched with awe and the magic of his beliefs.

'Since we're on bald statistics,' she said, and was rewarded with a touch of his hand on hers and a smile, 'How did they get the blocks of stone up? They didn't have bulldozers and cranes in those days.'

'You might ask how they cut the stone, much less carted it up. Those rocks, as you see, though perhaps you do not for there is nothing to compare them with out here, are half the size of a house. They were cut from a quarry on the eastern bank of the Nile, then put on rollers, guided down inclined planes to a boat and rowed across the river. Enough of this seriousness.' Omar loosened the reins and Mush bounded away. Susanne touched the flank of her mount and galloped after him.

They joined a track bordered by small, squalid dwellings. On the left was an ancient graveyard. Omar slowed until Hatshep had come abreast.

'That's the City of the Dead.'

'City of the Dead!' Susanne's imagination was stirred. She thought how inappropriate was the word cemetery. Then she remembered that English cemeteries were small, mainly tree-girded, often snugly encircling a church. They could never be called a city. Her eyes roved over the vast expanse of mausoleums and gravestones locked within stone walls that were the colour of the pyramids. A walled city of the dead. She imagined the wall as being there to keep in the restless spirits that might return down the Nile on their celestial barques in order to rove at night within their own designated city. She was awash with dreams.

Omar was watching her enigmatically. She felt he knew the sum of this strangeness that had filled her. He did not speak for a while. Then he stretched out an arm, pointing ahead. 'Over the horizon is the Western Desert where the allies fought in the second world war. You will know its history.'

She turned her eyes to the front where the sand dunes rolled away. The track had given way to sand. They were facing the vastness of the desert. She didn't want to think about English history. She wanted to stay with Egyptian enchantment. 'The stars know what is expected of them.' She turned the words over in her mind, thinking of the cultural fissure that lay between Omar and herself. Such a weight of strangeness she felt about her now. She let it lie there, waiting for what was to be.

As though he felt she needed reassurance Omar again reached across and put a hand over hers. The horses tossed their heads gently and snorted. Their velvet noses touched affectionately. 'They are very good friends,' said Omar. 'Not lovers. Not yet. But they could be. Would you allow Mush to give Hatshep a young prince of a foal?'

He was talking as though all this was real. As though the future was real, too. Susanne scarcely knew about reality any more. She was riding with the stars. 'Race you,' she shouted and Hatshep bounded away.

'Watch out for foxholes,' Omar shouted as on his stallion he pounded past.

She laughed and threw back her head. The shawl fell loose and swung out behind her. She felt like a desert maiden riding into the unknown.

CHAPTER THIRTEEN

They raced up a long hill. Hatshep galloped flat out but Omar held the stallion, capable of much greater speed, on a firm rein. When they reached the summit the horses were panting and sweating. Mush tossed his beautiful head and foam flecks, white as snow, flew from his mouth. Ahead of them now was a shallow basin and dotted over it a collection of tents, some as big as a marquee.

Susanne blinked. 'What's this? An army encampment?' Even as she spoke she knew the tents did not belong to the army for they were randomly placed.

Omar said, 'This is where we entertain our friends.'

She looked at him suspiciously thinking of jokey romantic novels of the twenties— Eleanor Glyn on her tiger skin; sheiks on fiery steeds sweeping the heroine up on the pommel of their saddles to gallop across blazing desert sands to a tent in the desert. But she was careful not to laugh because too many strange things had happened to stretch her credulity.

Omar pointed. 'That big one over there belongs to my family. It's where we hold our parties.' He nudged Mush into a walk and Susanne followed down the sand slope and across to a marquee that would easily hold a couple of hundred people. He led her towards a corner where the canvas flap was turned back revealing a bare brick floor. 'There is no need to dismount,' Omar said. 'There's nothing to see. If we left property here it would be stolen.' His eyes flickered. 'The *fellahin* would find a tent easier to rob than a tomb.'

'So, for your parties, can no one sit down?' Susanne laughed merrily.

He laughed with her. 'Our servants bring out rugs and cushions, and of course, tables. And the drinks and food. They transport it on camels during the day and then stay here on guard. I assure you, it's a very glamorous place to entertain.' She glanced at him, only half believing. His face held a kind of radiance. 'Imagine it,' he said softly. 'The moon and the stars up there, and the lamps in the darkness.'

Susanne felt lost. I am dreaming, she said to herself. Any moment now I will wake up and find myself galloping through Harvey's park with awful Nigel. This has to be a figment of my imagination. Perhaps I am ill. Perhaps I am dead. What she was experiencing was light years away from the world she knew. She shook her shoulders, her head, she closed her eyes then opened them again. The tent was still there, and Omar on his big stallion, smiling and saying,

'We shall have a party here to introduce you to my friends and family.'

She felt a sense of apprehension rising almost to fear. She remembered the rather battered car he drove, the only property, it seemed, that belonged to him. This fairytale life must be provided by his family. But, his father having warned her off, how could Omar hold a party for her? A party for which assuredly the family would be paying? Did he still believe, in spite of her protests, that she was rich? She remembered how the General had talked, scathingly, about English understatement. She remembered that he had not believed her.

Somehow, she had to get away. The situation had got out of control. This evening she would talk to Omar very, very seriously. She would make him understand. It would break her heart, but she was going to have to do it. She was going to have to say, 'I am poor, poor, poor. My mother and I have only what we earn. You've got to believe these designer clothes are not mine, and nor did we pay for the cruise. You've got to believe it!' She did not belong in his world. It was one thing to love a man, but quite another to allow him to lead her into this false position. Such a false position!

A voice said, 'You have a very expressive face. What are you thinking?'

She said in a tortured voice, 'You know nothing about me. I—'

'Only that I love you. What more is there to know?' And without waiting for a reply he reined his horse round, dug in his heels and set Mush to a gallop. Susanne followed. Omar stopped at quite a small tent several hundred yards away. Standing outside, watching them approach, was a large man in the ubiquitous *galabiya*. As Susanne reined in, Omar was addressing him in Arabic. The man came forward, Omar introduced them, and they shook hands.

He said in perfect English, 'I am very pleased to make your acquaintance, Miss Landseer.' He turned to call to two small boys who stood shyly watching them. The boys disappeared with alacrity into the tent and returned a few moments later carrying a tray on which stood two beautiful cut glass goblets each half-filled with ice. On the tray also was a bottle of whisky.

The man handed one goblet to Susanne and the other to Omar. He allowed the reins to fall on the stallion's neck, took the bottle in his free hand, splashed a measure of whisky into Susanne's glass and handed it back to her. Then he filled his own and put the bottle back on the tray. Gathering up the reins then, holding them in one hand, he indicated that they ride off together.

Susanne was thunderstruck. Hatshep stepped forward with the ambling gait of the Arab horse and the whisky in her glass sloshed giddily up to the rim and over her hand. Omar, with magnificent aplomb, lifted his glass to his lips and drank, apparently without losing a drop. 'Cheers,' he called. She raised her glass and received most of the contents in her face.

Omar was spurring Mush to a fast canter. Giddy with excitement, Suanne threw down the rest of the drink, inevitably losing most of it and getting an ice block down the front of her blouse. With the empty glass in one hand and the reins in the other, laughing weakly,

266

delightedly, a little hysterically, she raced after Omar. Mush was now swinging round in a big circle, heading once again for the tent. On the horizon the sun, like a vast blood-red orange, was sinking out of the pale evening sky. It dipped, and taking with it the remaining heat out of the day, slid from sight.

In her thin blouse and jeans, Susanne shivered, but it was only partly from the cold. The fact that Omar was descended from kings, that he dined with governors, had not affected her so strongly as this, her first glimpse into his private life. The homage he had received in the bazaar, his feudal treatment of his groom's family, this easy access to the hospitality of desert men of high standing, had shown him to her in a different light. A light that dazzled her, blinded her almost, but more than that, frightened her. Deep down inside her there was a growing feeling of panic.

As they approached the tent Omar's friend came to shake hands again. The boy took the glasses and they reined round for the return. A plethora of stars, coldly glittering, appeared in the velvet blackness of the sky.

'You are not afraid to ride in the dark?' Omar asked quizzically.

'No.' She was riding in the dark now. Had been for days. She felt disorientated. At least the warm horse flesh beneath her thighs was real. She smoothed Hatshep's silken mane with her free hand and felt comforted.

267

They sped back towards the pyramids. On the outskirts of Giza, near the City of the Dead, they slowed. Omar turned in his saddle. 'There is a friend of mine waiting on the track. Do you see him? He will offer us mint tea. It is necessary, out of courtesy, to accept. Unfortunately, he doesn't speak English.'

Susanne's eyes had accustomed themselves to the darkness. She could just see a large man in white robes out in front of them now.

'How does he know you are here?'

'The small boys. You call it bush telegraph, I think.'

Ah yes! The small boys. She should have known.

As they came closer they reined in and Omar introduced his friend as Abdel Gahbo.

Two boys appeared out of the darkness and took her reins as she dismounted, then led Hatshep away. Dimly, in the light of a bulb set in a wall, Susanne could see a low building near by. Stables? Omar explained, 'Abdel has a beautiful white stallion. He would like to show it to you.'

'I would love to see it.'

'But first you must have the mint tea.'

The two boys brought a tiny table with long, spindly legs, and with it two spindle-legged chairs. They placed the table on the sand and set the chairs at either side. Omar indicated gravely that she should sit. Two tall servants stood smilingly a few paces away. Omar spoke to their host in Arabic. In his turn he spoke to one of the small boys who hurried off and returned carrying a woollen shawl in his thin little arms.

'How kind,' Susanne exclaimed spontaneously. There was a patch of cold on the front of her blouse where the trapped ice block had melted. '*Shukran*,' she said to her host as she slid the soft garment round her shoulders. *Thank you*. Then turning to Omar, 'Why does the heat not stay in the air when the sun goes? In England, in summer, the evenings are warm.'

'Why? It is one of the secrets the desert keeps to itself. If you make friends with the sphinx perhaps it will tell you.' Omar seated himself in the chair opposite.

Susanne had a feeling of being on another planet. It wasn't possible that she was sitting at a tiny table on desert sand being stared at by small, dark-skinned boys with huge black eyes, waiting to be served with mint tea. That feeling of incipient panic came again. She tried to ground herself with light chatter. 'I think it's only friendly to people who can help it,' she said. 'But, since the prince has cleared the sand away I can't imagine what I could do to help.'

'It's possible it is only friendly to those it can help,' Omar replied softly.

She caught her breath as the magic of his words sank in. Then a boy came bearing a tray

269

with two little vessels made of fine china and placed them on the table. Omar raised his cup to his lips, indicating with a gesture that she do the same. The mint tea was sweet and strange. She took another sip, and another, listening to Omar's voice as he conversed with their host in Arabic. Idly turning her head she saw in the pale light of a hanging lamp on the wall a young Egyptian girl. She was slender, with thick, glossy black hair falling to her waist and she wore a long dress and pretty shoes. So they didn't all wear the long gown and headdress! Susanne smiled at her but the girl did not smile in return.

'Do you like the mint tea?' Omar asked, then when she did not immediately reply turned his head, following her eyes.

'Oh, yes. Yes, I do,' she answered, still caught in the girl's intense scrutiny. At that moment a young man strolled round the corner of the wall, glanced up, then ducked swiftly through an arched doorway in the wall. The girl followed him swiftly. Omar leapt to his feet, speaking rapidly to their host. Abdel Gahbo shrugged. Omar's angry words came snapping. Gahbo wrung his hands in protest, then resignedly he, too, crossed to the door, bent down and went through.

'What's the matter?' Susanne was startled.

'That girl has no right to be here,' Omar said. His voice was stern.

'Why? Who is she?' Susanne, too, rose to

her feet.

He did not reply. His eyes were on the open doorway. Their host came through and, following behind him, the girl. Her black eyes were deeply apprehensive, now. Omar's sternness melted away. He reached out and took the girl's hand. Though he spoke to her gently she looked extremely frightened. Their host had recovered his poise. He, too, spoke kindly to the girl, and then at length to Omar. Omar nodded then turned to Susanne.

'We will not have time to look at the stallion now,' he said. 'We must take the girl back with us. Abdul has been good enough to loan us a car.'

'What will happen to Mush and Hatshep?' Susanne was baffled by this turnabout. And she was also disappointed to miss the last part of the ride.

'They will be taken back to the stables,' Omar replied and Susanne was again aware of the way people did things for him. 'You are, anyway, going to the *son et lumière*,' he said. 'You must not be late. We will drop you at your hotel.'

We? He and the girl? She turned to their host and thanked him. He replied in Arabic, at length. Omar did not bother to translate, but then it was obvious, she thought, excusing him, that the man was simply observing the niceties.

A big black car purred along the sandy track and the three of them climbed in. The girl sat in silence. Who was she? Why did Omar not explain? Why had he not introduced her? Susanne had a very certain feeling he did not want questions. She felt left out. Humiliated. There was only one explanation, Susanne decided. She must be the girl his family wanted him to marry. But if he really did not want to marry her, then why should he be so concerned for her?

The car purred up the hotel drive. Omar stepped out, held the door open for her, shook hands formally, and without a word climbed back into the car. Susanne stood in the doorway, her heart like stone as she watched the big car circle the drive then roll away into the darkness. Baffled, bewildered and near to tears she crossed the lounge with dragging feet and climbed the stairs.

As she opened the bedroom door Vita jumped up, crying shrilly, 'Where on earth have you been? It's dark. It's been dark for ages. You know we're due to leave for the *son et lumière* in twenty minutes.' She looked distraught.

'I'm sorry, Vita. I really am sorry,' Susanne replied, 'I've been riding.'

'Riding? How could you be riding in this darkness? It's black out there. And it's so cold! You're shivering. Look, you've got scarcely anything on!'

Susanne felt unstrung. Vita's unexpected attack was pushing her over the edge. She said,

272

making a tremendous effort to keep calm, 'There's no time to talk. Why don't you go down and tell them I'm coming. I must have a shower.'

'What's the matter? I can see something's wrong. What has happened?' Vita's voice rose higher, out of control.

'Will you go? Please go. It won't take me long to change.'

'But where—'

'*Mother!*' Susanne said through clenched teeth. She thought if Vita didn't go she would scream.

Vita picked up her coat and went out of the room.

Twenty minutes! Susanne flung her clothes on the bed and went naked into the bathroom. The water was warm and soothing. There wasn't time to wash her hair, but she did. She was washing away the disappointment, the magic, the wonder; she was washing Egypt away. Was that a premonition she had had when, outside the tent of Omar's friend with the glass of whisky in her hand, she had had the feeling that she did not belong here; that she was out of her depth? Perhaps the girl's appearance was Fate's way of showing her the dream was over. She felt brittle. Dry and cold inside.

She stepped out of the shower and towelled herself roughly, switched on the hairdryer and equally roughly tossed her long hair around in the rushing stream of heat. Then she slipped into trousers and the Tomasz Starszewski jacket, flicked a pale lipstick carelessly across her mouth, picked up her bag and ran downstairs.

Through the big glass doors she could see the coach waiting in the drive. She strode across the lounge then stopped dead. Omar was standing in the doorway talking amiably with their Egyptian guide. The guide turned, acknowledged her presence, then went down the steps and climbed aboard the coach. Omar came towards her, smiling. She felt her knees give way.

'Come,' he said, just as though nothing untoward had happened. 'I am going to drive you and see that you are comfortably seated.'

Outside, the coach began to move. Dozens of pairs of curious eyes gazed down at them from the windows. She said, stupidly, 'What do you mean? Tell me what—' but she broke off as he butted in,

'No questions. Relax and let the evening happen.'

'But—'

'And then there is another surprise for you afterwards,' he went on. 'You must be accustomed to surprises, now.'

Oh, how I am that! she thought, but when he told her of the next surprise she was not ready. Not for one of such magnitude.

'My family is expecting you to dine with

274

them.'

Breathless with disbelief, she could only stare at him. Again, she had that sensation of her knees giving way. He took her arm and led her outside. He was laughing. 'You should see yourself. I told you you have an expressive face. My father is not an ogre,' he said, surprised that she appeared to think so. 'Of course he will be charmed by you when he knows you a little.' Omar was leading her down the steps and along the drive towards his car. It occurred to her that it looked rather out of place parked between two sleek black limousines. Like a poor relation. Nothing added up. She was trembling as Omar handed her into the passenger seat.

He bent to look into her face. 'Smile, please.'

She laughed shakily, holding the panic at bay, wanting to say the General hadn't been charmed by her when he met her at Aswan, holding that at bay, too. She was like Vita, out of control. She fumbled with the seat belt. Don't think about going into the lion's den. Don't think about the fact that you will be unwelcome. Think about the *son et lumière*, no further than that.

They sped down the drive and edged into the traffic. 'It's not far,' said Omar. 'We'll be there in a few minutes.' Out in front a procession of cars and tourist buses turned off down a side road. Omar took his place in the queue. Ahead and to the left lay a big car park. As they came up to the entrance he slewed round and drove straight on. Susanne frowned. Ahead the road was closed off by a rope. Omar drove right up to it then casually pressed the horn and with an air of smiling patience, waited. An angry attendant ran out of the sentry box then pulled up as he recognised Omar. He saluted, turned and swiftly unhooked the rope to let them through. On either side tourists were trudging along on foot from the car park, carrying cushions and rugs. Faces turned to look curiously at the single car making its way up the road. Susanne opened her mouth to say she felt like royalty then closed it again. Wasn't that how Omar meant her to feel? She thought, that's how he feels all the time.

'All those people are carrying rugs,' she said. 'Are we going to be out in the open?'

'There are plenty of rugs and cushions for hire,' Omar replied. 'One does not have to bring them.'

They sped right up to the stand. A group of men in dark suits broke up and several of them ran down the steps. One of them opened the passenger door and helped Susanne out. Omar came round and introduced the men. The remainder of the group joined them and were introduced. Dazed and dazzled, Susanne managed to respond appropriately. Her feet scarcely touched the ground. Someone came

276

forward with a rug. Another handed Omar two cushions. It was clear they did not expect payment and Omar did not offer, though, ' . . . rugs and cushions for hire,' he had said.

They were ushered into the building and escorted past tier upon tier of seats. 'This is the President's seat,' Omar remarked casually as they reached the front of the stand, 'but he is not coming tonight.'

Susanne wondered if the President's arrival would have made any difference. They sat down. The cold night wind swung in across the dunes. Omar tucked the rug round their legs, put his arm through hers and took her hand. 'I will keep you warm,' he said. Her fingers gripped his. In spite of the strangeness, she felt she was holding a lifeline of sorts.

Music rose. Lights played over the sphinx and the pyramids. Precise English voices brought Egypt's history to life.

'Sir John Gielgud, is it not?' Omar whispered, bringing his dark head disturbingly close.

'Yes,' she whispered back. 'And Sir John Mills, speaking now.' Their familiarity helped to peel away some of the strangeness. She settled back, feeling a little more at ease now. With her hand in Omar's hand she allowed herself to be transported through time and space.

Hours later, it seemed, there was a rustle and a murmuring behind them. The show was over. People were rising to go. Susanne came down to earth with a crash, remembering. No, she thought, submerged in a flood of panic, I cannot go to his father's home. I would not be welcome. Omar doesn't realise what he's letting me in for.

'I had better find Vita,' she said, speaking rapidly, not looking at Omar. The Colonel would get her out of this.

'She knows you are dining with me,' Omar said.

'How?' Susanne's voice was high and thin. 'How does she know?'

'I told her.'

The crowds were melting away towards the exit. Susanne felt isolated in a world that had suddenly become inhospitable and dangerous. Omar handed her the cushions and began folding the rug. 'It is a pity it's too late to include your mother and her friend this evening,' he said and began to move towards the exit.

One of the men in dark suits emerged from the crowd and reaching out took the rug and cushions from them. 'You liked our *son et lumière*, mademoiselle?'

'I loved it. Thank you very much for the rug. It kept us warm.' Someone had taken the car away. It crept in to meet them with a large, dark man at the wheel. Doors were flung open, hands extended to shake theirs. Susanne felt desperately uncomfortable. Who did these

278

men think she was? They showed no curiosity. Were they accustomed to meeting Omar with different women? Or was he on such a high political plane that he had to be treated with kid gloves all the time?

She settled down in the passenger seat. Omar slipped behind the wheel and the car began to move.

'My family live in an apartment now,' he said. 'We had many houses—five in fact—but that was years ago, before I was born. When the king was deposed our lands and our houses were confiscated by the state. We live in quite a modest apartment now. My grandfather was to have gone into exile with the king but he managed to convince the authorities of his good intent. As you may know, King Farouk was dissolute, weak and grossly self-indulgent. But my grandfather had never been involved in the goings on of court life. You may not know,' said Omar without rancour for the man who had brought the family down, 'but Farouk was a corrupt man. His reign was bound to end in tears.'

Susanne was fascinated. 'I knew he was deposed. We weren't into Egyptian history at my school.'

'I will give you books to read,' promised Omar beneficently. 'You must know the modern history of my country as well as the past, though that particular part, the time of my family's downfall, is not an era of which we can be proud. But it was short-lived.' He squinted into the traffic in front, made a face then shrugged his shoulders. There was a man herding a buffalo in the middle of the road. 'It is not romantic, our recent history. No warriors, no paintings, no barques on the Nile.'

She smiled at him. 'I'm sure I'll find it very interesting.'

'Yes, of course. Even quite shameful stories can be interesting.'

Modest was not a word that came immediately to Susanne's mind as they approached the Saheed apartment block. It was big and impressive, and it faced the river. Where else, Susanne thought nervously, but in the best part of Cairo. But perhaps the actual apartment was modest. One of the smaller ones, facing the back.

They drove up to the front door. A doorman appeared like magic to open the driver's door and Omar stepped out, dropping the keys into his hand. Then he hurried round to the passenger side to help her out. Somehow it seemed correct form to sit in her seat until that happened. The servant preceded them inside, pressed the button for the lift, saw them in then went back to the car.

Omar, if he noticed her nervousness, did not comment. The lift stopped and they stepped into a wide hall. He did not have to knock or use a key for immediately a door opposite opened and a man who was obviously a servant appeared. Accustomed as she was to the gaudily attired staff on the riverboat, Susanne was surprised to find him wearing a khaki coloured cotton garment closely resembling a night-shirt. His feet were bare. She took a deep breath and mustered all her courage though there was little enough available to her at that moment, and Omar led her inside. She had an impression of an enormous room with ceiling-high windows.

A tall, statuesque and exceptionally beautiful woman rose from a chair and came to meet them. It had not occurred to Susanne to wonder what Omar's mother looked like, or what kind of clothes she might be wearing. In the event she was elegantly dressed in a long kaftan of a wonderful shade of red, beaded and embroidered. Her light brown hair, only faintly touched with grey, had been swept softly back from her face leaving some wayward strands fashionably loose. Susanne's incredulous eyes went to the necklace she wore. Rubies! Set in gold! A necklace for a queen!

'My mother,' said Omar. His voice had taken on a particular intimacy and warmth. 'Mama, I would like you to meet Susanne.'

'This is a great pleasure,' Madame Saheed said, extending a hand. 'It is kind of you to come. And kind of Omar to bring you. He knows how I like to meet visiting English people.'

Even as part of her brain registered the fact that Omar had not told his mother this was the girl he loved, Susanne managed breathlessly, 'You're English!'

The woman smiled. 'Irish, actually, but that was a long time ago. I've been Egyptian for a long time now.'

Susanne threw a baffled look at Omar but his attention had been taken by a servant who was carrying a tray of soft drinks. He took a glass of orange juice and offered it to Susanne. 'You will understand,' he said solemnly, 'that in a Muslim household we do not dispense liquor.'

'Of course.' As he handed a glass to his mother she glanced round the room wondering if Madame Saheed knew that her menfolk imbibed spirits liberally in public places. On the walls there were tapestries as well as portraits set in expensive-looking gilt frames. There was one of Omar's father and one of Omar himself as a child, and then as a man. There were young men who could have been his brothers; a pretty girl. His sister? Two more servants were in the room now, all moving silently in their bare feet on the polished floor. The furniture was dark and heavy, elaborately carved and upholstered. There were scattered Persian rugs.

And then the General walked in. Susanne saw him first. To say he appeared shocked would be an understatement. In a split second he wiped the shock from his face and advanced upon the little group with all the dignity and poise his son had inherited. He kissed his wife, then extended a hand to Susanne.

'We are always glad to entertain visitors to our country,' he said urbanely, speaking to her, but looking at his son. Susanne saw their eyes, the black and the blue, spark in a clash like steel on steel. 'What is she doing here?' he was asking with those steely eyes. She felt that so familiar rush of panic and asked herself the same question. She had an overwhelming desire to drop her glass and dash out of the door.

Madame Saheed was saying in her tranquil voice, 'I understand you met my son in Aswan.'

Susanne cleared her throat. Even so her voice emerged gritty and thin. 'He came aboard our boat. Our captain manager— invited him.'

'Do sit down, Miss Landseer.' Madame Saheed indicated one of the heavily carved and upholstered sofas that stood against the outer wall and Susanne sat down with a thump, glad to take the weight off legs that had become unreliable. The orange juice rocked dangerously in her glass. 'Do you travel a lot?'

Now was the moment to say she did not travel at all. That she lived in a tiny rented cottage and rode a friend's horses. That she had won this cut-price cruise in a competition. She threw a panicky look at Omar but he

283

seemed to be examining some interesting mark on the toe of his shoe. She felt abandoned, and dreadfully frightened. She took a large mouthful of orange juice and wished it was a slug of gin. 'Not much,' a voice was saying, emerging from inside of her. She tried to add she could not afford to but the voice wasn't up to that. 'I work,' she added. 'So this is rather a treat.' And then the voice, quite beyond her control, changed the subject. 'Do you ride, Madame Saheed?'

Omar's mother laughed. 'Indeed no. I don't do anything clever.' She moved to a gilt-framed chair standing near the sofa on which Susanne sat.

'She has brought up six children,' said Omar, losing interest in his shoe.

'My family is my greatest joy,' she replied looking up at him fondly.

'Do you go home?'

She smiled easily, it seemed. The question amused her. 'This is my home. I scarcely think I would fit in, in the western world, now. Women would think me lazy, and spoiled. I suppose I am. I have forgotten how to do anything for myself.' Again, that smile. Gentle, and quite beautiful. It lit up her face and her eyes. She turned to her husband, though appearing to address the room, 'It is very nice to be an Egyptian wife.'

'But as the English might say, not every woman's cup of tea.' The General's voice was

284

cool. A warning-off voice, Susanne thought. 'Modern English girls are accustomed to a type of freedom that my wife does not want.'

Omar's face was still. But was that a nervous tic in his cheek? He said, 'You have not told Susanne about your daughters,' then without waiting for his father to speak added, 'My sisters each have a university degree and though they are married, they work. It is different for the new generation,' he said with an air of confronting his father though he did not look directly at him. 'Perhaps my mother is the last of the lovely ornamental wives.'

Madame Saheed, relaxing comfortably against a silk cushion said, 'I am glad I am not of the new generation.'

'And so are we,' said Omar lightly then waited for his mother to laugh with him. As though she had begun to feel the tension between the two men she looked apprehensively from one to another of them then without speaking rose and went to the door that was standing open at the end of the room. Perhaps a servant was waiting just outside for she spoke to someone, then turned to face the room again.

'Dinner is ready.'

The dining room was peculiarly Eastern, and strangely ornate. They ate at a long table with heavily carved legs, sitting on gilt tapestry chairs with high backs. There was a great deal of gold in the room; an enormous gilt-framed excerpt from the Koran dominated the end wall. There were golden ornaments on small tables and in cabinets. Omar's mother seemed herself to be a thoughtfully presented part of the decorations where she sat at the foot of the table in her beautiful gown, her jewellery glittering in the light from a magnificent chandelier.

'I do hope you won't find the food too spicy,' she said. Her manner towards her guest was considerate; charming.

Susanne hoped so, too, but in the event she found the piquant flavoured meat and vegetables delicious and said so, then spoilt the compliment by biting accidentally into a pickled pepper. Tears sprang to her eyes, she coughed, and had surreptitiously to get rid of the offending object in her napkin. Everyone, even the general who had been eating in silence, his face set in a frown, allowed himself a crusty laugh.

'You said you have a job, Miss Landseer?' Omar's mother was the perfect hostess, intent upon putting the guest at ease. Susanne wanted to ask her to use her first name, but did not dare.

Omar stepped in saying casually, as though the matter was of no great importance, 'Call her Susanne, Mama. You don't have to be formal.'

Susanne turned her head to smile at him. Was he sending her a message with his eyes?

286

To relax? To be careful? Something she could not read lay in their blue depths. She took a deep breath and said, 'Unlike your daughters, I haven't got a university degree. So I haven't got what you would call a career. I do PR work. But I've been made redundant. That's why I was able to come on this holiday. Immediately I go back I shall have to look for a job.' She swallowed, lifted her gaze to her hostess' face and said deliberately, 'I have to work. We're not at all well-off, you know.'

The General said cynically, 'It is the cry of the British.'

His wife smiled tolerantly. 'My husband has never accustomed himself to the English and, for that matter, Irish habit of understatement. My father used to "cry poor", as Youssel puts it. He thought he must reach into his pocket and buy my family some food. Then he came to Ireland and found we lived in a castle. He was very angry. It was not easy to make him understand. I am not certain he understands now.'

Susanne licked her dry lips. The pepper had left its mark. 'We do not live in a castle,' she said.

Her hostess nodded, though barely noting her comment. 'He could not see,' she went on, 'that what my father said was true. He could not sell the castle and neither could he afford to make it comfortable. In fact, we were poor. Now here I am sitting on a beautiful gilt chair in an expensive dress and—'

'Mama,' Omar broke in, gently touching her arm and giving her a wry look.

She smiled indulgently. 'Yes, of course, I must not discuss our family affairs, but it is true that I always feel very rich when I look at my late mother-in-law's jewellery and remember that as a child I ran wild in Ireland.' She raised her fine eyebrows and with a droll look prepared to shock. 'In bare feet, very often,' she said.

Susanne glanced automatically at the bare feet of the two servants who waited patiently in the open doorway, then embarrassed, glanced quickly away.

Omar laughed. 'It is as well they do not understand.' Susanne, not knowing what to do, laughed also though her cheeks were hot. Madame Saheed smiled at her comfortingly, an expert at putting people at ease.

They had delicious honey cakes for dessert, then strong coffee. Susanne wondered if it would keep her awake but she had not the confidence to turn it down. They had started dinner very late and it had lasted a long time. As they left the table she turned to Omar and said *sotto voce*, 'I think I should go soon.'

The General, overhearing, acted with alarming speed, 'I will have you driven back to your hotel, Miss Landseer,' he said just as though her remark had been addressed to him. 'My son and I have some important business to discuss this evening.'

'I am taking—'

But his father did not allow Omar to finish. 'It is necessary that we talk now,' he said, using the voice of a General issuing an order to one of his subordinates.

Susanne glanced at Omar, then turned away quickly. This time he was not trying to hide his feelings. His eyes were cold and defiant, his mouth set in a straight line. 'It's all right,' she said hurriedly. 'I will be quite all right.' She turned to his mother. 'Thank you, Madame Saheed. I have so enjoyed my visit.'

'It has been a great pleasure,' she replied graciously.

Susanne knew then, recognising a tone of finality in Madame Saheed's voice, that Omar had told her nothing of the love between them. To his mother she was just another tourist passing through, to be given hospitality and treated with courtesy. She felt a cold sensation in the pit of her stomach, as though a stone had fallen there.

'I really will be all right,' she said turning to Omar, though not daring to look into his eyes. Her voice sounded in her own ears thin and high. He made a slight movement towards her as though, in spite of his father, he was going to escort her. Frightened, she turned away sharply. 'Good-bye, General,' she said, not offering her hand for there was no point. She knew, quite certainly, that he had dispensed

289

with courtesies. He only wanted to get rid of her, now.

'Good-bye, Miss Landseer,' he said.

CHAPTER FOURTEEN

Her mother had borne the silence stoically as they showered and dressed. Susanne knew that she had to say something. But what? Most of the night she had lain awake, aching, defeated, thinking of Omar's devotion to his family. Of his family's strength. Of his father's power.

Of treachery.

'Aren't you going to tell me what happened last night?' Vita asked at last, tentatively.

'I don't think so.' She knew she was being rude. She couldn't help what she was saying. If she weakened, softened, allowed herself to become human, her emotions were likely to splay all over the place.

Vita was silent as they sat down at the table. A little tight-lipped. Unhappy. The Colonel, wending his way towards them, read the expressions on their faces and swiftly turned away. Susanne jumped up and went over to ask him to join them. He was a sensitive man, unlikely to ask questions, and he would be a comfort to Vita, as well as acting as a catalyst.

The two of them chatted inconsequentially while Susanne ate her breakfast in near silence. They made no effort to include her in their conversation, and for that she was grateful. The food and strong coffee put a little courage back into her. She began to feel more in control. When Peter came by she was able to put a smile on her face. He paused at the table looking down at her uncertainly.

'Good morning, Peter.' She managed a smile.

He appeared to take heart. 'Are you coming to the museum?'

Omar had said he would take her to the museum. She kept the smile firmly on her face. 'Yes, of course.' Her voice was brisk, cheerful. 'I'm looking forward to it.'

His face lit up. 'Will you, er, would you come with me? Share my taxi?'

'Yes, why not? Thank you.' She pushed back her chair and stood up, keeping her eyes above head height, avoiding the curious stares. It was natural that they should all be wondering about last night. They had been seated when she was swept in with Omar accompanied by the important looking men in blue suits. And now, here she was leaving the dining-room with Peter! She felt their eyes on her back and wanted to run like a rabbit but she made herself walk sedately to the door. 'See you,' she said lightly and sped upstairs for her handbag.

The museum exhibits were magnificent. Fabulous colours. Elegant forms. Gilded

291

wood. *Look at those sculptured stone sarcophagi! Look at that headdress! The vulture and cobra attached to it are symbols of Upper and Lower Egypt. That beaten gold mask was made to conceal the dead Pharaoh's face.* Peter's facts slid across her brain. She was thinking how short on facts were Omar's stories. He would have told her the whys. Why the vulture and cobra were symbols of Upper and Lower Egypt. Why the face should be hidden by the gold mask.

Her mind drifted to the trackless desert of the Bedouins; to the sandstorm and the beauty of the changing sky. The warmth of Omar's hands returned to taunt her.

She started when Peter said, 'Now for the perfume shop. Is everyone here?'

She went obediently with the crowd as they trooped out into the road. Lively, courteous young Egyptians anxious to make sales produced low stools and served them with tiny cups of black coffee. *This is the most famous perfume shop in Egypt, you know. We send our perfumes all over the world. You will buy this, Madame? This?*

She shook her head. All around her the women of the party were enthusiastically trying out exotic scents, dabbing glass stoppers on their inner wrists, exclaiming excitedly. *I like that one. That's too strong. What about this one?* She felt distanced from them.

'Madame? You have not tried our beautiful

perfumes!'

'No, thank you. No, thank you.' She had to get away. She felt hemmed in by these predatory salesmen with their guilt-provoking, hurt expressions. She put the coffee cup down and, rising abruptly to her feet, went to the door where she stood watching the crowds. Such a multitude of red fezzes, brown faces, white *galabiyas*. Such an overwhelming number of people all scurrying like ants about their affairs. She watched a spruce-looking man in a tailored suit and a young girl climb out of a long, shiny, chauffeur-driven car and cross the pavement. She stepped aside to allow them to enter the perfume shop. Then she did a double-take. Surely this was the girl who had been at the stables of Omar's friend yesterday? The girl he had taken home.

Without consciously making a decision she found herself following them inside. They were standing at the counter now. She moved closer. The girl, as though aware of being watched, looked round and smiled shyly. Susanne went deliberately right up to her and held out her hand. 'Good morning,' she said.

'Good morning,' the girl returned her greeting.

Susanne stood by in startled silence while the girl spoke to the man in Arabic. He turned, holding out his hand. 'I am Rahman Malif,' he said. 'My daughter tells me you met yesterday.'

Susanne introduced herself. 'We did meet,'

293

she said, 'but as your daughter appeared not to speak English, we didn't have any conversation.'

The man's eyebrows rose. 'She is shy, but of course she speaks English.' He smiled at the girl tolerantly and she nodded and said something to him in Egyptian. He turned back to Susanne. 'She tells me you know her fiancé, Omar Saheed.'

The air in the perfume shop grew hot and distinctly oppressive.

'Nermeen and Omar are to be married shortly,' the man said. 'We have come this morning to buy her some perfume. Will you sit down and take coffee with us?' Susanne made an effort to reply, but could not. 'You seem surprised,' the father went on. 'Did you not know there is to be a marriage in the Saheed family?'

Susanne managed a glassy smile. 'If I looked surprised it was because . . .' what on earth could she say? She improvised, 'Nermeen's, er, so young. I mean—young to be married.'

'It is the way of things here,' the father replied. He looked fondly at his daughter. 'She has been promised to Omar since she was six. She is now seventeen and it is time for them to marry.'

Susanne's mind was in chaos but she managed, 'I hope you will both be very happy.'

Out of the chaos Peter's voice came to save her. 'Time to go.' The party began to move

294

towards the door.

Nermeen's father held out his hand. 'Good-bye, Madame. I am always glad to meet a friend of the Saheeds.'

'Practising your Egyptian?' asked Peter with unexpected wit, coming up beside her as they filed out into the street.

'I met them yesterday.'

'Did you?' He looked taken aback. 'You certainly get around.' He spoke with a touch of resentment, as though she had no right meeting people outside of their party.

She moved over to the edge of the crowd. A boy in T-shirt and jeans slipped past her. Startled, she looked again. Wasn't that the same young man she had seen yesterday with Nermeen at the stables? He was standing in the doorway now, craning his neck over the heads of the crowd as it washed round him. A moment later he stepped back, looking scared, and flattened himself against the wall. Then Nermeen's father came striding out, grasped the boy by the elbow and spoke to him angrily. The boy snapped back and for a startled moment Susanne thought they would come to blows. Then Malif swung the boy round and let go of his arm. He went, shuffling his feet, his face drooping with misery.

As Malif turned he came face to face with Susanne. 'That boy is a nuisance,' he said. 'He follows my daughter everywhere.' Then he repeated irritably, 'He is a nuisance, that boy, I can tell you.'

So that was the reason Omar had been so disturbed yesterday; why he had been sharp with his friend Mr Gahbo. Perhaps this boy had followed Nermeen and Omar, jealous, thought Gahbo should have sent him away. What did it matter now? She thought numbly it looks as though Nermeen is to lead the sort of sheltered life Madame Saheed leads, while Omar indulges in lighthearted affairs as his fancy takes him.

Maybe it's all a game. She remembered the men imbibing whisky in the hotel, the soft drinks served in their home. Perhaps Omar wanted one last flirtation, one final fling, before losing his freedom ... Some of his freedom? Bitterness crept into her heart.

'Hey!' said Peter brusquely. 'Are you in a dream, or what? We're all waiting for you.'

*   *   *

The afternoon was free.

Peter paused at her table as lunch was coming to an end. 'What are you going to do, Susanne?' His face was bright, hopeful.

'I think I've seen enough,' she said.

'Cultural indigestion?'

'Something like that.'

'Let's go riding, then.' She looked at him blankly. 'I can ride,' Peter said, grinning. 'There are horses for hire out by the pyramids.'

'But what are the horses like?'

'Horses. Four legs, mane and tail.'

She laughed. 'Well, it'll be an experience.' She pushed her chair back. 'I'll get into some jeans.'

They walked together through the bright, scented gardens, past the swimming pool and up the road to where little groups of tourists were photographing camels and taking short rides on them up to one of the pyramids and back.

'How about a camel?' Peter asked.

'No thanks.' She smoothed the mane of a bony, leggy old mare wondering what it ate, and how often. It shook its head cantankerously as though it hated this life it led and the people who rode it.

'You want ride?' eagerly enquired a small boy who was clutching the horse's reins.

'Yes. I think so.' She spoke doubtfully. What kind of a ride would this poor creature give her? She turned to look for Peter and saw him already astride another sad horse. He looked very pleased with himself. Oh well! She allowed the boy to leg her up.

He immediately leaped on to a bare-backed mare and bending down, snatched up her reins. She protested. 'Let that go. I can ride.'

'This wild horse.'

'Rubbish,' she retorted, laughing.

He let go of the reins but immediately

297

moved his mount directly in front of hers, blocking her. She tried to rein the creature round without success. It had evidently been trained to follow for it tossed its head, rattling the loose bit, and refused to budge. They ambled along in single file.

The boy looked behind. 'Trot? You wish trot?'

'Yes. Okay.' She had never had such a rough ride. The track was stony and the horse, too apathetic to look where it was going, tripped on stone after stone. If it was capable of moving faster than a bumpy trot she never found out for the boy riding in front effectively blocked the way. The sun was miserably hot, the saddle uncomfortable. She was glad when their escort turned and they picked their way joltingly back to base.

'I can always say I've ridden an Arab steed,' said Peter cheerfully as they dismounted.

That evening as the sun went down they sat in the gardens sipping drinks. Susanne had her back to the sunset. She felt she never wanted to see it again. Peter said, 'Let me move your chair. This is the last time you'll—'

'I'm perfectly comfortable,' she snapped, then as his pleasant face fell she added apologetically, 'I'm sorry, Peter. I'm so tired I scarcely know what I'm saying or doing.' It was not true that she was tired, only that there was no spark of life in her to hold her up. He fingered his glass, brooding, and she knew he

298

too was thinking of Omar, and wondering what had happened last night. Wondering, too, no doubt, why he had disappeared. She was grateful to him for not asking questions.

As darkness fell round them with the extraordinary suddenness of the East she rose and excusing herself went into the hotel to change. On this, their last night in Egypt, they were being taken to a nightclub. Peter caught up with her at the door. 'Susanne . . .'

She turned. 'Yes?'

He looked shy, shorn of the familiar brashness. 'Would you wear that pretty gold dress? You know, the one you wore the first night we were at Aswan?'

He was asking her to wear the gown she had on when Omar came down to the quay at Aswan, when their eyes met across time and locked. When they recognised each other and knew . . . 'Yes,' she said curtly, 'Yes. All right. And I'll wear the necklace, too.'

Peter's puckered frown stayed in her mind's eye as she went up the stairs. Why on earth had she said she would wear the necklace? Yet even as she asked herself the question she knew it was a kind of exorcism.

Vita was in the bedroom, already dressed. She was standing at a table looking down. She picked up a letter as Susanne came through the door and handed it to her. Susanne said, speaking slowly and distinctly, 'He's going to marry someone else. I found out today.

Perhaps you would like to tear that up.'

Vita took a moment to recover. 'I'm sorry,' she said. She looked back at the letter then at Susanne's face and said compassionately, 'I cannot live your life for you. You must tear it up yourself, if that is what you want to do.' Then she went out of the room closing the door behind her.

Susanne looked down at the letter for a long time. No, she said to herself. I will not read it. What is the point? It is over. Quite over. We were a couple of ships that passed in the night. The rest was a dream. And now I am awake. She dared not open the letter knowing that if it said Omar was coming for her tonight, even knowing what she knew, she would wait for him.

The coach was due to leave at eight. There were not more than a dozen passengers. Most of the older members, conscious that they had to be on the plane for take-off at five in the morning, were turning in early. Vita and the Colonel sat together at the back, pretending they hadn't seen Susanne and Peter come aboard.

It was not far to drive and there was nothing to see except a few street lights, oases in the desert night. They turned in at a big courtyard already half full of parked cars. Their guide took them to a table for six. The rest of the party gathered round. Peter spoke to the waiter in an aside, 'We want a table for two, please.'

'Sorry sir,' he replied, 'these two tables for six have been reserved for the party.'

Peter began to argue but the man was not to be swayed. 'I am prepared to pay,' he said then. 'I insist upon a table for two.'

The man went reluctantly to see what he could do. Susanne said, 'Let's sit down with the others. Let's not make a fuss.'

She was aware of curious glances; surreptitious looks. Of course the rest of the party would be entertained, watching her bouncing back and forth like a yo-yo from one man to another. You can tolerate anything for a few hours, she told herself. Tomorrow it will be all over, the pain, the awkwardness, the unbearable sweetness.

'They can easily bring out an extra table,' Peter said. 'I'm going to stick out for it.' An important looking man in a dark suit came bustling up and led them to a corner where a boy in a *galabiya* was already setting up a tiny table. Some notes changed hands. Susanne began to protest but Peter had taken over. He pulled out her chair.

She sat down thinking resignedly that perhaps this was her own fault. It could be said she had co-operated with him in wearing the gold dress.

Eerie, romantic eastern music filled the room. Cymbals and drums. 'Come on,' said Peter jumping up, holding out his arms to her.

She wanted to wait until there were some other couples on the floor, but Peter, it was clear, was equally concerned to be out there where the party might see that on this, the last night, he had, over all the odds, won. She wended her way slowly through the tables and because theirs was at the back of the room they were, after all, not the first. Peter swung her on to the floor with an air of exhibiting a trophy. He was a good dancer and they were well matched. When the music stopped and they went back to the table his good humour was restored.

'You dance well.'

'And you.' She smiled at him and he responded, embarrassingly, by grasping her hands across the table. Her first instinct was to pull them away, then she relaxed. Did it matter? He was harmless enough, and she didn't have to see him again.

He asked, sounding puzzled and hurt, 'Did you have to wear the necklace and bracelet that chap gave you?'

'Why not? If a strange man, whom I'm never going to see again, likes to waste his money on me, that's his problem.'

'You're harder than I realised,' Peter said critically, though still holding tightly to her hands. 'I thought, when I met you, that you were sweet and soft. And . . .'

'And what?' She was curious to know how he saw her.

'Vulnerable,' he said, looking embarrassed. 'I really thought that. But after what I've seen—'

'After what you've seen,' she broke in, 'I'm surprised you insisted on blocking me off from the rest of the party.' She wished she could say, let's face it, we've nothing in common. We could never make a couple. But that would spoil his evening. And why not, she thought, then. He's doing his best to spoil it himself. Yes, he is right. I have become hard. I am quite, quite different from the girl—woman, she thought now—who glowed in Omar's presence. She felt the tears welling up inside her.

'Belly dancers!' said Peter, letting her unfriendly remark pass and swinging half round so that he faced the little square of dance floor. She took the opportunity to take a tissue from her bag so that it would be ready if the tears overflowed, but they stayed in her heart, weighing it down.

The dancers were plump and lithe in their shimmering, bikini-like costumes made demure by a partial screen of floating veils. Men whistled. Peter said boyishly, 'Phew!' The lights were lowered. He stood up the better to see the girls as they gyrated to the beat of the drums. Susanne remained sitting. She could see as much as she wanted to. The room became noisy with wolf-whistles and laughter. Everyone was enjoying themselves. One of the

303

tourists joined the belly dancers. And then another.

Peter looked down at her. 'Do you want to have a go? How are you at this?'

'Not at all good, I'm sure. I think they've got enough volunteers, anyway.' There were people getting up all over the room and running on to the dance floor.

Peter looked round as though seeking someone to join him. Susanne saw him stiffen, saw an expression of sharp anger tighten his face, and with a jolting heart, somehow knowing, she followed his eyes. Omar was standing by a pillar near to the door watching them, his falcon's head high and his blue eyes narrowed.

Peter grasped her wrist and swung her out of her seat then led her between the tables, sliding, half-running towards the centre of the room. Susanne began to dance, wildly, frantically, as though her whole life depended on the speed of her movements. The beat quickened. Faster, faster. She kept her eyes down so that she might not see Omar. She willed him to go away. Faster. Faster. She looked up at Peter's face and heard him say breathlessly, 'Oh God!'

She never afterwards knew exactly how it happened. Did Omar wait for the music to stop in order to produce the greatest effect? Or did the band stop playing to watch the drama played out? Certainly if there was sound she did not hear it, and nor was she aware of movement in the crowd. It was as though the whole world waited.

Omar stepped right up to her. 'Come with me,' he said.

She lifted her head high. 'No,' she replied. 'Please go away.'

He took her by the wrist and jerked her towards him.

Peter protested, 'I say . . .'

A voice, perhaps that of the Colonel, said, 'Look here, young man . . .' Rising murmurs of anger. Gasps of incredulity. The crowd moved back. Omar's arm slid round her waist, iron hard. She was aware of a large man in a dark suit—two of them—standing close by, watching, not intervening. Just watching it happen.

She seemed to lose all sense of reality, then. Did she go with him? Did he drag her? She only knew she was whirling through the room, her feet scarcely touching the floor, and the crowd had parted to allow them to pass. Then they were outside in the black night with the moon risen, golden in the sky, and the diamond-bright stars winking down.

'What are you doing with me?' She was aware that the courtyard was empty. That no one was coming to her aid.

'Why did you not wait? You knew I was coming for you.'

She jerked herself free. 'Because I am not a

chattel for you to do what you like with,' she flared. 'I don't jump every time a man pulls the strings. I'm not Nermeen.' She spat the name at him and as she did so she jerked with all her strength and broke free. He easily snatched her arm again. 'How dare you! Let me go!'

'I dare because you are mine,' he said. 'How dare you sit in the darkest corner in there with that . . . that . . .'

Nincompoop was the word that came to Susanne's mind. She felt he would have used it had his English run to it. 'How can you say I am yours when you are set to marry that girl we found at the stables? Nermeen. I talked to her today. And to her father. You are to marry her. You are to marry her soon, Omar.' Her voice broke. 'Don't deny it. Why did you not tell me?'

'I did not want to hurt you,' he said.

She was outraged. 'You thought you could have a wife and keep me on the side!'

He strode across the forecourt dragging her with him. She fought like a tiger. 'Where do you think you're taking me?' They were leaving the car park behind.

'You'll see,' he returned grimly and a tremor of fear ran through her. She remembered that a room full of people had seen Omar carry her off and not one of them had come after her. They were in an outer courtyard now. In the light from the moon she could see two horses tethered to poles and in an instant recognised

306

the mare and stallion that they had ridden the day before. Mush and Hatshep.

'Right!' said Omar. 'You're on your home ground, now.'

In spite of her predicament, a tremor of excitement ran through her. But, 'I can't ride in this,' she cried looking down at her long gown.

He lifted her bodily into the saddle. She heard the delicate material of her skirt tear at the seams. As he went to untie the mare she flung herself over the other side and made a run for the door but Omar was too quick for her. 'All right. You asked for it!' he said fiercely, and gripping her wrist with one hand, he untied his stallion with the other, flung the reins over his neck and once more picked her up in his arms. Then she was on the front of his saddle and he in it, heading out into the darkness.

They galloped through the star-bright night, the only sound the muted thud of the horse's hoofs on hard sand. At first Susanne was half-hysterical with fright, but as the wind caught at her hair and filled her lungs she gave herself up, exultantly, to what had to be.

Turning, she looked up into Omar's face. He bent his own head and kissed her. The horse thundered on.

This was mad, crazy, it could not be happening! She would wake up in a moment out of a dream. Heaven alone knew how long they sped over the sand and through the star-lit night. Heaven alone knew how Omar found the way for there could surely be no track. And then she remembered that horses would always remember a route, in spite of darkness, if they had gone that way before.

'Look!' Omar had reined in.

She turned her head. Out in front now where a shallow valley lay the pale misty forms of tents showed in the moonlight. In one of them, bigger than the rest, a light glowed.

An explosion of excitement burst inside her. 'Omar,' she breathed.

'Susanne,' he mimicked and bending down kissed the nape of her neck.

A man in long cream robes and swathed headdress came out of the tent as they approached. They slid down and he took the horse. Mush had flecks of foam on his withers and his mouth. His beautiful coat was gleaming with sweat. 'Abdullah will rub him down and cover him,' Omar said, giving the stallion an affectionate slap.

Susanne looked down at her dress. Saw it was split from hem to waist. 'Omar, how can I appear like this?'

'You will have to be more careful with your clothes, won't you?' He affected to be stern.

'How can I face people?' Briefly, she thought this extraordinary man was going to wave a magic wand and produce another gown for her, but he only asked calmly, 'What

308

people?'

'You mean—'

'Why should we share your last evening?' he asked lightly as he led her into the tent.

She looked round, breathless with wonder. It was softly lift from a row of tiny lights high up in the roof. There was an enormous Persian rug in the centre of the wood floor, a low table set with silver and china, some covered dishes, a pair of tall candles in gilt sconces, and some small urns piled with red hot coals. On the floor were fat, coloured cushions.

Susanne's breath gradually came back. 'You went to all this trouble and I spoiled it. If I had only known!'

'You had my letter?'

'I'm sorry,' she said. 'After last night, and then Nermeen today, I . . . it seemed better not to read it. You hadn't been in touch.'

'I am not my own master, you know that. I expected you to trust me.' He was smiling at her, his almond-shaped eyes glinting. 'I trusted you, and yet I found you in a dark corner with another man, wearing my necklace.' Then he said softly, exultantly, 'But I have won, after all.'

There was champagne on ice to drink from beautiful glasses, followed by mutton kebabs and strange, spicy vegetables, exotic fruits and sweet, honeyed dessert. They relaxed on the cushions while the servants, silent on their bare feet, carried the table away.

'Of course you know you cannot go home tomorrow,' Omar said.

The horror of her situation bore down on her. 'Omar, we must talk about this girl, Nermeen. You are to marry her. She has been waiting to marry you since she was a child.'

'It is the way in Egypt.'

'Omar, darling, how can you sit there and say that so calmly,' she cried distractedly, 'and then tell me I can't go home. What do you want of me?'

'I want to love you.'

'I cannot just be loved—like that. I cannot play second fiddle to a wife. Your mother would understand that.'

'You would not be second fiddle to Nermeen.' He touched her cheek, and she felt that now familiar fire rise up in her. He kissed her and her head reeled. Then she felt Omar's gentle hands pushing her from him with infinite tenderness. 'This is not the place to lose our heads,' he said and indeed it was not, for at that moment one of the servants moved silently across the open doorway, his robes a light shadow against the velvet sky. 'Tomorrow this matter will be resolved.'

'But how can it be resolved? I have told you I met Nermeen's father this morning in a perfume shop. You have allowed them to go ahead with plans for the marriage.'

'I do not wish to hurt them,' Omar replied.

'But . . .' She could not go on. She did not

310

understand. She wanted to ask why he had not broken the engagement, but his grave gentleness made the question sound callous. 'Omar, you have not told your mother about me. She treated me as a tourist passing through.'

'I did not want to draw her into what was essentially between my father and me.'

'Why did you take me to meet her, then?'

'I wanted to prepare her.'

'And what of Nermeen?'

'In dealing with young girls it is necessary to be even more delicate.'

She remembered the big, chauffeur driven car and burst out, 'Nermeen is rich. Your father said—'

He cut her off. 'Nobody in Egypt is rich these days.'

She looked at him earnestly in the candlelight, watching his eyes. 'You do know I have nothing, don't you? Only what I earn. You know, because I told you, that the horses I ride don't belong to me.'

He looked amused. 'To whom do they belong?'

'A man called Harvey Bevin. A well-known racing man who is a neighbour of ours. My mother rents a cottage from him.' She hurried on before he could react, 'Did I tell you,' she was so upset and confused she couldn't remember, 'that neither my mother nor I could afford this cruise. I won it in a competition.'

He bent to kiss her lightly on the cheek. 'Clever as well as beautiful,' he said. 'Now we must go. It is two o'clock and your plane takes off at five. The coach will be leaving for the airport at half-past three. You must be there to talk to your mother. And we must not hurry Mush. He has had enough galloping for one night.'

'Omar . . .'

'Yes?'

'What is to happen?' He had said 'your plane' and earlier, were the words a figment of her imagination, or had he really said, 'Why should we share our last evening?' Her brain was clearing. She recognised she was dealing with a man of a different culture, with different standards. Even a different sense of humour.

'I have a plan,' he said, 'but I cannot tell you. Dare not.'

'And what am I meant to do?'

'You will wait at the hotel. We will ride to the stables now, pick up my car, and I will deliver you back. Then, later, I will come.'

CHAPTER FIFTEEN

As she stood between Vita and the Colonel in the foyer beside their luggage, waiting for the coach to pick them up, Susanne forced her mind to go blank. Everyone was sneaking surreptitious glances at her, and avoiding her eyes. Nobody, not even Vita, had asked questions. She had been only too relieved at her arrival, safe and sound. Vita had not slept. Had not even gone to bed. The coach slid in and staff bustled round collecting the bags. She took a seat at the front where people could not turn round and stare at her. Vita sat down beside her and unexpectedly took her hand.

'Don't,' she said in a choked voice, terrified that the tears in her heart would rise up and overflow. Vita's hand slipped down between them, staying close in case it should, after all, be needed.

*   *   *

The green fields of England looked particularly beautiful after desert brown. Susanne was up early on the day after her return, exercising the horses.

'Good holiday?' Nigel tossed the question carelessly in her direction as he strode past.

'Very good, thank you.'

He mounted the beautiful Silver Penny that Harvey had wanted her to ride. Harvey was not in attendance that morning, nor the next nor the next. Surprisingly, he had not crossed the fields to share a drink with them, though he must have known they were home. Vita, too, thought it odd. She contemplated telephoning, then decided against it. Susanne went up to London to look for a job, staying with a friend. Wonderful, she said when people asked her how the holiday had gone. Out of this world. And that was true. So very true.

She came back on Friday evening to find a big car parked in front of the house. Vita met her at the door in an untypical state of excitement. 'Susanne!' she exclaimed, 'I thought you'd never come. Didn't you get my message?'

'What message?' She turned, indicating the vehicle in the drive. 'Whose car?'

'Rupert is here.'

'Why Vita, you're blushing!' she cried. 'Wait 'til he sees you in wellies and jeans! What a shock!'

Vita smiled tolerantly. 'I'm not blushing. But I am excited. There's a surprise. We're invited up to Harvey's.'

'So what's the excitement about? Apart from the Colonel's presence?' It was no big deal being invited to Hammer Place. They had been there often enough before. 'Is he having a party?'

Vita hesitated. 'It's about . . . horses.'

'What about horses?' She put her bag down on the hall table. The Colonel appeared in the doorway to the drawing-room and in their greeting Vita's answer was lost. 'Better hurry and get changed,' she said, breaking in. 'We're late now. You can talk to Rupert later.'

She bounded up the stairs, had a swift wash, changed into a light dress and ran down again. They were waiting for her in the car with the engine running. She slid into the back seat. 'Aren't you going to tell me what this is about?'

'I told you. Horses.'

She settled down to wait, baffled. Vita apologised for the rutted track. The Colonel said it didn't matter at all, he would drive slowly. They came out on the road and a moment later were turning in at the drive leading to Hammer Place.

There was only one other car so clearly there was no party. Vita turned round. 'You go on in,' she said. 'It's your surprise. We'll follow.'

'Don't tell me Harvey's got a horse tied up in the hall!'

'Go in, my dear,' the Colonel said. 'You'll see.'

Susanne climbed out and walked across the gravel to the door. It was standing open and there in the big square hall was Omar looking distinctly out of place, as though dressed for a

315

board meeting in a formal suit. But then, as she thought afterwards, an Egyptian was scarcely likely to have a wardrobe full of country tweeds. At the time she could only think she was hallucinating. She blinked, trying to blink him out of her fevered mind because this was madness, to conjure up a person who could not possibly be there.

He came forward saying reproachfully, 'You ran away from me. You should have known you could not do that.'

She managed to find a whisper of a voice. 'How did you find . . . ?' And then she could not go on.

He put his arms round her. 'You mentioned it was Harvey Bevin's horses that you rode. Did you forget you were talking to a man who moves in the racing world? I have not met him before, but I knew him by repute. He was very easy to trace. Why did you run away? Why did you not trust me?'

The tears were running down her cheeks. 'You didn't say . . . I didn't know . . . I mean . . . You told me nothing. And there was Nermeen.'

'Ah, Nermeen. She and Jarkas are with our host, in the drawing room, I think. Or maybe they are walking in the garden,' he said casually, watching with smiling eyes for her reaction.

'What!'

He laughed, enjoying her astonishment. 'I

316

believe you may have seen Jarkas. There was some sort of fracas at a perfume shop?'

'Oh yes. Nermeen's father chased him away.'

'She and Jarkas have been in love for some time.'

'Why did you not tell me?'

He held her away from him, looking tenderly into her puzzled eyes. 'I could not,' he said regretfully, 'without risking things going wrong. People cannot keep secrets, you know. A chance glance, a guilty look, and an intelligent person is suspicious. If I had said to you, "This girl Nermeen is in love with a boy who is shortly to come to London to study and she wishes to go with him. I am trying to work out a way to help them and at the same time free myself from this arranged marriage," you would have met my mother, who is a very discerning woman, with stars in your eyes. And, as you would say, the cat would have been out of the bag.'

'Omar, they surely couldn't force you to marry her! At your age!'

'No, they could not force me,' he agreed. 'But we are a very close family and I do not want to cause hurt. I have my own methods of getting my own way. I do not like disruption, or ill-feeling. When a thing is done, it is done, and they will accept what they cannot undo. I have abducted Nermeen,' he said, smiling like a mischievous small boy, 'and in a manner of speaking, I suppose I have abducted Jarkas, though he was to leave next month anyway. Now Nermeen is here her father will consider she has been defiled, so he will rush after her and insist she marry the boy. Meantime, your friend Harvey Bevin has agreed to look after them.'

'Oh, Omar!'

'Oh, Susanne!' he mimicked her. 'Now, shall we find the others?'

They were indeed in the garden. Vita and Rupert had gone round the side of the house to join them. Harvey came forward and gave Susanne a hug. 'So,' he said in his benevolent way, smiling down at her, 'you've captured a famous rider. I'm very proud of you.'

'Excuse me for correcting the English of an Englishman,' said Omar with impeccable good manners, 'but I think the word is captivated.'

They all laughed appreciatively.

Nermeen, pretty and shy in a white dress with a demure neckline came forward and shook Susanne by the hand. 'I have to thank you,' she said. 'I always wish to marry a younger man,' she added ingenuously, and they laughed again.

Susanne turned to Omar, her face bright with happiness, 'So it's not true you have to marry for money?'

'Oh yes. It would be better. Very much better,' Omar said gravely. 'I love my father but I cannot please him in all things. He will have to put up with my being poor.'

Susanne thought of the castle in Ireland and the fabulous jewels his mother wore so casually for dinner when entertaining a visitor of no importance and she smiled in her heart, thinking that perhaps there was not so much difference between them, after all.

We hope you have enjoyed this Large Print book. Other Chivers Press or G.K. Hall & Co. Large Print books are available at your library or directly from the publishers.

For more information about current and forthcoming titles, please call or write, without obligation, to:

Chivers Press Limited
Windsor Bridge Road
Bath BA2 3AX
England
Tel. (01225) 335336

OR

G.K. Hall & Co.
P.O. Box 159
Thorndike, Maine 04986
USA
Tel. (800) 223-2336

All our Large Print titles are designed for easy reading, and all our books are made to last.